The 13th Street
HABERDASHERY

ISBN   Paperback: 979-8-9994918-0-0
ISBN   Hardback: 979-8-9994918-1-7
ISBN   eBook: 979-8-9994918-2-4

Library of Congress Control Number: 2025915796

Published By:

BOOKMARC
A L L I A N C E

The 13th Street

HABERDASHERY

JEFFERY LEE LEMIRE, SR.

CONTENTS

CHAPTER 1

Billy Patterson was a woodsman of the first class. Everyone who knew him knew that he was much more comfortable in the woods, swamps, and mountains than he was in a room full of people, even family and friends. He could move through the woods like a ghost. It wasn't necessarily a matter of pride so much as a matter of fact. With people it was a different story. He could never really catch social cues very well. Too many things had happened in his life that caused him to pull away from people rather than confide in them. He just was not very trusting with his emotions. He had his friends, but even with them the relationships were not normal.

Billy wasn't exactly a kid any more. He had wondered if people were ever going to stop calling him Billy and start calling him Bill. He had originally thought that when his father "Old Bill" passed he would become Bill, but that didn't happen. It was twelve years ago that his dad had passed and folks still called him Billy. He didn't really care, but thoughts just cross your mind. That's the way it is.

He was quite excited because he was getting to hunt an area on the north end of Patterson Lake, a lake around which his family owned more than half of the land. There had been three dry years in a row and the swamp on the north end of the lake had nearly dried up. Billy had been exploring it for about a year now hunting rabbits, squirrels, deer, and whatever presented. He had seen a bear down in there, but had not shot at it. The State so strictly regulated the bear population that he didn't want to take the chance. Normally Billy did just as he pleased, but with bears, turkeys, and water fowl, he was more careful because he suspected that the State Game Commission tagged some of them and he didn't want to be caught with a tagged animal in his freezer. As he worked his way through the swamp in an area he had never explored before, he sat down to take a break. It was really tough going through the marsh and he wasn't exactly a spring chicken any more. In fact he was fifty seven years old. He had let himself go after his wife passed. She was the light of his life, but had passed away after three years of marriage. Billy now looked like an old time mountain man. He just didn't care what anybody thought. He was just himself. He didn't eat well and he drank too much. His jacket had never been cleaned. It had started out a medium tan, but was now from dark brown to light tan depending on the stains and sun bleached parts. He couldn't see much point in changing. This one still served him well. There were folks that wished he'd change it before going to town. Nobody knew the last time he had trimmed his beard and his moustache was trimmed just enough to stay out of his food. Nobody had ever caught him getting a haircut, but it did get trimmed up now and then. Who did it and when it got done was a mystery.

As Billy sat there looking around him, he noticed something red up ahead. He stared at it trying to figure out what it was. His initial reaction was one of disgust, thinking that someone had thrown trash into the lake that eventually found its way through the brush to this spot in the marsh. Finally, when he was finished resting, he got up and walked over to it. There was an oddly shaped hump sticking out of the soil. He noted that this spot was normally two to three feet under water and surrounded with heavy brush. Billy bent over to get a closer look and was mystified as to what he was seeing. He reached down and brushed the dirt and vegetation away and then stood there with a stunned expression on his face. He sat down rather suddenly and heavily. What he had just seen changed assumptions that he had been living with for fifty years. Buried in the mud at his feet was his sister's 1968 Ford Mustang that had disappeared fifty years ago. Three young girls from town had disappeared suddenly. The police had finally concluded that they had run away in Cassie's 1968 Mustang and headed for California or who knows where. The late '60's were times when young people "dropped out" and were never heard from again. This was the first time in fifty years anyone had seen a trace of them or the car.

After a long pause, Billy pulled his cell phone out and dialed 911. He heard, "911, what is your emergency?" He hesitated and they repeated the question. He said, "Yeah, I'm here. This is Bill Patterson and I'm out on the north end of Patterson Lake marsh and I think that I have found a fifty year old crime scene!"

Billy was still sitting in the same spot when the police began arriving. Memories were washing over his soul as he sat there. He remembered his only sister, Cassandra Sue Patterson. She was the pride and joy of the family; a truly beautiful, highly intelligent, daughter and sister. Billy was seven years old the summer she disappeared. In fact, his seventh birthday was forgotten in the horrible nightmare that followed the disappearance. He would never forget it; he *could* never forget it.

The first person to arrive was the County Sheriff, Mack Becker. He was on the team that had investigated the disappearance of the three girls back in 1968. The investigation had extended through '68 and into '69. He had told everybody else to hold back. He wanted to see the car before anyone else did. The case was closed "unsolved". The majority conclusion was that the girls had run off together, but Mack had never believed it. He had argued for forty- seven years that something had happened to them, but almost nobody would listen. They had interviewed nearly everyone that had even the most remote contact with them. There was just nothing. Everyone had an alibi. There were just no suspects. The car had never been found. They had put out a nationwide bulletin, but there was just nothing. He remembered the helpless feeling of knowing there was something that they just could not see. Now, after all these years, there was a break in the case. Mack had been a twenty-one year old rookie deputy fifty years ago when the girls disappeared. He was now seventy-one and was planning on retiring after this term as Sheriff. It would be very satisfying to put this case to bed after all these years. He felt like he could retire in peace after that. The case had always haunted the recesses of his mind.

Sheriff Mack, as everyone called him, trudged through the underbrush to the place where Billy was sitting and waving at him. Mack and Billy had become friends during the time of the investigation. Although Mack was much older, he noticed that Billy seemed to get lost in the shuffle so he tried to pay him extra attention. They stayed quite close over the years. When Billy lost his wife, he had sort of slipped off the grid and Mack had lost touch with him for a time, but recently they had reconnected. Billy was waiting for him. He said gruffly, "Found Cassie's car. It's there in the mud. Fifty years ago, this was full of water. This is the first time in fifty years this marsh has been exposed for this long. I'm probably the only person who has been out here in a hundred years or more. I just stumbled onto it while wandering around in the marsh." Mack replied, "We'll have to pull it out and confirm, but it looks like you're right. I never believed they ran off in the first place." Billy said, "I know you didn't. Neither did I. Our family was way too close; she never would have done that!" "I know," said Mack.

Soon the place was crawling with State Police, County Deputies, and even FBI lab folks showed up because of the high profile and time factor. It was felt that they would have the best chance of finding anything useful. If anything useful was even there. Getting the car out of the mud proved to be a major undertaking. Because the soil was unstable in the marsh, it was unsafe to bring large equipment down to the car. The wrecker drivers got as close as they could to the edge of the lake where the soil was solid and ran their cables out as far as they would reach. They then had to add chains to reach the car. The workers had to dig by hand down to the back wheels to hook the chains. Then, because of the suction of the mud, the wreckers could not budge the car. The workers had to continue to dig almost to the front tires before the suction was broken enough to pull it out. They brought lights and worked into the night. Somebody came up with the idea of using a large tree near the car as a crane. They ran a cable over one of the stronger looking limbs. With one wrecker pulling back and another pulling up, they were able to break the car loose and haul it out. Once they got it out of the hole, a single wrecker was able to pull it up the hill and onto the farm lane leading to the road.

Mack did a quick survey inside the car expecting the worst, but it was empty. "They're not in here!" he announced. "We have the car, but still have no idea what happened to the girls." He was both disappointed and relieved. He wanted this to be over, but he didn't want to find the remains with one of the family members standing there. By this time, there were family members from all three of the girls milling around.

CHAPTER 2

The discovery of the car in the Patterson Lake Marsh nearly fifty years after the fact was the biggest thing that had happened since the day the girls went missing. All of the old discussions were hauled out, restated, and rehashed. Once the authorities got the car to the State Police lab and started going over it several of the theories had to change. For one thing, the keys were in the ignition and another, the gear shift was in drive so it seemed that somehow it had been driven into the lake. How and by whom was a mystery that so far remained opaque. They also found the girls' overnight clothes and overnight bags in the trunk, so the idea that they ran off seemed to diminish in probability.

Cassie Patterson, Pauline Franklin, and Esperanza Chavez had been planning on leaving for the Chicago area to meet their boyfriends who were in a rock and roll band that was finishing up a summer tour in the Chicago area and would be heading home on Monday. They had been seen in several places in town the morning of their disappearance. Nobody could remember seeing them after lunch that day.

Jack Franklin was Pauline's brother and Esperanza's boyfriend. He was the drummer in the band. He was called "Crazy Jack" but not because he was really crazy, but because of his antics on stage. Jack was a better than average athlete and an honor student. His short term plans were to keep playing in the band for a few years, then go to college and get a degree. He and Esperanza planned to get married. It seemed like the future was so very bright for them and it was, until it wasn't.

Mark Bellingham was the lead vocalist and rhythm guitar player. He was probably the brains behind the band. He wrote most of their songs. They had charted with a couple of songs, although they had not broken the top ten. Truthfully, they hadn't broken the top forty, but they were having fun. They were excited about their prospects; things looked good for the future. He was madly in love with Pauline. They were talking of a future together. Mark was a really good high school athlete. Some thought he had potential to play at the college level but felt he was wasting his time with his music. He, too, was an honor student and planned to further his education someday. His attitude was that the colleges would always be there and that was true.

Then there was Willy Hill. He was a wild and crazy one. He played lead guitar and did back-up vocals. In fact they all did back-up vocals. His main squeeze was Cassie Patterson. His best friend was Cassie's older brother Peter. Pete played keyboards and bass. On occasion he played with the band, but did not want to commit to it full time. Peter did not have a girlfriend. In fact it turned out that he never would. When it became okay to come out of the closet, he let the world know that he was gay and that was that. He wound up in Hollywood as a moderately successful actor. He originally went out there thinking he could find the girls, once the police decided that they must have run off to California.

The band had formed while the kids were in the sixth grade. At first they were really awful, but had a lot of fun making noise. Little by little they improved. They all started taking private music lessons from Mrs. Appleton, the school music teacher. She taught keyboards, chord structures, the proper way to sing, and how to sing harmony. Without Mrs. Appleton, the band would have never been. The boys really loved music and were willing to work very hard, but they were lost in the woods without their teacher. She recorded their practice sessions so they could hear how they sounded. She also allowed them to practice in the music room after school, on weekends, and during the summer.

Mrs. Appleton was only about five years out of college and full of ideas and ideals about teaching music. Her husband was a Captain in the Marine Corps and was deployed in Vietnam. He had been deployed less than a year and had some time left on his assignment. She had moved from North Carolina where they had been assigned and taken a job close to the area where she grew up so her family would be nearby. She lived about fifteen miles from her parents and her extended family was all around. She had grown up as Abigail Jensen. Her students loved her and the boys in the band owed most of their success to Miss Abby's training and advice. They really appreciated the guidance and help that she had given them.

The band had gone through a metamorphosis of name development until they had landed on the name "First String". It sounds very sophomoric and it was. In fact, they were still in high school. They were coming home from summer tour and putting the band on hold until after football season so they could play their senior year. After football season, they would start writing and getting ready for a tour that would begin right after graduation. They already had a couple of songs that Mark had written that the recording execs were sure would chart. They were just waiting for them to finish football season. They would record the songs during the winter so the songs would be ready for release in the spring. Their plans were made and their careers were about to take off. Everything was falling into place.

CHAPTER 3

Beau Bellingham was Mark's younger brother. He was about the same age as Billy Patterson. Beau and Billy had never been what you would call buddies, but they were very close in a strange way that only trauma and tragedy brings. Even during the days after the disappearance when people were at each others' throats for any and every little thing, Billy and Beau weren't antagonistic. They sort of found each other during that time. They were two little boys lost in the shuffle of a really traumatic loss. People didn't seem to be mindful of Billy's loss. He had lost his only sister whom he adored. Beau sort of became Billy's sounding board and comforter during those months and years. In high school, they sort of drifted apart, but always had a special "thing" between them. Beau had seen Billy crying his guts out when nobody else seemed to notice, but had kept his friend's secret for years. Beau had never even told his wife.

Once the car was found, Beau immediately called Billy. They hadn't spoken in months, but with them it didn't seem to matter. When Billy answered the phone Beau said, "Billy, Beau here. Are you okay with all this that is going on?" Billy replied, "Beau, thanks for calling. To be honest, I was shocked when I found Cassie's car in the marsh. Who would have ever thought that it would turn up after all these years? I surely didn't." Beau replied, "You must have been gut punched when you realized what you were looking at." "That about describes it," responded Billy. "You know that area is usually under around three or four feet of water and because of the thick underbrush, boats never get in there. Had the marsh not dried up, we never would have found the car." Beau said, "That is a fact. Now the question is how did it get there and who put it there? I think why is fairly obvious. Somebody did something to those girls and wanted to cover it up." Billy said, "That's what Sheriff Mack thinks. He wants to find somebody who was not involved in the original investigation to put fresh eyes on this to see if there is something that was missed the first time through. He is convinced that there has to be a clue somewhere." "You know," Beau said, "my brother Mark retired from the FBI about ten or twelve years ago. He spent his last few years with the FBI heading up a unit that looked at high profile cold cases. They had a pretty good solve rate considering the trails were all ice cold. Maybe Mack should talk to him. He doesn't live far from here." Billy replied, "I'll mention it to Sheriff Mack. He may think Mark is too close to the original investigation. We'll see. By the way, thanks for calling. You were always there for me." Beau nodded and replied, "Like old times." They said their goodbyes and hung-up the phones.

CHAPTER 4

Cassandra Patterson

Cassandra Sue Patterson was the only daughter of a prosperous farmer by the name of William Patterson. He was known as Old Bill because he had named his youngest son William, Jr., and he was called Billy. Cassie had an older brother, as well. His name was Peter. Pete was different and had always been that way. Back in 1968, they weren't so quick to label people. It turned out that Pete was gay, but it was not until he moved to California many years later and came out that his family knew for sure about him. Suzanne Lilly Patterson was Cassie's mom and she was the glue that held the Patterson family together. Everyone called her Lilly. Her love for her husband and children tended to overrule any conflict that came up while they were growing up. Old Bill knew that something wasn't right about his oldest child, but his wife kept him from causing an irreparable rift. She always brought them together and kept peace in the family.

All of the Patterson children were good students, but Cassie was really exceptionally quick as a student. In fact, it seemed like she never had to study to get good grades. She had an excellent memory and could remember the classroom explanations and didn't need to really study. She normally had her homework done before she left the class so rarely did she bring work home. Her little brother Billy just thought that she was the smartest big sister in the whole world. She certainly was in his world.

The Pattersons attended church every Sunday morning and evening. They also went on Wednesday evenings. The adults had Bible Study and the kids had youth activities. Cassie and her mom sang in the choir. Pete played piano and organ depending on what was needed on any given service.

Along with getting straight A's, Cassie was involved in all kinds of extracurricular activities. She was in the school choir, the band, the drama and musical productions, cheer-leading, and 4-H. Every year, for the past four years, Cassie had raised the prize steer for the County 4-H Fair. She was considered the one to beat if somebody was going for the title. Old Bill was quite the expert on cattle and he imparted much of his wisdom to his daughter, whom he adored.

Cassie had been quite the tom boy growing up but when she was fifteen going on sixteen she suddenly started changing. She became more aware of fashion in both clothing and hairstyle. She started going with her mom to the beauty shop to get her hair trimmed and styled. She also started catching the eye of the young men in town. She had dated a few guys and flirted with a few more. Recently, she had been seeing Willy Hill and it seemed like a steady relationship. Old Bill was not sure how he felt about that, but knew Willy and his family. Willy was a hard working kid who played sports, studied hard enough to make the honor roll, and played drums for the First String. They were successful and were already making a lot of money for kids in 1968. That impressed Old Bill enough that he stayed out of his daughters affairs. Besides, Lilly had spoken and he knew his place.

Cassie loved her life. She loved her family. She loved her school. She loved her friends. She loved her teachers. She loved her church. She loved the Mustang her daddy had bought for her. She had asked him for a car so she could get back and forth to all her activities. He had picked the Mustang. And she really loved Willy Hill. That was about to become a problem because Cassie was pregnant. She had not, yet, told anyone about it. She had no idea how she was going to tell her mom and dad. In fact, she had not even told Willy. She didn't even know how she hoped he would react. She was in a very confused place in her life and didn't know where to turn. She hadn't been to the doctor about the pregnancy yet. She would have to tell her parents before going to the doctor. The biggest reason that she hadn't gone to the doctor was that she just didn't know how to break the news to her parents. She knew it would break their hearts and she didn't want to do that. It was a little bit late to be thinking along that line, though. She knew it was true. It was a big burden for a seventeen-year old girl to be carrying around. Her best friends Esperanza and Pauline noticed that she wasn't her normal bright happy self and asked her what was wrong. She just always blamed it on their senior year coming up and all the changes that were going to take place. She always said to them, "After this year things will never be the same." There was way more to it, but she couldn't tell them. They usually talked about everything, but this was different.

She was going to have to spill the beans soon though because she would be showing before too much longer. Cassie's dream was to be a lawyer. She saw that dream slipping away and that made her sad. She did love Willy and she was confident that he loved her, too. She felt like their senior year was ruined and somehow she thought that it was her fault. That was a lot of stuff to push around.

CHAPTER 5

Pauline Franklin

The way her grandfather described Pauline Janene Franklin was "as fresh and bright as a spring morning". She was a blond haired, green eyed, tempest of joy and happiness that infected her world with the zest for life that she possessed. She was popular because of who she was and how she treated people, not because she tried to be. She was a truly nice person. She loved her life and the people in it and she was not shy about letting it show.

Her father was the Honorable Josiah Paul Franklin, a local attorney who had been appointed to the bench around five years before. He was Judge Franklin and the title fit him. He had a dignified reserve that made him a good fit for the bench. He was friends with and a college classmate of the governor which did not harm his case or career at all. A look at Pauline's mom and one could tell how Pauline would look in her forties. She was an exceptionally attractive, blond haired, green eyed lady. Some would have said she was beautiful and few would try to dispute the claim. She was, however, unassumingly humble and thoughtful of others. Pauline was like a carbon copy of her mother.

There were two brothers, one older and one younger, and one younger sister. Pauline was seventeen. Her oldest brother, Josiah, Jr., was nineteen. They called him Jack. He was tall like his dad and quite athletic. Their father had not been an athlete, but their mother's brothers were very athletic in their day. Both of their uncles had played college ball. Uncle Mike played baseball and Uncle Franky played basketball. Neither of them was good enough for the pros, but didn't really care. The next brother was eleven year old Mikey. He was the family outdoors-man. He loved to be out in the fields and the woods. He loved to hunt and had been hunting squirrels, rabbits, and other small animals since he was able to pull back the bands of a sling shot. He was pretty good with it. He had begun hunting with a bow and arrows, as well. His dad had promised him a.22 rifle for his twelfth birthday and he was counting the days. The youngest and the princess of the family was Kerry. She was six years old and quite precocious. She was as cute as a button and really funny. Like many slightly precocious children she was funny when she was trying to be serious so she would make everyone else laugh and then she would cry because their laughter offended her. Then they would laugh all the more. Mrs. Franklin's name was Marlene and she loved her husband, her children, and was devoted to them.

The Franklin family was very active in community activities. The children were all active in church, 4-H, youth sports, scouts, and whatever else came along. They had three cars which was a bit unusual for the times. One was for the Judge to take himself to the court house each day. Marlene had her car for her errands and they had bought a car for Pauline. She drove to school and helped drive her siblings to various scheduled activities. Both Pauline and her mom were busy about town during and after school and all summer long. The Franklin family led a busy, active life and they loved it.

Little Kerry loved her big sister. She was quite certain that the sun rose and set somewhere in the general vicinity of "Paulie's" room. She was a true believer. She believed her sister was the smartest, the prettiest, and the best at everything. Sometimes it was bothersome. For instance, when Marlene was preparing breakfast and Kerry wanted Paulie to do hers "'cause she does it better". Pauline contributed to the situation by spoiling the child something fierce. Pauline always said, "She's my only little sister and will soon be grown up and won't think I'm so cool anymore. I'm going to take advantage of it." Marlene thought of those words many times after Pauline disappeared and was so glad that she had made her sister feel so special. It just made you wonder.

Pauline was one of those students that just "got it". It didn't seem like she ever had to study but always got straight A's. She had the ability to remember things she heard, even detailed explanations, but she also did the work that it took to grasp the material. Difficult math concepts that were so hard for many to master looked easy to her because she could remember the explanation. She always did her homework and turned it in on time. She did not fall behind. It was something her father taught her. Catching up is harder than doing the work when it is assigned. Her work ethic made school look easy to people watching who had no idea how hard she really worked. She reasoned that sometime down the line, she may get into a class where either she didn't understand the explanation or the teacher was not a good enough communicator to get the point across clearly. So she did her homework all the while making it look like "a piece of cake" to those looking on. She had taken the SAT last year, her junior year, and had scored ridiculously high on it. She was getting letters from some great universities, most of which she was pitching in the trash. She did have a letter from Harvard which she had kept and one from Stanford. She doubted that she wanted to go that far from home, but one never knew. She was more interested in staying in the Midwest. Her dad had gone to the University of Cincinnati for his undergraduate work and then to Notre Dame for law school. She wanted to stay closer to home and go to Notre Dame Law School just like her dad. She had even toyed with the idea of politics. Her unspoken, secret goal was to be the first female Chief Justice of the Supreme Court. She was afraid people would laugh at her so she didn't talk about it. Girls didn't commonly dream such dreams in 1968.

The romance between Pauline and Mark was unexpected, but then that's the way love is. It seems to snag you when you're not looking for it. Their relationship had developed slowly considering Mark and her brother, Jack, were lifelong friends. There is something to be said for propinquity. The fact that they were together so much even though she was a pesky little sister until she wasn't, probably led to their blossoming interest in one another. They had become very close in the past year. Neither Mark nor Pauline had given up their goals; they just began to think of a different context for them. They were very careful so that she didn't wind up pregnant. That would have really thrown a monkey wrench into the mix. They were looking forward to their senior year of high school and whatever came after. Pauline loved her life. She thought it was pretty much perfect.

CHAPTER 6

Esperanza Chavez

Esperanza Luisa Maria Chavez was the raven haired beauty of Pleasant Valley High. She had thick, wavy, jet black hair, and flashing black eyes. She caught the eye of everyone, but only Jack Patterson caught hers. Esperanza means "Hope" in Spanish. She went through a period in the sixth and seventh grades where she tried to get her friends to call her Hope. Her family called her Pera which was the traditional Spanish nickname for Esperanza. Some of her close friends heard that and picked it up. Others, including Willy, called her Esper. She finally surrendered to the name. When her parents spoke her name using their Spanish, it had such a lyrical beauty and rhythm that she couldn't help but love it. The problem was that it was not as pretty in English, she thought. All of her friends thought that it was a beautiful name and loved to say it. They tried to learn to say it with the Spanish accents and rolling R's, but never could really get it right.

Esperanza came from a large family. Her parents had six children. She was in the middle of the pack, but was the oldest girl in the family. She had two older brothers. Her oldest brother, Manuel, Jr., or Manny, was twenty-one and in the Marines. He was one of the fortunate ones. Rather than going to Vietnam, he was assigned to Embassy Guard duty in Panama. He was upset that he had not been sent into combat. None of his family was sad about it, however. Umberto or Beto was nineteen, almost twenty. He had graduated high school and was finishing up a trade school to be a diesel mechanic. He still lived at home and helped take care of the family. He was already working part time while he finished his training and was already making good money. At seventeen, Pera was the apple of her father's eye, (her older brothers as well) and her mother's pride and joy. After Pera, came Pedro sixteen, Elizeo fourteen, and Lucinda or Lucy who was eleven going on twenty-one. They were a happy, hard-working family who had been in the Pleasant Valley area for three generations, now.

Manuel Chavez, Sr.'s family was originally from Mexico. His grandfather, Adelberto, had come to Texas as a young man to work on a Texas ranch. He was an outstanding horse trainer. He broke the half-wild horses on the ranch and trained them to be cow ponies. In his line of work, he had broken several of his own bones. It was rough work. As a man in his late twenties, he had followed a herd of cows north and never returned to Texas. There had been farm land available for people who were willing to work and he was. He got himself a piece of land and carved out a nice farm for himself. He found another family of Mexicans in the neighborhood who had a lovely daughter which was the biggest reason that he never returned to Texas. They married and raised crops, kids, and horses. Adelberto Chavez's horses were well known for their quality and training. His grandson, Manuel, still lived on the old farm and raised some horses, although mainly for his own benefit. His main business was a construction company that his father "Beto" Adelberto, Jr., had started. The business had its ups and downs, but the name Chavez was known for integrity so they always seemed to have some work. They weren't among the movers and shakers in Pleasant Valley, but they were probably as well off as any family in the area in an understated way. The Chavez family did not feel that they had to prove anything.

Unlike most of Esperanza's friends, the Chavez family attended St. Anthony's Catholic Church in town. The only one among her friends that was Catholic was Willy. They had tried to date, but nothing came of it. Then she noticed Jack and buds of romance sprouted and began to blossom. The kids had not looked beyond their senior year. They had no idea that it made little difference who she dated in high school. Unlike her parents, she had no intention of marrying at eighteen and becoming a mother immediately thereafter. She had made up her mind that she was going to college and she was going to be a pediatrician. Her dream was to discover the cure for childhood cancer. She was already working hard on her goals. Her preparation included taking the required classes so that she could qualify academically and working on weekends as a volunteer in the pediatric department of the Pleasant Valley Memorial Hospital.

The disappearance of Pera had temporarily wrecked her family. They started coming apart at the seams but then Lucy reminded them that Pera was the glue that held them together and she would not want them to fall apart. She said with tears in her eyes and a quivering voice, "When my sister comes home, she will need us to be her family like we have always been!" That started the change that helped them to pull together. They supported each other and held each other during the horrible days following the disappearance. They held it together as the pain dulled and days became weeks, and months, and years. They continued to talk about her and taught their children about their Aunt Pera who had gone away, but was expected back any day. Even though that day had not come, it had served to hold them together and focus their emotions on a more constructive goal rather than tearing each other apart.

CHAPTER 7

Nobody even knew the girls were gone until the guys got back from their tour. It was late Monday when they rolled into town in their rented tour bus, horns honking with lots of hullabaloo. For some reason, they always pulled into the high school when they returned to town which they did on this occasion. Maybe it was because they were all athletes and the team bus always did that, too. As they rolled up the street, a caravan of cars pulled in behind them. In a small town, these guys were a big deal so people wanted to see them and hang out for a few minutes. In the line of cars was Esperanza's brother Beto. He asked Jack Franklin where the girls were. Jack told him that they had never showed up at the concert or at the hotel later that night. The band had just figured that they changed their minds and didn't come. Beto showed mild concern, but did not see any cause to worry. He called the families of the other girls and none of them had heard anything but they all agreed that the girls were dependable and would turn up.

By Tuesday morning people were starting to get worried. There had been no word from them and there was a cold knot of fear in the breasts of those who knew and loved Cassie, Pauline, and Esperanza. This was not like them at all. These were three responsible, dependable young people.

The families agreed that they should call the authorities and report them missing. They did that and an investigation was started. It started with the police in the town of Pleasant Valley. They did not have many resources and quickly asked the County Sheriffs Department to assist. As it turned out, over time, the Sheriffs Department took over the investigation. They, in turn, called in the FBI to consult thinking they may have a kidnapping. As time went on and there was no demand for ransom, that idea sort of died on the vine. What was left was a strange, very strange, disappearance. It was as though they had disappeared into thin air.

The Sheriff at the time was one Wilbur Gaston. He was an experienced lawman and as good as any at investigation. There was just nothing to investigate. It was as though as of noon on Friday, a red 1968 Mustang and three young girls disappeared from the face of the earth. They interviewed nearly everyone in town. Nobody could recall seeing the girls after lunch or early afternoon at the latest. They were just gone.

There were all kinds of theories floating around. Some believed they were abducted by aliens. They were sincere about it. How else could they disappear so completely? Good question. Others believed that they were taken by some cult and forced to become wives of cult members. Their car was just hidden in somebody's barn somewhere. Sheriff Gaston was pretty sure that they had searched every barn and vacant building in this and several other counties. They had also checked with every off-the-wall cult and weird religious group they could find. There was just no trace. Some also thought they were grabbed and sold into prostitution. As ugly an idea as that was, it did hold some possibilities. If that were the case, the chances of ever finding them were slim to none. Many believed that they were dead and even tried to have séances to contact their spirits. Finally, after three-plus years of active investigation, the Sheriff's office officially classified it as a cold case and put it on the back burner. After ten years, they closed the file and put it in storage. The storage required one entire ten by ten room for all of the interview files and evidence tagged. It all pointed to nothing. The official position was that the girls had decided to leave town and headed for California and whatever kind of life they could find out there. For forty years the file had laid dormant. For fifty years the mystery had thumbed its nose at the authorities.

Mack Becker had been a twenty-one year old rookie the summer of the disappearance. That is what the case became known as, "The Disappearance". Everyone knew what that meant. Mack Becker never believed that the girls ran away. Girls like that didn't run away. They were all from stable families that loved them. They were honor students and church going kids. Kids like that didn't just run away. One might, but three together wouldn't. Even if they did, they would not go away and never call, write, or return home. Something about this case would just never leave him alone. Now he was seated at his desk looking at the lab report on Cassie Patterson's 1968 Mustang. Finding that car blew lots of theories and opinions clean out of the water.

Sheriff Mack's next task was to find someone to go through this file and see what they had missed before. There had to be something. He wanted fresh eyes. He needed somebody who was not involved in the investigation before, but was familiar with the incident. He thought that he knew just the person.

28

CHAPTER 8

The First String never played another note. They never practiced and never recorded their songs. Something had gone out of them that they just could not get back. For them, it was truly "the day the music died". Mark Bellingham sold a few songs and actually raised enough money to pay for college and law school. The football team made the play-offs, but got knocked out in the second round. They were just proud that they made it that far. Mark went on to college and graduated with a degree in criminal justice. After college, he joined the Marine Corps and trained as a Marine sniper. He served six years in the Marines and was honorably discharged. After the Marines, he worked for one of the three initial agencies of the government. At the ripe old age of thirty-three, having completed a law degree and having passed the bar, he joined the FBI. He had retired a few years before, at the mandatory retirement age of 55. He was now doing consulting and freelance work as a security specialist and private investigator. Business was good and life was comfortable. He and his wife had bought a place on a lake around thirty miles from where they grew up. He had even gotten to the place where he had stopped thinking about the disappearance every day. Sometimes, he went an entire week without it crossing his mind. When he heard the news of the discovery of Cassie's car it was like his heart was torn out all over again. He felt like the eighteen-year old kid who had lost the love of his life and didn't know how or why.

Mark told his wife, Sarah, that he had to go see what was going on. She quickly grabbed a sweater and jumped in the car with him. He said, "You don't have to do this." She replied, "If you are going, I'm going. You should not face this alone. Those girls were my friends, too. Remember?" Mark replied, "Of course I remember. How could I forget? We were all just a bunch of kids who had gone to school together since kindergarten." They drove in silence. The radio was playing softly.

When they arrived at the Patterson place there were lots of cars. Billy was in the front yard; Mark and Sarah got out of the car and walked over to Billy. Billy said, "Mark! I am so glad you are here." Mark replied, "We had to come, Billy. How are you holding up?" Billy responded, "I have to admit that this tore some scabs off that I thought had healed." Sarah hugged Billy and said, "Some wounds never really heal; you just learn to live with the pain." Billy nodded, "I think you are right. Oh! By the way, Jack Franklin and Willy Hill are in the house. You might want to see them." Mark replied, "I would love to; I think I'll go look for them."

As Mark walked toward the house, Sarah stayed with Billy for a while. Billy and Sarah were the same age. In fact, Sarah and Billy's deceased wife had been best friends so there was a bond between Sarah and Billy. Mark stepped into the living room of the house and saw Jack and Willy in conversation across the room. They spotted him at about the same time and headed over to where he was. The three of them embraced like the old friends that they were. They had kept in touch over the years and even talked of playing together again, but nobody had their heart in it. Willy was the first to speak, "Marky! How are you anyhow?" Mark said, "I'm fine. Maybe I'm a little bit in shock, but okay; how about you?" Willy was always the emotional one and had a tear in his eye as he said, "I gotta be honest; this really blindsided me. It was the last thing that I was expecting. In fact, I was not nor ever would have expected it." Jack chimed it, "Yeah, it was a real kick in the head. I had to sit down to avoid falling down when they told me that Billy had found the car. Poor little Billy!" Mark grinned, "He isn't exactly little Billy any more, but I'm sure it was stunning to him when he realized what he had found." Jack said, "Mack told me that when he got down into the marsh, Billy was setting on a mound of ground and didn't look like he had moved since he made the call. He still had his phone in his hand." Willy interjected, "Well, what would you do? Finding that car after fifty years, most of which were spent thinking they were off somewhere in California, rich and famous or whatever!" Mark rejoined, "My years with the FBI did not make be a believer in happy endings. There were a few, but they were not normal. I figured that we would never know anything. Does anybody know how they are going to move forward?" Willy replied, "I think Mack has a plan, but he hasn't shared it with me."

Mark saw Sarah approaching and turned to her. "What's up, Darlin'?" he asked. She replied, "Billy said that Mack Becker would like to talk with you. He will be here in about a half hour. Do you want to wait for him?" Mark replied, "Sure, let's wait. There are lots of people here that I'd like to say 'hi' to anyway, how about you?" She smiled, "Yeah, me too. It's like a reunion in a way."

Sheriff Mack arrived and found Mark Bellingham chatting with old friends. When it was convenient, the two of them broke away for a private conversation. Mack said, "Mark, I don't know how to even begin investigating at this point. Most of the suspects are dead or senile. All of the evidence is in boxes and will take days to sort out and re-inspect. I hear that you have done some cold case work. What should we do?" Mark gave the Sheriff a thoughtful look and said, "What you should do is hire me and a team of people to go through the evidence. I believe the answers are still available. They are probably in those boxes. Our perception of what we see is always tinted by our experience and expectations. A different view point is almost always helpful." Sheriff Mack relaxed, "I was hoping you would say something like that. How much will it cost the County?" "Well, I would give you my friends and family rate," replied Mark. The Sheriff chuckled and said, "Should I be scared?" Mark replied, "I usually get a minimum of $150.00 per hour plus expenses. I'll do this for $50.00. I'll keep the expenses down by calling in personal favors as much as possible. You will probably have to pay the team standard rates because many of them are not retired like me. I have other streams of income, Mack." Mack looked at Mark and said softly, "That's generous of you, Mark." "Let's just say it's personal," Mark said. "When do you want to start?" "Come by my office on Monday. I'll have a contract for you to sign and you can take a look in the evidence room and look over the space we'll have available for you to work. Is that okay?" "That's fine," Mark replied. "See you Monday."

After another hour or so of chatting with old friends, Mark and Sarah headed for home. Mark explained to Sarah that he had accepted an assignment to re-investigate the disappearance. It was probably the coldest case he had ever taken on. She was in agreement. They both agreed that it would be emotionally stressful and that they needed to keep lines of communication open for the duration of the case.

As they were walking toward their car, Mark saw Pastor Fogarty. He asked Sarah, "Isn't that Pastor Fogarty over there?" Sarah looked and replied, "I believe you are right. Let's go say hello to him." "Okay," replied Mark. They had to wait several minutes for Pastor Fogarty to finish the conversation that he was conducting as they walked up. When he was finished Mark greeted him and had to identify himself. Pastor Fogarty was pleased to see him and remarked, "Mark, I don't think that I've seen you since you left Pleasant Valley after graduating college." Mark replied, "No, I guess that it has been that long. You are looking well." The pastor chuckled, "You mean for a man my age, right?" Mark laughed, "No, I didn't mean that. You are just looking well. You must be close to eighty, aren't you, since you brought up age?" The pastor acknowledged that he was seventy nine and holding, as he said. Mark asked, "Do you still pastor the church here in Pleasant Valley?" Pastor Fogarty replied, "No, I left that appointment about five years after the disappearance. I have been here pastoring the Black Creek Community Church for the last forty-some years. We bought a place out on Black Lake." Mark replied, "How about that. We live over there, as well. We bought a place on the lake after retirement." Pastor Fogarty looked surprised, "You are retired already?" "Yes," Mark replied. "FBI has a mandatory retirement age of 55 for field agents. I would have had to take a desk job to stay active and I didn't want to do that." He gave Mark and inquisitive look and asked, "Do you ever play music anymore?" Mark dropped his head and said, "I pick up my guitar now and then, but I have never played with anyone else since the summer of 1968." "That's too bad," the pastor commented. "I recall that you played well. It's too bad to waste such talent." Mark quickly said, "I am so sorry. This is my wife Sarah. You may remember her as Sarah Swainson." "Oh, yes!" He replied. "I do remember. It is so nice to see you again." About that time another parishioner came up and asked the pastor for a moment of his time. "Please excuse me," he said, "I need to deal with this." They said their goodbyes and went their separate ways.

On the drive home, both Mark and Sarah were quiet. Finally Sarah asked Mark, "Are you going to ask Mack to be a part of your cold case team?" Mark grunted and then said, "I think I would have to put him in jail to keep him away. He has never believed the consensus report that was put out back in 1978. He never believed that the girls ran off. He said then that they were not that kind of girls. It looks like he was right. He nearly got his butt kicked off the department because he was so vocal in his dissent over the report. You have to give the guy props. All these years he has carried a torch for some kind of foul play and it looks like he was right. Crazy!" Sarah replied thoughtfully, "He must feel vindicated in a way." "Yeah, maybe," replied Mark. "Mostly I think he is pleased that he finally got what he always wanted, a chance to re-investigate this case. He never really stopped anyway."

CHAPTER 9

Billy Patterson was drunk. He'd been doing that way too much recently. He felt like life just was not fair and truthfully he was right, but it never has been and probably never will be. The discovery of Cassie's car was just too much for his mom. She had held on all the years since the disappearance to the hope that one day the phone would ring and it would be Cassie checking in after all these years. It was unreasonable, but what about this whole mess was reasonable? Lilly Patterson had not been well anyway. It just seemed like all hope went out of her when Billy told her that he had found Cassie's car. Everybody knew what that meant; Lilly just stopped pretending at that moment. She was gone within two days.

It crushed Billy. He felt like, although totally unreasonable, that he had not been able to protect his sister and now he had killed his mother. There was no truth to either feeling, but he felt what he felt and was very drunk as a result. His brothers tried to talk with him, but he wouldn't give them much attention. Beau Bellingham was the only one that could talk him down when he got drunk and belligerent. He did get belligerent. He wanted to take on the world. He fought at the drop of a hat and he would drop the hat.

He was full of anger and aggression. He spent about as much time in jail as he did out. Only the fact that Sheriff Mack understood what was behind the downward spiral shielded him from serious charges and prison. Nobody wanted to press charges and make Billy's pain worse than it already was. Beau had talked Billy into going into a rehab program in order to dry out and get some help. He hated shrinks, but was at a point where he was going to have to accept treatment or prison. He opted for treatment.

He was seated in a comfortable room with a therapist who was trying to get him to talk. Things weren't going really well. Billy was willing to talk about fishing, hunting, baseball, football, or just about anything else except his family. He for damn sure wasn't going to talk about his feelings. Dr. Neely was wishing that Billy would wear a different jacket to their sessions. It wasn't the odor; it was just so unsightly. It looked like blood on it from field dressing game. It seemed like he could wear something more appropriate. Billy was thinking about what a waste of time it was for him to come here. The insurance was footing the bill or Billy would not have agreed to do it.

After a few seemingly wasted efforts at starting a conversation, Dr. Neely asked, "Billy, why do you fight so much?" Billy looked at him with a startled look and grinned, "Because I'm good at it," he replied. "Why do you think you're good at it?" Dr. Neely asked. Billy gave the doctor a sardonic grin and said, "Maybe because I do it so much." That caused both of them to laugh. "Seriously though," the doctor asked, "do you really enjoy fighting?" Billy gave him a long, sad look and said, "No, not really." Dr. Neely tilted his head to one side and asked, "Well, then why in the world do you do it? You have a choice, you know." Billy responded, "I know. It's something that I can control. I have never been beaten in a one on one fight." Dr. Neely gave Billy a long, searching look and recapped, "So what you are saying is in your life where so much is out of your control you fight because that's one thing that you can control. You can predict the outcome?" Billy replied, "Exactly! Maybe that's why the only place I ever really fit into was the Marines." "Maybe," the doctor replied.

Dr. Neely was an experienced psychiatrist, but Billy was a challenge even for him. He wondered what the key might be to helping Billy turn his life around. He asked Billy an off-the-wall question, "Billy, why do you think you have never lost a one-on-one fight? Don't say because you're good at it." Billy thought about the question for a moment and replied, "Maybe it's because I have more bottled up anger than the person I'm fighting, along with being really good at it. I just do not quit. Pain does not affect me because the pain inside is still greater than the pain outside." As he spoke those words, a single tear slid down his cheek into his beard. "If it would make the pain inside go away, I would gladly take a beating," he said sadly. Dr. Neely realized in that moment that Billy had taken a giant step forward. He sat back in a moment of awe. Billy just sat. He had no idea what had just happened. He just knew that for the first time in a very long time he felt better than when he came in to see the doctor. After that day, therapy began to be more productive for Billy.

C H A P T E R   1 0

After Mark Bellingham's meeting with Sheriff Mack, he got really busy with the funeral of Lilly Patterson and other matters. It was a couple of weeks before he was able to assemble the team that he wanted to work on the case of the disappearance of the three girls. Nobody needed to tell him what an uphill fight he had, to figure out what had happened to them. His brother Beau had kept him up on what was going on with Billy. Mark felt badly for Billy, but that was not his problem right now. He had his first team meeting this morning and that was what was on his mind.

There were five of them seated around the table. They were all cold case specialists. The place at the head of the table was open. He walked it and sat down. "Good morning team," he said. "I hope that you have some time, because this case has been around for fifty years and it could take some time to sort it all out. Anybody have any pressing problems?" They all shook their heads. To Mark's immediate left was Willie Parker. Her name was actually Willamina Parker. She was a tall, well put together African American/Native American woman. She had competed in the multiple track and field events and nearly made the Olympic team. She had been an alternate that was never called up to serve. She was an experienced cold case investigator who had a knack for noting things that other people missed. She was Mark's number one choice for reviewing the old files. He was very pleased that she had decided to join the team. She had recently retired from the FBI as well and had not, yet, taken a position with anyone else.

Beside her was Tex Bosley. Tex was short and as inelegant as Willie was elegant. He resembled a toad. He wasn't really fat, but was short and thick. He looked like he didn't have a neck. His eyes were always busy and they missed nothing. He was the best in the world, in Mark's opinion, at analyzing old evidence and making relevant observations. He was there because Willie was there. They were best of friends. Nothing going on there as far as Mark could tell, but they were close. They were secretly known as the "Odd Couple".

At the far end of the table was Quigley J. Crane. He was a bit of a dandy. He always dressed to the nines and spoke with an affected culture. He was a kid from Ohio whose parents ran a hog farm. They did well and sent him to the best of schools where he learned to disdain them because they were so common. Mark did not like him, but admired his ability. He could listen to taped interviews and tell by the voice inflections if people were lying. He was rarely wrong. Everyone called him Jay which he hated. He wanted to be called Quigley J. It was too much. Out of self-respect, people did not give him the satisfaction. When he introduced himself, he would say, "I am Quigley J. Crane. People call me Jay; I prefer Quigley J." Something about the way he said it made one want to default to Jay and let it go. He had an air about him.

On the side of the table opposite Tex was one Victor Villa. Victor was an absolute genius at securing things that were needed. It didn't seem to matter what it was, Victor had a way of finding it. He brought new meaning to the phrase, "I know a guy". Mark was convinced that he knew every guy everywhere. In the nearly twenty years that Mark had known Victor, he had never come up empty. If they were having a hard time getting documents or whatever, somebody would say, "Call Victor." Soon the needed material would be in hand. The other positive fact about Victor's work is that no case had ever been thrown out over his methods of acquisition. Mark could not think of a time that his methods had ever been questioned. It was good that he was on board.

Last, but by no means least, there was Gina Wilson. Gina could organize a roomful of evidence in such a way that she could put her hand on any requested document in a matter of seconds. Nobody knew how she did it and the secret would die with her. He felt like she was an essential element of the team.

Mark said, "Good morning to all of you and welcome aboard." There were mumbled responses and they were off. "I want to introduce you to what I think will be the most challenging case of our lives. It involves the disappearance of three high school senior girls in 1968…"

After the briefing, the team entered the evidence room and all assisted Gina in beginning to lay the file out in whatever way worked for her to be able to do her thing. Mark had worked with her on several cases over the years and still could not figure out what her method was. What looked to him like chaos was her bread and butter. Once the file was set up by her method, they could ask for any document, interview, or whatever and she would produce it in seconds. Rather than stay in hotels, the county had rented a house for the team. It was a big old house with eight bedrooms and six baths. They were only using five of the bedrooms, as Mark was going to stay at home, so they set the file up in one of the spare bedrooms. The other spare bedroom was set up with their computers and communications equipment. After a couple of days, it looked like an FBI operation center writ small. It would work quite well for the team, it was thought.

CHAPTER 11

Mark thought that the first task that they should undertake was to try to establish a time line of the day that the girls disappeared. It was August 13th, 1968. Just reading the date took Mark back. The memories were so vivid. The First String was playing that Friday night in a suburb of Chicago. They were actually expecting the girls to arrive in the afternoon. That had been the plan. When they didn't arrive when expected, the band just thought they had been delayed or decided not to come. Cell phones were not yet invented and communication was more difficult so they really couldn't check to see what happened. The end of tour after-party put thoughts of the girls out of their minds until the next morning.

In the morning when they were loading up to leave for their last date and then home, Willy spoke up and said, "I wonder what happened to the girls? I thought they were coming down last night." "Yeah, me too," replied Jack, "maybe they changed their minds or something happened to Cassie's car." Willy looked at him with slightly bleary eyes and said, "Maybe. What do you think, Mark?" Mark replied, "I don't know. If they don't show sometime today, we'll see them when we get home. It's a bit difficult to get a hold of us. If they don't show up tonight, maybe we can call and find out what happened." In the rush of the final concert of the tour and the after-party, no call had been made. The band arrived at home to find that the girls had just dropped off the edge of the world, or so it seemed.

As they reviewed the file, a timeline began to emerge. It seemed that the girls were seen in town starting at around ten in the morning and did some shopping. They were seen having lunch in the Wascally Wabbit, a local diner and major hang out for high school kids. The place had a Bugs Bunny theme and did a thriving business. Witnesses placed them there having lunch at around twelve thirty until around one fifteen. The conversations were flowing freely and witnesses said that the girls had expressed that they would be leaving for Chicago at around three thirty. Nobody could remember seeing them after lunch. It was like they drove away from the Wascally Wabbit and left the world behind. Those who remembered seeing them leave the diner said that they were heading toward the city limits but had no idea if they had actually left town. That was where the girls disappeared and the speculation began. There was just no verifiable information to place the girls anywhere after they left the diner.

The investigators had done an amazing job of investigating. It looked like they had spoken with every person who had been in town that day. The tapes and transcripts were nearly endless. It was going to be important to scour every transcript and review every tape. Jay had his work cut out for him. Every person interviewed had an alibi that had been verified by at least one person. This was a close town; people noticed each other and were on friendly terms.

It was remarkable that the disappearance drew the people of the town closer together. Things like this often drove people apart and divided communities. These people just could not imagine that anyone in town would hurt those girls. That attitude was probably partly what contributed to the final disposition of the case that the girls had just run off.

After a couple of weeks of reviewing the file, digesting the information, and comparing notes, the team sat down for a formal review. They all agreed that they could not recall a more thorough investigation of a case. They looked at everyone. Every town had its shady characters and this one was no different.

One such person was Phillip Bass. Phil was not a bad guy per se. He was just looked upon with suspicion because he wasn't like everybody else. For one thing he was simple minded. The people of the town would look at each other and grin and circle their ear with their finger as a sign that Phillip just wasn't as smart as they were. Of course, that was way before schools actually specialized in helping the marginally intelligent and mentally disabled. Phil had been left in the dust so he had not graduated high school. He could only work at odd jobs and seasonal work. He didn't drink or spend a lot of money on cars and fancy clothes so he actually did alright working like he did. It did leave him with quite a bit of time on his hands though. As a result, he hung around a local news stand because he loved comic books. When he was a kid, it wasn't a big deal, but in 1968 he was thirty-six and was instantly under suspicion. He had been in the Wascally Wabbit the day that the girls disappeared. He was seen laughing at something one of them said. That really made people suspicious. They thought that he was eaves-dropping. It never occurred to them that he might have just overheard something that amused him. They were sure that he had something to do with the disappearance. It turned out that he had a rock solid alibi. He had spent the afternoon fishing in the river with one of his cousins. His cousin being a very responsible, reliable person; they had to leave poor Phil alone. They grumbled about it though. The whispers were something like, "I mean he is the kind who could do something unpredictable!" "Right?" " I know!" It seemed that nobody tried to explain how one, feeble minded man, would make three healthy teenaged girls disappear without a trace and make a red 1968 Mustang vanish into thin air. It was a preposterous theory, but in 1968, they were grabbing at anything to try to explain and cope with the horror that was the vanishing of three of the town's most precious citizens.

Another suspect was old Frank Persons. Frank was the custodian and handy man that worked as the janitor at the high school. There were other custodians, but Frank was the only black man on staff. It turned out that he did not get the third degree because he and his family were in Pittsburg, where he had grown up, visiting relatives. Mark could remember the venom that people had about Frank until they realized that he wasn't even in the state at the time. No doubt some were ashamed of themselves, but white people didn't apologize for their behavior in 1968. Racism was endemic and acceptable on a certain level. Society has changed, but at the time that's just the way it was.

The team sifted through interview transcripts of over a hundred people who all ended up being alibied out of suspicion. Most of the original suspects were dead by now. The team looked at one another across the table. Mark asked, "Anybody have a comment?" Jay spoke up saying, "It looks like they found everyone who didn't do it. But somebody must have been in town that day that nobody noticed, don't you think?" "Or, somebody is lying," replied Victor. Mark rejoined, "Those do seem like the probabilities. So where do we go from here?" Willie spoke up, "I think that it might be useful to go over all of the physical evidence adding to it what was found in the car. It might reveal something heretofore unnoticed." Mark studied the papers in front of him and finally replied, "That is a good suggestion. I feel like anything else would be spinning our wheels. Let's do it starting first thing Monday morning. Take the weekend off and get some rest. I feel like we have been wearing ourselves out and making no progress. See you Monday. On second thought, everyone is invited to my place tomorrow evening for a cookout. Steaks on the grill sound good?" They all responded positively so it was on the books.

CHAPTER 12

Mark looked over his team on Monday morning. It was only seven o'clock in the morning and they were all there and ready to tackle whatever came at them. Mark and Sarah had gone to church on Sunday. It was the first time that they had been in church in quite a while because they were normally out-of-town on weekends. They had reestablished contact with the Reverend Mr. Fogarty. They had fallen out of the habit of attending church in the past few years. This new project had Mark emotionally raw. Sarah had been very supportive knowing that there were going to be some raw memories coming up as the work progressed. She hoped he would find some comfort in church. If it didn't help, at least it did not hurt.

They had the physical evidence laid out, but there wasn't much. Two of the girls had kept diaries. Both of the diaries had been copied and were laid out on the table. They started reviewing Cassie's personal thoughts. It felt intrusive and rude, but had to be done. Much of her writing was about different boys and what she thought about them. Much of it was not very complimentary. Mark concluded that it was a mercy that we could not read peoples thoughts. A little over a year before the disappearance, she and Willy had started dating. At first it was clear that she just dated him because it was exciting to date a guy in "the band". Her feelings clearly began to change and love began to blossom. It was both beautiful and heartbreaking to read it. It was clear that they had crossed the line from dating to becoming lovers. In fact, in her last entries, she was worried about being pregnant. She was trying to figure out how to break the news to Willy, if there were indeed any news to break. There was nothing in Cassie's diary to even remotely presume that she was thinking about running off. Her major conflict seemed to be if she was going to college or having a baby.

The other diary that they had was Pauline's. Mark was more apprehensive about reviewing this one. He felt that he should tell the team that he and Pauline had been close and that they had been talking about a future together. Mark had not been planning on college because his music career seemed poised to really take off once he had time to really invest in it. In fact, opportunities had presented themselves to him during college to expand musically, but somehow the fire had gone out. He told the team what he had to and tried to move on, but they were curious and started questioning him. Finally, he told them that he had written a few songs that had sold. One had been a number one hit for a friend of his from the old days. When they found out that he had written that song, they treated him differently and he didn't like it. "Look," Mark said, "that was a long time ago and has no bearing on here and now. It was a lifetime ago and a thing that never happened, so, if we could, let's move on. Okay?" They all sat back and relaxed and said a collective, "Okay! Let's get to work."

As they reviewed Pauline's diary Mark was relieved that she was a little more level headed about their relationship. Always practical, Pauline wrote like she thought that her children might someday find and read her diary. That thought caused a stab of pain to Mark's heart. Pauline's diary left no impression that she was about to jump ship to go seek fame and fortune in California.

After about an hour of reading diaries, Tex spoke up and said, "I have no idea where they (speaking of the original investigative team) ever came up with the conclusion that the girls took off for California. There isn't any evidence here that they were even thinking that in their most remote imaginations." Mark replied, "I know that seems to be a reach, but those guys worked this case as an active case for three years and then had a skeleton team on it for seven more. It was a live case for ten years and without the story they finally told, they had nothing. It had to be really tough." Jay shook his head sadly, "They didn't even know the car was five miles away in the marsh. Whoever did this was brilliant or extremely lucky, maybe both." Gina sat there staring through sad eyes and said softly, "Such a waste of youth and beauty!" Everyone agreed. Then Gina looked at Mark and said, "You really loved that girl, didn't you?" Mark smiled, "Yes, I did; inasmuch as an eighteen-year old kid could love, I did. But that was a lifetime ago, Gina. Now we need to figure out what happened to them for the good of all concerned." Willie asked in almost a whisper, "What if we never figure it out?" There was almost a feeling of awe and reverence in the room until Tex busted in with, "Why are we whispering?

This is just another case, isn't it?" Mark said emphatically, "Yes! It is just another case. It's just a very old, very complicated, well investigated and unsolved case. We need to solve it! There has to be something that has been overlooked by the original investigators and by us. Let's go over it again. Let's list every person mentioned in the interviews against the list of persons interviewed and see if we can find someone who slipped through the cracks." Victor said, "That'll take a week!" Mark replied, "Then we had better get started unless you have a better idea."

Over the course of ten days of meticulous reviewing and cataloging of statements and listing names, the team came up with four names of people who had not been interviewed. One was owner of the candy store across from the high school. His name was Wilfred Orell. It turned out that he died during the investigation before anyone could get around to talking to him. Everyone was asked not to leave town, but exceptions did have to be made occasionally. The second was a lady by the name of Wendy Jones. She lived across from the high school and for some reason she had not been interviewed. She too, was long since gone and could not be interviewed. The third person was one Elliot Fogarty. He was the new pastor in town in 1967. He was just out of seminary and in his mid-twenties at the time. Mark explained to the team that Pastor Fogarty was the same one who was pastoring the church where he and his wife had gone on Sunday. He had been the pastor of the local church where two of the three girls attended and participated. He lived a few towns over, but he was still in the vicinity and still alive. Mark said that he would make contact and set up an interview. The fourth person who was mentioned, but never interviewed was Mrs. Appleton, the music teacher. Mark remembered her very well. She had been their music mentor and friend. He remembered that her husband, a Marine Captain, had been killed in Vietnam. He couldn't remember exactly when, but it was while he was still taking private music lessons with her. That was a long time ago. Sometimes it seemed like a quick look in the rear-view mirror, though. Sometimes memories were so indistinct and fuzzy and sometimes they were so vivid. It's funny how that works.

Mark remembered reading somewhere in the file that Abigail Appleton had been out of town over the weekend. He asked Gina to locate that document which she did in a matter of seconds. It seemed that one of the investigative team had interviewed Mrs. Appleton and she had stated that she was out of town that weekend. She had gone to visit her grandparents who lived a couple of hours to the west. The note said that her alibi was confirmed but did not say how. The person signing the report was Deputy Mack Becker.

CHAPTER 13

Mark was sitting in the foyer of the church waiting for Pastor Fogarty to get free. He had asked him to block out at least an hour, if possible. The pastor had promised to do his best. Within about fifteen minutes, the receptionist/secretary asked Mark to go on in. The pastor was quite cordial, but that was his stock it trade. Mark couldn't tell offhand if it was his professionalism or if he really was that warm person that he projected.

Pastor Fogarty walked into the room with his right hand extended and a big smile on his face. He certainly looked sincere. "Good morning, Mark," he said, "it's nice to see you again so soon. What brings you here?" Mark replied, "Good morning, Pastor Fogarty. I have to tell you that this is not a social call. I have some rather unpleasant business with you." The pastor frowned, "What kind of unpleasant business?" Mark said, "Well, you, may or may not have heard, but since the discovery of Cassie Patterson's car in the Patterson Lake marsh, I have been hired by the county and state to re-investigate the disappearance of those three girls fifty years ago. We're now looking at it as a homicide more than a mysterious disappearance, since it would be highly unlikely for three people to disappear while their car remained here." Pastor Fogarty said thoughtfully, "I see what you mean, but why talk to me?" "We have gone over the file five or six times since starting the work. The last time through, we listed every name mentioned by any witness and cross-referenced to see if anyone had not been interviewed. Your name came up along with a couple of others," replied Mark. The pastor looked at Mark quizzically and asked, "Looking for a missing piece?" Mark smiled and replied, "That is exactly right! It's not that you are a suspect, but you were not interviewed and we have no suspects. We'd like to know what you remember even though it has been a long, long time ago. Do you have time for an interview?" "I guess I do," said Pastor Fogarty, "Should I have an attorney present?" "You have that right," replied Mark, "but this is more an effort to find something that may have been missed the first time around." "It's fine." said the Pastor, "Let's do it." "Great!" replied Mark, "Please just let me set up my recorder." After setting the recorder, Mark started, "This is Mark Bellingham interviewing Elliot Fogarty in reference to an incident that occurred on or about the 13th of August, 1968..."

"It had been a real hot spell even for August. Tempers were a bit frayed from several days of excessively hot weather. I remember because back then, the church was not air conditioned. During those times there was a Friday morning Bible Study group in the fellowship hall. It was a ladies' Bible Study and was led by Karen Brown, who was long since passed. The Bible Study broke up at around eleven-thirty and most of the ladies left. Jenny Albert and Sandra Smith stayed to help get the music ready for Sunday. We were there working on that until around twelve-fifteen. When they left, I drove to town to grab a quick lunch. I stopped by the Wascally Wabbit for a bowl of chili. The girls were in there finishing up their lunch. In fact, they left while I was still in there. They were planning on heading for Chicago soon after lunch. I overheard them telling their friends. They waved at me as they left. Two of them were part of our congregation. Cassie and Pauline both attended the church in Pleasant Valley since they were children. I guess that I didn't know them all that well; I'd been their pastor for less than a year. I arrived here in November of 1967. They had always been very active until a few months before they disappeared. They had starting drifting away a little, but still were there on Sunday mornings."

Pastor Fogarty continued, "For your information, I got married along the way. My wife Cheryl has been with me for over forty years now. She started coming to church about a year after the girls disappeared. She involved herself in the music program and other church activities. We began dating and about a year later, we were married. She has been a great help to me. In fact, she directs the choir here at Black Lake. She is really a fine musician. You know sometimes churches don't have a lot to work with in terms of talent for a choir. Cheryl always manages to bring out the best in the singers. It's a wonderful talent. Mark replied, "I knew someone like that once."

Mark asked the pastor, "Did you see the girls after lunch?" Pastor Fogarty replied, "Actually, I did. Well I didn't actually see them, but when I drove past the school on my way out to see Jason Black, I saw the Mustang at the high school." Mark felt a bit of a rise of excitement. This was the first new information in fifty years on the subject. Mark followed up, "About what time was that; do you remember?" "Yes, I do," replied the pastor. "It was just a couple of minutes before two o'clock. I was supposed to meet Jason at two fifteen and was congratulating myself on the fact that I was going to be on time." Mark asked, "Were there any other cars around the school?" The pastor replied, "I do not remember seeing any other cars around at that time." Mark started to ask about the school being open, but remembered that the school was often open during the day. The three girls were all honor students and honors band members so would have had access and nobody would have thought anything of them being there. He thanked Pastor Fogarty and ended the interview. After a bit more small talk, Mark took off. He realized that except for the person who killed them (he was openly regarding this as a homicide now) Pastor Fogarty was probably the last person to see any sign of the girls.

As Mark drove back to the investigation headquarters, he pondered the fact that the only new person that he knew of that he needed to interview was Mrs. Appleton. He wondered if she were still around or had left the area. He would have to see if he could locate her. Mark remembered her as being the kind of person that could light up a room with their personality. She was bright, vivacious, and always fun. Well, almost always. He recalled when the news came that her husband had been killed in action in Vietnam. It was a big deal. The entire town rallied around Mrs. Appleton, Abby, as she was known to her friends and peers. Mark remembered her coaching of the band and how helpful her ideas were. Mrs. Appleton was part of the reason Mark and his fellow band members had come to love music so much. She helped them learn to play, but also inspired them to create. His memories of her were always good. She had been very supportive when Pauline disappeared. She kept saying everything would be all right and that time would ease the pain. She was right. He didn't forget, but the searing pain eventually became a dull ache. Now, fifty years later, it was an occasional stab like arthritis that flared up now and then, but mostly didn't hurt any more. Maybe it was more like the thing that someone said long ago. The pain of the loss does not go away; you just get used to it after a while. Mark didn't know which it was, but felt there was truth in most of what people said. Anyway, Mrs. Appleton had helped him through a very tough time in his life. Mark hoped they would be able to locate her and get the interview, but he was also looking forward to reconnecting.

CHAPTER 14

On the way back to the office, Mark stopped at the Wascally Wabbit for some lunch. He was hungry. When he walked in he was struck by the fact it felt like a time warp. It was as though nothing had changed. It looked exactly as it did fifty years ago. He had heard that the place had been renovated and figured that they updated the décor. That was most assuredly not the case.

When he walked in, he was greeted by people whom he had known as a kid. It made him feel like a kid again. Jack Franklin waved from the back and indicated that Mark should join him which he did. They talked about old times and the people that they had known. Some of them were passing on. Jack commented on the fact that they were now the older generation. Mark laughed at how absurd it felt although true. Jack and Mark had always been close. They had gone to school together since kindergarten. They had played on the same sports teams and competed against each other for positions and records. Mark was the quarterback; Jack was the point guard. That was the way it seemed to go with them. There was true affection between them. Then there was the fact that, if things had gone as planned, they would have been brothers-in-law. Mark and Pauline were pretty sure that they were destined to be together. Life had thrown a monkey wrench into those plans, however.

Jack was about halfway through one of the Wascally Wabbit's famous hamburgers. They were mammoth and delicious. Jack looked as though he may have ingested a few too many of them over the years. Mark ordered a bowl of the soup de jour which was a cheesy potato. If it was as good as it used to be, it would be great. It had always been one of Mark's favorites. Jack asked, "How's the investigation going?" Mark replied, "While unable to provide specifics, I can say that we are making progress. We have managed to dredge up some new information and we are still digging through what the car may tell us. We're hopeful that we'll be able to find a suspect. The chances of them being alive after all this time are very slim, but we'll keep looking." Jack stared at him, "I'm amazed that there could be any new information to be found after all these years and after the first investigation." Mark rejoined, "That was one of the most thorough investigations that I have ever reviewed. It was clear that the head detective and his team took it seriously and personally. Having said that, you'd be amazed at what is still there. Also, modern forensic techniques allow us to look at things that they had no ability to even think about knowing." Mark knew that would be true if they generated any physical evidence. That had been woefully in short supply since the beginning of this investigation. Jack, who had finished his lunch and was preparing to leave, said, "Well, keep me posted." Mark grinned at him and said, "You can read about it in the papers." That was a line from a play that they had done in high school that had become like a catch phrase. Jack looked shocked and then started laughing, "You remembered the old days!" Mark replied, "I have forgotten nothing." They parted laughing, but there was a hidden meaning in Mark's parting quip. This investigation was tearing the hide off old scars. Sometimes he felt like he was stepping on a grave.

CHAPTER 15

When Mark arrived back at the office, he sought out Victor. "Hey, Victor, I need for you to do a deep dive on some people for me." "Okay," he replied, "who might they be? Mark said, "I would like a background on all of the school employees from fifty years ago. Focus on those still living, but don't overlook the deceased. The dead may yet speak to us." "That's a large order," said Victor. "That's why I gave it to you!" replied Mark, "I would like weekly progress reports, please." Mark then sat down with Jay, handing him the interview for voice analysis and transcription.

Willie and Tex were in the office reviewing the data on the car. Mark asked them, "Is there anything remarkable about the evidence taken from the car?" Tex looked at him and said, "There is quite a bit of stuff to analyze. I'm not sure what it might tell us, but we're going over every piece individually." Mark replied, "I know one thing for sure; if there is anything worthy of note, you guys will find it." Willie looked up with one of her half-smiles and said, "I'm glad you are confident. This is one of the most difficult cases that I can remember. The first investigation was remarkably good. In fact, they left no stone unturned that I can see. Clearly they missed something, but we're missing it, too, and we're pretty good at what we do." "Just the best is all," Mark replied. "Maybe next week, we'll take the time to go over the car ourselves. If the forensic team has done all that they are going to do, maybe we should take a crack at it. I'm not thinking that we are better than them, but I remember that car. Maybe I'll get some of the old crowd to go over it and see if there's something out of place or whatever. It would take only one anomaly that others missed to turn this case. Let's think about that." "Sure thing, Boss," Tex replied, "I don't see what it could hurt, as long as they don't touch anything."

Mark decided to knock off early since it was Friday afternoon. He drove home to find Sarah working in her flower garden. He gave her a hug and kiss then asked, "Could I interest you in some dinner?" She looked at him with an arched brow and asked, "What do you have in mind?" He smile into her eyes and said, "I was thinking Italian. What do you think?" She answered, "That sounds delicious to me; are you in a hurry?" "No, take your time," he replied. "There's no big rush." Sarah gave him a big hug and said, "Gimme a half hour." "You've got it," he replied. She went into the bathroom and he sat down on the porch swing to enjoy the late afternoon air. While he was waiting the phone rang and it was Jay. "What's up, Jay?" Mark asked. Jay said, "I have just finished reviewing the pastor's interview and I feel like he's hiding something. Something doesn't ring true." Mark replied, "Do you suspect him?" Jay came back with, "I don't know what to do with it, yet. It's more like he's hiding information that he doesn't want people to know, but I don't know." Mark replied, "Jay, the recording is being transcribed. Once that is done, please mark the areas on the transcript that raise suspicion so that I can review them. I would very much like to review them as soon as possible. Are you okay with that?" "Sure, no problem. See you Monday." "See you then," Mark replied.

Dinner was great. Mark could feel himself relaxing. After dinner Mark and Sarah walked along the river, as the restaurant was close to it. When they got home, Mark turned his phone off and they went to bed. The next morning while they were sipping their first cup of coffee, Mark told his wife, "I'd like to go to church tomorrow, if you don't mind." She replied, "That's fine with me. Is there any particular reason why you suddenly want to go to church?" "Well, yes," Mark replied, "there is. We found out that there were only two people even mentioned in the original investigation who had not been interviewed. One was the pastor of the church in town at the time. He is none other than Pastor Fogarty, who now pastors here in our town. I interviewed him yesterday and Jay reviewed the recording and feels like he has been less than forthcoming about something." "Do you think that he did it?" she asked. "I don't know what to think to tell you the truth, but I'm not going to name a suspect, yet. I'd just like to observe him." "Let's do it!" Sarah replied. Mark cautioned her, "We have to be careful not to tip our hand. He cannot suspect that we are watching him. We don't want to put him on his guard." "Right!" she said. "Just be normal."

Church was uneventful. The sermon was unmemorable. The music was remarkably good, though. The choir director was a lady that neither one of them recognized. They had never really gotten a good look at her, since she was always up front and they sat near the back of the fairly large church. She had a remarkable knack for bringing music out of people. The choir was unusually good for a local church in a small town. He had meant to try to greet her and compliment her on the music, but in the crowd at the end of the service, the opportunity never presented itself.

CHAPTER 16

Mark spent the afternoon on the porch reading and dozing. He was remembering how it was in 1968 and 1969. The political world was in turmoil; America was a nation fighting a very unpopular war. Kids were declaring their freedom to do as they pleased. Women were trying to liberate themselves. Husbands and fathers were trying to figure out how to deal with the changes taking place. It was a time of upheaval. It seemed like the American culture was in upheaval and nobody seemed to know how it would work out. Some were predicting the end of the world and others were trying to usher in a communist utopia.

The civil rights movement was in full swing. Young people were dropping out. They were rejecting the materialism that they saw strangling the life out of their families. The drive to have the latest and best was tearing families apart as mothers were going to work full-time in order to afford the things that were supposed to make leisure time special, but there was not leisure time because they were working so much. Kids were coming home from school to an empty house. Kids were experimenting with booze and drugs. Hair got longer; clothing styles more casual and sloppy. Hippies were everywhere. Drugs were flowing freely and in the middle of it all was a generation of kids trying to grow up in a world caught in a culture clash.

The First String really believed that they had it all figured out. They saw themselves as rising stars in the music world. Mark now realized that as fast as the music scene changed, that the chances of them coming back after their senior year were much slimmer than they had thought at the time. It was his thinking that the record label had made them a bunch of promises because they didn't want them to jump ship to another label. As it turned out, none of that mattered.

Pauline Franklin was a beautiful girl with blond hair and laughing green eyes. She was intelligent, but was also a hard worker who applied herself to study. She was an honor student. She was a year younger than her brother Jack and his two best friends, Mark and Willy. She was almost always around when they were hanging out at the house or the Wascally Wabbit. She was with her own friends, but always around. It was natural that she would catch the eye of the guys. She was beautiful with a body that would catch the boys' attentions. She was a cheerleader, played flute in the band and orchestra, sang in the choir in school and church. She was a good, all-around American girl.

She and Mark were friends before he and Pauline ever dated. They couldn't remember when they fell in love. They had been together in so many situations. Mark was in the band and high school choir. When Jack, Willy, and Mark started playing music together in the sixth grade, she was around for many of the jam sessions. She was there when they started playing Mark's compositions and she was very impressed and proud. They were often together at the Wascally Wabbit just because their groups came together so often. Then Mark asked her to go to a movie with him. She said a slightly flippant, partly serious "Okay" and it began. She was fifteen when they started dating.

Over the next two years, they were pretty much inseparable. That is not to say that they spent every waking hour together. It is more to say that they were "going steady" within a few months of starting and neither one of them was looking any further for someone to love. They thought that they had found it. After Prom, their junior year, they consummated their love and were as committed to each other as two high school kids could be. They were careful to avoid pregnancy as both had plans before marriage. Pauline was going to college and Mark was hitting the road with the First String. The road ahead looked perfect from where they stood the summer of 1968.

Cassie was not so fortunate. She and Willy Hill had started going together since just before Prom. Willy had asked her out and she accepted. They knew each other because Willy and her brother Peter were friends, but they didn't do sleep-overs and stuff like that. In 1968, that was mainly a chick thing. Cassie and Willy hit it off right away. They went to Prom together and had a great time. The chemistry between them was noticeable. They were soon sexually active; very active. It seemed like they were going at it whenever and wherever they could without getting caught. Their unbridled passion resulted in Cassie missing a period. She was pregnant, but not showing yet. In fact, she hadn't told Willy. The only other person who knew was Pauline who was sworn to secrecy. Cassie was not sure how she was going to break the news to Willy and then her family. Telling her daddy would be the toughest part. She was really dreading that. Were it not for finding Cassie's diary, nobody would have ever known that she was pregnant.

Esperanza was the third oldest of six children of their parents Manuel and Rosa Chavez. When she was small, they spoke almost exclusively Spanish at home. When she was in the fourth grade, she came home insisting on speaking English. She told her mother, "Mami, if you are going to learn to speak English, you have to practice. You have to watch American TV and speak English at home." Manuel agreed so they started speaking English at home to the extent that the youngest of the children hardly knew any Spanish. They were convinced that their future was in the USA so felt it a small price to pay. They did not lose their food culture. The Chaves house was legendary for the great tacos, enchiladas, tamales, caldo de rez, and de pollo.

Esperanza wanted to be a pediatrician and had the brains to do it. She was an honors student in the honors classes. She and Jack Patterson had recently started dating. She was still a virgin and intended to remain that way until marriage. Jack was accepting of her choice. He was constantly stunned by her beauty and grace. She was the most beautiful girl he had ever seen including the movie stars. None of them could hold a candle to her in his opinion. The truth was that even though his vision was filtered by a deep love for her, he was not wrong. She was an exceptionally beautiful girl. He felt so lucky that she would date him. Jack got along great with her family. They all loved him. He and her dad worked on cars together.

Jack was a bit of a wizard, mechanically. He could fix anything and there were lots of things around the Chaves household that needed fixing. With so many children, money was always short so Jack made a great impression. In fact, a man that owed her dad money had given him a pick-up truck that he said needed a new engine. He owed her dad a couple of hundred dollars. They were so excited when Jack looked it over and found that the vehicle would be serviceable with a fairly minor repair. He was going to finish the repair as soon as the band got back from tour on Monday.

Sarah came out onto the porch and found Mark dozing. The sound of her settling herself into the porch swing roused Mark from his nap. They smiled at each other and Sarah asked, "Hungry? There are cold cuts and left-overs. Grab whatever you want." Mark replied, "I'll eat in a few minutes. Let's just sit here together for a few minutes." Sarah looked at him and asked, "Is this case bringing up a lot of old pain?" Mark made a rueful face and said, "It really doesn't feel like old pain. It still feels pretty fresh. I'm forced to go over stuff that I haven't thought about in this detail for many years. It is not easy to handle." "No," she replied, "I'm sure that it isn't. I was a freshman at the start of the fall in 1968. I remember that year so clearly." Mark said, "I thought that I had finally gotten over it. Sometimes I wish Billy had never found that car!" Sarah nodded, "Me, too!" She whispered. They sat a few more minutes nursing their private thoughts and then Mark wandered into the kitchen to find something to eat.

CHAPTER 17

As Mark drove to the office on Monday morning, he noticed the town. In 1968 it had been a busy place. All of the main street businesses were thriving. There was a new area of business developing out on the highway north of town and things were booming. There had been three car dealerships, two hardware stores, a furniture store, three or four drug stores, five or six restaurants on main street, plus a busy bar and grill out on the highway. He remembered the old downtown hotel and bar that had been there forever. His grandfather remembered having a beer in the old bar after World War I. The main street was packed with small businesses that were thriving on the backs of the other larger businesses and a couple of small factories in the area. The local farmers were thriving. People drove to other cities around the area to work in the larger factories making all kinds of things. Gas cost around twenty-five cents per gallon then. The town seemed to be always busy with traffic and noise.

Fast forward to 2018 and the town was quiet on a Monday morning. There were a few cars on the streets, but not many. Many of the main street buildings were empty and deteriorating. Some of them had apartments in the upstairs which was the only reason why they had not been torn down. If given time and more of the apparent inattention they were presently getting, they would likely fall down. The town was not at all what it had been when Mark grew up here. It made him feel a little sad. Life was like that, though. Time changed everything. Economic priorities and fiscal realities built towns, roads, and bridges. The changing economic realities brought about the deterioration of one in order to give birth to another. Just like people, civilizations were born with an expiration date. Mark guessed his little hometown was not expiring just yet, but was certainly well past its prime. Again, he wished that Billy had never found that car. In some ways it would have been better to leave things as they were. Once the car was found, though, the law dog in Mark and others made them need to know the truth.

When Mark arrived at the office, Sheriff Mack was there waiting for him. Mack apologized, "Sorry, Mark, I should have made an appointment, but it seemed like such a formality." Mark shook Mack's hand and said, "Mack, you don't ever need to make an appointment to see me. I will be available to you unless it is just impossible. What's up?" Mack looked at Mark with a rueful expression and said, "I was shocked to discover that we missed anything in the original investigation. We thought that we were really thorough." Mark replied, "You were very thorough! It took a lot of digging to find the two people that had not been interviewed. The only reason we noticed is that we were searching for something that was missing or out of place, and that was all we found. It was one of the most complete investigations that I have reviewed in my career." Mack sat back, "Well, that makes me feel somewhat better. Do you think anything will come of it?" "I don't know," replied Mark. "I have interviewed the preacher and nothing that he has said leads us anywhere on the face of it. My voice inflections specialist has advised that he has some reservations about the pastor's statement. He is going to give me a report this morning to show the areas where he thinks the subject may be evading a direct answer. It could mean nothing. In fact, at this point in time, we would have to be very lucky to find anything that would be significant." Mack nodded, "You are right about that. I just feel like we missed something the first time through. I really hope we get it right this time." "Yeah, me too," agreed Mark. Mack looked at Mark almost apologetically and said, "I need to tell you something and I hope you don't think I'm crazy." "I can't promise you what I will think, but I promise not say so even if I think it," replied Mark with a reassuring smile. Mack replied, "I have had this dream that has recurred over the past forty seven years. In it, the girls are sitting in Cassie's Mustang in front of the school. Cassie and Pauline are just sitting there, but Esperanza is looking at me and saying, 'Help us'. I can't hear her, but I can read her lips. That is why I have never believed that they ran off. The dream has never gone away." Mark leaned back in his chair and picked up his coffee cup. It was cold. "Mack, did you ever tell anyone about this? Because that is quite bizarre," Mark replied. Mack said, "No, I didn't want people to think I had lost my mind. Also, I was a rookie deputy the year of the disappearance. Who would have listened? It would have just caused problems." Mark agreed, "You are probably right about that. With the Sheriff retiring in 1971, he just wanted to clear his docket so he came up with the runaway theory so he could close his file." Mack thought for a moment and then said, "He talked himself into believing it and then talked others into believing it. Some of the families even agreed that that must be what happened. The Patterson boys never agreed. Peter went to California and made his fame and fortune, but he never stopped looking for the girls. He called me every month for twenty years. He still calls about every six months. He's still looking. Billy never believed it either. He says his sister would never leave him like that. One of the bonds that Billy and I have shared over the years is that neither one of us ever believed that they ran away. Still don't." Mark dropped his head for a long moment and then looked Mack in the eye and said, "It looks like you were right and for the record, I do not think you are crazy. Your instincts seem to be right on. Maybe Esperanza is communicating with you because she felt she could trust you. There is much we don't know. I have seen too many strange things happen in life to discount anything." Mack replied gruffly, "Thanks, Mark. That means a lot coming from you." They said their goodbyes and Mark got himself a fresh cup of coffee.

The rest of the team started filtering in with all of the earmarks of a Monday morning. Mark couldn't help but chuckle a bit. The last one to walk in was Willie at exactly eight o'clock. These people were not accustomed to showing up late and they did not today. Mark called them together for a team meeting.

"Does anybody have anything new this morning?" he asked. Nobody had anything new. "I think we need to figure out ways to broaden our search," Mark stated. "What are you suggesting?" Tex asked, with a Monday morning attitude. "Tex," Mark replied, "did you get drunk this weekend?" Tex eyed him suspiciously and growled, "Why do you ask?" "We have known each other for a long time, Tex," Mark replied, "and I know what you do when you think you've hit a wall. We're not ready for that, yet." "Okay, " Tex mumbled, "I'll keep it dry from now on until we crack this thing." "So you were drunk," Mark said with a grin. Tex shrugged, "You caught me. What are you suggesting?"

"We have tried to run down all of the adults that were in town. What about kids. There is no reference in the file to any conversations with kids. I'd like to canvass people who would have been seven to fourteen-years old at the time of the disappearance. What do you think?" said Mark. Victor mused, "That could potentially bring in a bunch of new information. Kids often get overlooked because they often don't talk about what they have seen unless they are asked. How would we go about it?" "What do you think?" Mark asked. Willie spoke up, "We should probably run a request on TV news, radio news, and other media such as Facebook, Twitter, and the like. Do you think that would work?" Mark responded, "What would we say to catch the reticent outlier?"

As the meeting was breaking up, Mark looked at Victor and asked, "Vic, how is the progress on the deep dive into school employees?" "I have started," Vic replied," but this is going to take some time. All of the records have long since been archived. Some places are cooperating in digging the paperwork out, but some are telling me that I will have to come and go through the files myself. If I do that, I will need some help." Mark nodded, "Thanks for the update. If you need someone to go through files with you get with me and we'll set up a team. I'll go, if I can. If not, we'll get someone on the team to help out."

CHAPTER 18

Mark asked Jay to meet with him and he came in and sat down in one of the office chairs. "Jay," said Mark, " I am interested in why you think the pastor is hiding something. It seems a bit strange to me that he would have anything to hide." Jay replied, "Well, most of the questions brought very matter of fact responses from him. I don't think he knows anything for sure. It's like he suspects something, but didn't want to say it." Mark scowled in thought and said, "I wonder what that might be. Pastors hear things and they have immunity from divulging confessions even though they are not Catholic. It could be something like that. What do you think?" "I think that you are most likely right," replied Jay. "At any rate, I don't think that this is the time to raise his suspicions by going back for clarification at this time. I would be more comfortable if we continue to pursue the new leads that we have and see what comes of them. Also, I like the idea of asking a general question of the public to see if anyone saw anything that was not gleaned in the initial investigation. Kids often see and overhear things that at the time do not seem significant. The kids get overlooked. Maybe we can stir up something from those who were kids at the time." Mark replied, "That's a good idea."

When Jay had left his office, Mark sat back in his chair. As he sat, his mind went back to the events of his younger years. He remembered how Willy, Jack, and he, had been literally inseparable as kids. They took the same classes, played the same sports, and liked the same cars. They had graduated from bicycles to mini bikes to dirt bikes to cars, together. They had discovered their mutual love for music when rock and roll really took off. They played hard, worked hard, and dreamed big. They did not think about the hardships of getting there; they just assumed that they would be successful. They thought that they were well on their way to that perfect life they imagined for themselves.

The first big hitch in their perfect town, perfect life, came when Marine Captain Appleton was reported killed in action. Their beloved music teacher was distraught. His death occurred while school was closed for the summer of 1967. The students all rallied around Mrs. Appleton. Nearly the entire town attended the funeral. They had to hold it at the football field. There was no auditorium in town large enough for it. None of the townsfolk knew Captain Appleton, but they knew and loved their young music teacher. They went all out so that she could feel the support of her students and colleagues. The 1967-68 school year was tough. Several times students would find Mrs. Appleton crying alone. They always tried to comfort her but there was only so much they could do.

As time went by, things got better, but they were never the same after that. Mark remembered the day that he had found Mrs. Appleton crying alone after school. He wrapped his arms around her to try bringing her some comfort. As he held her tight, something changed. He couldn't really identify the moment, but there was suddenly something sensual in the embrace. They both felt it. He wondered what he should do. He looked into her eyes and saw acceptance so he did not move away. Things were never quite the same after that.

Mark called Mack to see if he wanted to collaborate on a public appeal for information. Mack's attitude was that they had done everything they could do back during the original investigation. He acted a bit irritated as though the new team was second guessing the original work. Mark assured him that they were just looking for any loose ends that might be left hanging. Mack finally said, "Well, then knock yourselves out!" and hung up. Mark was sorry that Mack was taking such an attitude but deep down inside, he didn't blame him. Even though the original investigation was not Mack's, he had been involved and appeared to be taking it quite personally. Mark decided to try to keep Mack more in the loop. He sent him an email inviting him to their morning report/skull sessions each morning at nine o'clock.

Mark then headed for lunch. He drove to a local bar and grill that had not existed back in 1968. It was called Barney's and was reputed to have good food. When he walked in, he saw Willy and Jack at a table in the back. They waved at him so he walked back and joined them. Mark asked, "May I join you?" They gave him a disgusted look. "You have to ask that?" they said together and they all started laughing. When they were young they had been so close that they often finished sentences for one another. They looked around the table at one another and started laughing again. It was almost like old times. Then there was silence. Willy spoke up asking, "Do you guys ever get your instruments out and play?"

Jack replied, "I still have my drum kit and yeah, I hit it now and then." They both looked at Mark. He dropped his head and looked up at them, "When I retired, I started getting the old Stratocaster out and working it some." The others were amazed. "You still have that old beauty?" Willie asked. Mark grinned, "Yes, I do. I would never willingly part with the old girl." "Do you have a name for her?" asked Jack. "Well, not officially, but although I have never said it out loud, I do," replied Mark. "Tell us!" they both demanded. Mark said, "Suffice it to say I just think of her as Miss P." Saying it out loud for the first time in his life caused him more pain than he expected. He was silent for a moment trying to corral his emotions. Then he said, "First love, you know."

As they ate their lunch together, they talked of many things that had happened during their growing up years and in the intervening years. Some they had shared some they had just heard about. Then Willy asked, "Do you guys remember the old fishing hole down on the river?" Both Jack and Mark affirmed that they remembered it. They had discovered it when they were in the sixth grade. They had made a pact to never share the spot with anyone else. It was their special fishing spot. Mark, Jack, and Willy were often referred to as "The Three Musketeers" or "The Three Stooges" and on occasion "The Three Blind Mice", depending on the situation. They were almost always together and were notorious for their pranks on each other and nearly anybody else in town. They were really harmless and they never really hurt anybody although they pissed a few people off over the years. Most of their antics were things that people laughed over now.

Willy asked, "Did either one of you guys ever tell anyone about the old fishing hole? "Not me," replied Mark. "Me neither," replied Jack. "Still our little secret," stated Willy. "That is really something. All these years and nobody but us knows about it. We sure had a lot of fun down there, though, didn't we?" "We sure did!" the others agreed. "We should get ourselves into a flat bottomed boat and see if the small mouth bass still like to hide in that old hole." They all agreed that it would be great to do it again.

Mark looked down at the empty plate in front of him and said, "It's time for me to get back to the office. I have work to do." Willy looked at him questioningly, "How's it going, Mark?" he asked. "Well, believe it or not we are actually developing some new leads. We have found a couple of people that the original investigators did not interview and are in the process of locating them and interviewing them. We are also going to try to find out if there were any kids from that time who saw something and just didn't come forward or felt that nobody would listen to them." Jack raised his eyebrows, "You have really become good at what you do, haven't you? That's really a good idea. Have you thought of using hypnosis to bring out repressed memories?" Mark replied, "We haven't done that, yet. Hypnosis is not always really reliable, but in extreme cases you do what you have to. This case could become extreme, if we don't develop something positive soon." Mark stood to his feet and said, "Gotta go. I have enjoyed myself more than I knew that I could. You guys are good medicine for me." Willy looked him with almost pleading eyes and said, "Do you think that you would ever consider playing again?" Mark looked at Willy and then at Jack and realized that these guys had talked about this. "I don't know," Mark said, "I would like to do it sometime, but can't seem to make myself do it. I'll tell you what I'll promise you. If we actually crack this case and find out what happened, I will break out Miss P and we'll go at it, if you still want to; fair enough?" Mark saw the old light in their eyes and they both responded with a hug, but no words. There really were no words. They just said, "Oh Man! Oh Man!"

CHAPTER 19

Days passed into weeks and weeks into months and it seemed like they weren't making any meaningful progress on the case. Their appeal asking anyone who had seen anything coming forward just had not born fruit. Mark still needed to speak with Abigail Appleton. He wasn't really putting it off, but he did have some misgivings about doing the interview. They had been so close so many years ago and it might make it difficult to be objective. He was thinking about having somebody else handle the interview. She had been their music teacher, mentor in making First String a reality, as well as the girls cheerleading coach and sponsor. Mark called Willie into the office and asked her if she would handle the interview. She agreed to do it so he left it with her to do it on her own schedule.

The holiday season was soon upon them. Mid-November was nearly upon them. Mark decided to give his team the option of taking six weeks off to include Thanksgiving and Christmas through New Year's Day. They would meet back in the office on the first Monday after the New Year. Everyone could use a break. They were the kind of people who invested themselves in their work and took it personally when they could not solve a case. They were not accustomed to being stymied on a case, at least not for long.

Mark managed to work in a couple of days of deer hunting. Billy had invited him to go with him and Mark had accepted. They bagged a couple of bucks and had a great time. Billy asked Mark how things were going and Mark was very frank with him. "Billy," he said, "we have hit a wall. We are going to interview Abigail Appleton. She's not a suspect, but we noticed that she was never interviewed like everyone else was after the disappearance." Billy gave Mark a funny look and said, "You didn't know?" "Didn't I know what?" Mark asked. "Since she married the preacher, she has started calling herself Cheryl. I guess it is her middle name. She doesn't go by Abigail anymore." "Really!" replied Mark, "I didn't know that she was still around. I never heard that she had married the preacher, not that it was any of my business. We just lost touch after… you know." "Well," replied Billy, "when she married the preacher she started calling herself Cheryl. Her full name was Abigail Cheryl Jenson Appleton. She quit teaching once she married the pastor. After a few years, they moved over to the church they're pastoring now in the town where you live." Mark didn't think anything could surprise him anymore, but that did. He was quiet for long enough that Billy asked him, "Are you okay?" Mark replied, "Yeah, I'm fine. That just took me by surprise. It's curious that she would change her name, don't you think?" "I never really thought about it. Do you think it's important?" asked Billy. "I mean," said Mark, "she didn't really change her name. Maybe she likes Cheryl better than Abigail. Maybe her new husband liked her middle name. It isn't a big deal, but I can't afford to overlook anything at this point. We aren't generating that much new evidence. I always thought she was an outstanding teacher. She sure taught us a lot more than music." Billy responded, "She sure did." Mark gave a Billy a suspicious look, but said nothing.

Billy dropped Mark off at his office and told him that he would cut and package the meat from his deer. "No need to pay the professionals to do it; I do a better job than they do, anyway." Mark responded, "Billy, let me help you." Billy looked at him and said, "Nah, you'd just be in the way. I have my ways of doing things." Mark grinned at him and said, "Well, thanks for the hunt. Nobody in this state can find game the way that you can and that's a fact." Billy agreed, "That's a fact."

Mark had called Sarah to let her know he'd be home for dinner so they ate dinner soon after he arrived home. After dinner Mark helped Sarah with the dishes. When he sat down in his recliner, the weeks of endless work and a day of being outside in the fresh air caught up with him and he was asleep in a matter of minutes. At around eleven o'clock Sarah got up to go to bed. The normal noises of the house did not awaken Mark so she just threw an afghan over him and went to bed. She thought that he hadn't slept like that in weeks. She told Bowser, their big, black mutt to watch him and she went to bed.

Sometime during the night, Mark had a dream. In his dream, he was walking on the sidewalk in front of the high school. All the cars were old. It felt weird because he knew that he was going back in time, but couldn't seem to control it. As he walked down the sidewalk, he saw a red Mustang coming down the street. He could see Cassie was driving and Pauline was in the front passenger's seat. They were both stone faced. Their eyes didn't move and they weren't talking. As the car passed, he turned and watched it go by. Then he saw Esperanza in the back window. She was frantically saying, "Help us! Help us!" There was no sound, but her lips were clearly saying, "Help us!"

Mark came awake with a start. His heart was pounding and he was in a cold sweat. He then realized that he was still in the living room. He looked at the time on his phone and it was four o'clock in the morning. He had slept at least six hours in his chair almost without moving. He got up and Bowser nudged him to let him know he was there. Jack ruffled Bowser's ears and then went to the bathroom. He then went into the kitchen and got a small glass of orange juice which he sipped a bit and then gulped it down. He didn't think it would do any good to go back to bed so he made coffee. At four-thirty, Mark started sipping coffee and going over the dream in his mind. He knew it was weird because it was Mack's dream. He wasn't sure all the details were the same, but the message was the same. He was going to try to talk with Mack about it.

At six-thirty, when Sarah got up, he had French toast with eggs over easy all ready to eat. As they ate breakfast, Mark told Sarah about the dream. Sarah got tears in her eyes and said, "You have to figure out what happened to them." "You know that I fully intend to do just exactly that, right?" Mark replied. "Of course I do," she said, "but that just intensifies the need to solve it. Those girls can't be at rest until you figure it out." Mark said, "I have to talk with Mack. He has had a similar dream that reoccurs. He's been having it for years since the investigation was closed. I don't know whether or not spirits have the power to manipulate circumstances in time and space, but it is almost like they caused the drought so that Billy could find the car and re-open the investigation." Sarah looked at Mark for a long moment and finally said, "Do you really think that?" He replied, "Honey, I don't know, but you have to admit that it certainly is strange. After all these years with me here and access to the most successful cold case team in history, how can it be coincidence?" "When you put it like that, it does make you wonder," said Sarah. "Have some more coffee?"

CHAPTER 20

The rest of the Christmas season was both quiet and relaxing. Mark had no more dreams or nightmares. In fact, he started sleeping through the night again. He did meet with Sheriff Mack and they talked about their dreams. At first it felt a bit awkward, two experienced law dogs talking about their dreams, but as they got into the details it was almost chilling. The dreams seemed identical in every detail. That was unnerving because Mack had never divulged the details of the dreams to anyone. In fact, Mark was the only person that he had ever told about them. Mark said with a chuckle, "It's like they're contagious."

"By the way," Mark stated, "I have located the other witness that was overlooked back during the original investigation." "And who was that?" asked Mack. "She was the music teacher, Abigail Appleton," replied Mark. "She is now Cheryl Fogarty. She started using her middle name when she married Elliot Fogarty." "What did she have to do with it?" asked Mack. Mark replied, "Nothing that we know about. She has an alibi; she was visiting her grandparents. Unfortunately, we cannot confirm her alibi and there is no indication in the file that anybody did originally, although it's a detail that may not have made it into the file. She might have seen something or someone. You know that a small detail that seems insignificant to everyone can mean everything to the right someone. In this case, she may have seen something that when plugged into the composite that we are putting together, could complete a picture that we couldn't see without that piece." Mack agreed, "You are right about that. When are you going to interview her?" "Not sure just yet," replied Mark. "Soon I hope. I have asked Willie, a member of my team to do the interview. I think I might be too close to the witness to be subjective."

Mack stared at Mark for several seconds and then said, "You know, Mark, the highway running through town was a main truck route back in 1968. They had not completed the interstate this far at that time so all of the traffic going farther north had to drive right through here." "I remember that," Mark said. "What are you thinking?" "Back when it happened I wondered if a trucker could have grabbed them, but the logistics of grabbing three young girls seems to discount that theory. It would just be too hard to control all of them. They were strong, athletic girls. I doubt one man could control all of them," said Mack. "Well, unless he threatened to harm one of them if the others did not comply," replied Mark. Mack said, "I'll bet that would have worked. Those poor kids would have been so scared that they would do about anything to protect each other. I just believe that something really bad happened to them. How could somebody take the car way out there and get back while keeping the girls under control. The guy had to have an accomplice. It's the only way. It's a five mile walk back to town from where we found the car." Mark raised the question, "What if he had already done whatever he was going to do with the girls and wasn't coming back to town anyway? Maybe it was a driving team. A two guy team makes more sense than one lone guy. Don't you agree?" Mack agreed, "That is a very real possibility. If it's true, the chances of them being alive today are slim to none. We'll probably never know." Mark said with a determined look, "I'm not ready to concede anything at this point. I think they were murdered and I am going to continue investigating as though I am sure the killer is still here, although I don't have the slightest notion as to the identity of the person or persons."

CHAPTER 21

Billy Patterson was drinking again. The discovery of Cassie's car then the subsequent death of his mother was too much for him. The pain of the loss of his sister was revived by the discovery of the car and the loss of his mother, but now it was compounded. After Cassie's disappearance, there was a period in which Billy felt forgotten. Later, though, he and his mother became very close. They clung to one another. He was her baby and she needed some comfort. He was vulnerable because he was so young so they held on to one another through the darkest days that a family could know. They had cried together, reminisced together and finally learned to laugh again together. They had lived through the dark days and finally saw life's sunshine again. Now she was gone. It had been really hard to bury Old Bill, as everyone called him. Burying his mom was killing Billy.

On top of reliving his dad's passing, Billy was reliving much of the pain and agony of Cassie's disappearance. He remembered crying until the tears were gone and there was nothing but a fiery ache of agony in his chest and constant painful memories parading through his mind. He felt alone, like he did before he and his mom found each other following that fateful day in 1968. He did not know the fire that had burned in those days could be rekindled, but here it was. He was trying to drown it in whiskey, but it just seemed to feed the fire. The worst part is that he was having dreams.

The dreams started soon after his mother passed. His brother had come home from California and Beau had been there for him. Between Pete and Beau, he did pretty well for a few weeks. Then Pete went home to California and Beau sort of disappeared back into his own life and Billy was left alone to face the ghosts of his loved ones. It wasn't that they were frightening, he just felt so *alone*. He had always been a loner, but this was different. Being a loner and being alone were vastly different. Now he was alone. His life felt empty. The dreams were so vivid, too.

The first dream was at a football game. Cassie was a cheerleader. In fact, she had been selected as head cheerleader for her senior year. She was really excited about that. In the dream, Billy was just arriving at the game. It had always been permitted that when the Patterson family arrived at a game whether football or basketball, Billy was permitted to run out to the cheerleaders. Cassie would always give him a big hug then all the other girls would hug him. He was like the little brother to the entire cheerleading squad. He felt so loved at that moment. Then other dreams came.

Billy began spending hours in Cassie's room. Nothing had been moved from where things were the last time she left it. Her dirty clothes had not even been picked up. For fifty years his mom had cleaned around them. She dusted without moving anything. Billy would just sit on the end of Cassie's bed like he did when he was small and she was there. They would talk and laugh. Billy knew that his sister loved him and he had nearly worshipped the ground she walked on. A couple of times he fell asleep on her bed like he did when he was small. The second time it happened, he awakened in his own bed when he clearly remembered falling asleep on Cassie's bed. He remembered how she used to carry him to his bed and tuck him in after he fell asleep in her bed. It made him wonder, but that was impossible. Besides he wasn't a kid any more. He was probably just blacking out from drinking so much, but it was curious. And, there was the sense of security and well-being he had felt when he awakened that morning. That was really unusual. Then there was the dream. The one he could not forget.

Billy found himself at a funeral. He was seven years old again and his whole family was there. In fact, the whole town was there. His mother was weeping and sobbing. His father looked so very serious. He saw his brother Pete. His eyes were red from crying. He couldn't see who the deceased person was. He spoke to his mother, but she acted as though she didn't hear him. He asked his father, "Daddy, who died?" His father acted like he wasn't even there. He tapped on his brother's arm and Pete did not react. Finally, Billy walked up to the casket so he could look inside. He was stunned to see his beautiful sister Cassie. She just looked like she was asleep. As he stared at her, she opened her eyes. It was strange, but Billy felt no fear. Cassie spoke to him. Her voice was just as he remembered it. Her words were a bit curious. She said, "Billy, thank you for finding my car. I hope you can help find us so that we can come home." Billy asked her, "Where are you? Can you tell me?" Cassie said, "In a dark place, Billy. There is no light in here." Then she said a word that he didn't understand. He asked her to repeat it, but she just smiled and closed her eyes.

Billy awakened in a cold sweat. The dream didn't make sense. They didn't even know that the girls were dead for sure. As he thought about it, though, he realized that he had suspected it for years. Everything in his dream was information that he had in his head. He wondered if his subconscious mind was trying to make sense out of the situation. He made up his mind at that moment that he was going to stop drinking so he could keep his mind clear and sharp. He didn't really believe that Cassie had communicated with him, but he didn't discount the possibility and wanted to have a clear mind in case she did.

He wondered if he should talk about his dream with anybody. He decided that at least temporarily, he would keep it to himself. He didn't want people thinking that he was crazy or something, after all. He figured some people were thinking that anyway. He surely did miss his mother at times like this. She always seemed to understand him.

CHAPTER 22

Mark and his team were beginning to seriously think about a team rather than one person as a perpetrator. It did not seem plausible that one person could control three 18-year-olds, kill them, and dispose of their bodies. The more they thought about it, the more they leaned toward the concept of abduction. The girls were probably spirited out-of-town and the car dumped in the swamp. Two men could have handled three teenaged girls with little trouble, especially girls who were not trained to deal with that kind of trouble. Young people were so naïve in 1968. The world was starting to change, but kids in rural America were not prepared for the darkness that was descending upon their culture. Serial killers were largely unheard of in 1968. They existed, but had not become the media stars that they would become.

They started trying to identify any local truck driving teams from fifty years ago as well as identify any trucking lines that had regular routes through the area. Their efforts not too surprisingly generated lots of information but very few suspects. They were able, with the help of trucking company records, to identify thirty-two driving teams that circulated in and out of the area in and around

1968. There were sixty-four individuals named. Of the persons named, forty-nine of them were deceased. All of their heirs were asked whether or not they had kept any of the stuff their dads had accumulated over the years. All, with the exception of three, said that they had long since disposed of everything that their dads had collected during their driving years. Of the three who had boxes of the stuff their dads had collected, none of them yielded anything that might have been a trophy of conquest.

There were fifteen of the drivers still living. The team found, through their efforts to contact them that seven of them were in various stages of dementia. Four of them were in fairly good health and were available for interview. Three of them had just disappeared from the face of the earth. Their families had no idea what happened to them or how to contact them.

The good news was that the team was able to interview at least one person from each team identified. They remembered the disappearance, but denied any knowledge of it other than what was on the news and what they picked up from locals when they had lunch at one of the various bars, diners, and restaurants in Pleasant Valley.

One driver, a man by the name of Henry Wilson, said something curious in his interview. In fact, he said that it had not occurred to him in years. He said that he had seen a red Mustang convertible turning onto the road that went out past the north end of Patterson Lake on the afternoon of the disappearance. He said that the top was up and he couldn't see who was driving. He was asked how he knew that road led past the north end of Patterson Lake and he said that he and some of his friends used to come on weekends and fish the local lakes. He had been on Patterson Lake a year or so before the incident. It raised some suspicions but nothing could connect him with the disappearance. Besides, they knew where to find him. When he was asked why he never mentioned that before, he replied that nobody had ever asked him and he didn't even know that they were looking for a red Mustang. They pressed him as to whether or not there was anything else remarkable. He said, "No, not really, well except that the trunk was open and there was something in the trunk that was too large to allow it to close." When questioned about what it was, he wasn't sure. He thought it looked like a wheel chair or something like that. He thought it was between five and six P.M.

His statement really puzzled the team because it did not seem to fit with anything else. In addition, it put a wrinkle in the time line, as well. It was clear that if his memory was reliable that the girls were still in town much later than anyone thought. Why had nobody seen them?

Mark called Mack and invited him in for a briefing. Mack was there within fifteen minutes. Mark laid out the latest information that they had generated. Mack was silent for a long time. "It's not much, but substantially changes the time line that we thought we knew back in 1968. Do you think that the girls ever left town?" "I don't know what to think," said Mark. "What do you think about a wheel chair? That seems a complete misfit to the rest of the narrative, doesn't it?" he said. "It does," Mack replied. "As far as we know, none of them required a wheel chair and there was no wheel chair found in the car or around it in the swamp. We dug that up pretty well. We would have found it," said Mack. Mark nodded his assent. Mack continued, "You have stirred up more new information that I would not have believed was available. That is good police work. Where do you go from here?" Mark replied softly, "I don't have much new material to cover. I have one or two leads and then I'm going to have to either let my team go or get lucky." "For my part," said Mack, "I hope you get lucky." "Yeah," replied Mark. They shook hands and took their leave of one another. The Sheriff thanked Mark for keeping him in the loop. Mark parted with this request. "Mack, let me know if anything pops up no matter how insignificant it may seem." Mack nodded, "Will do, Mark."

CHAPTER 23

The world in 1968 was a so different than the present time. In the spring of 1968, Martin Luther King, Jr. was assassinated. Later in the year, Bobby Kennedy was cut down by an assassin's bullet. There was unrest around the country, but in Pleasant Valley there was little impact except the outrage in some circles and the quiet, knowing nods in others. The different viewpoints weren't discussed in public or in the editorial page of the local paper.

America was still the industrial power in the world and the goal of many high school seniors was to get a job in one of the local manufacturing plants, work until they could retire, raise a family, enjoy their grandchildren, and move on to make room for the next generation. That was more or less the cycle of life. There were some whose families were farmers or business owners. They, of course, would work for their family business until it was their turn to take over. They would then run the business until their children were ready to take over. The economy was strong and the future was bright. There were no major storms on the horizon.

The war in Vietnam was on everyone's mind as the news media put it before the nation's eyes every evening. There were demonstrations and protests in the streets of nearly every major city. There were anti-war demonstrations manned by thousands of young people who did not think that it was our war and that we should not be fighting it. The radical groups were taking advantage of the chaos to agitate. The Weathermen, Black Panthers, Students for a Democratic Society and other such militant groups were threatening violence. There were, in fact, several incidents of bombing and fire fights that fed the rumors that there was an impending civil war coming. What many did not realize was that the civil war was taking place in the classrooms of our universities. The generals were radicalized professors who were preaching anti-American rhetoric and promoting left-wing ideology. They were extolling the virtues of Fidel Castro and the iron-fisted, totalitarian government of the USSR. The Democrats' quadrennial convention held in Chicago turned into a riot, inside and out. The Chicago police, under orders from Mayor Richard Daly brutalized protesters outside of the convention center. The action on the floor of the convention became so violent that a reporter was knocked to the floor by the crowd. It seemed that disorder had conquered and the orderly lives that Americans had enjoyed were cowering in the shadows.

While the rest of the world was still struggling with these convulsive issues that were changing America, the folks in Pleasant Valley were grappling with the unexplained disappearance of three of their own. The upheaval elsewhere in America had little, if any, immediate impact on Pleasant Valley. They were grief stricken, horrified, mystified, and suspicious all at the same time. They were grief stricken because even though they were constantly reminded by the authorities that there was no evidence of foul play, something had happened to those kids. They weren't the kind to just go away and never contact their loved ones. They were horrified to think that three people could just disappear from under their noses without anyone noticing anything. They would look at one another and wonder, "How in the world…" They were mystified because there was just no evidence that pointed to anyone. Usually there was something, but there was just nothing. It was mystifying. And they were suspicious because of the possibility that the person who made those girls disappear was still among them and the frightening possibility that they could and would strike again. It took years for the people to relax and start acting normal again. Slowly but surely, the good people of Pleasant Valley started to relax. They started allowing their children to have a normal childhood again. The fear that had gripped them slowly ebbed away to leave them cautious but not as militant as they had been.

Willie completed the interview with Abigail Cheryl Jensen Appleton Fogarty. Mark read over the interview transcript and found no surprises. She was out of town that weekend to visit her grandparents. She had returned on Monday to find the town disquieted over the missing girls. She remembered the agony of the following weeks and months. It was terrible. She actually shed tears as she talked about the loss of the three girls. She said that she had loved them like they were her own children. Yes, she had changed her name to Cheryl when she married Elliot because he preferred it to Abigail. There was nothing incriminating or really very interesting in the transcript.

Mark walked out to chat with Jay. He had reviewed the tape and did not note any red flags. It was another dead end. Mark was not surprised. He didn't really expect anything significant to arise from her statement. He was curious about the name change and briefly thought about asking her, but decided to wait for that.

CHAPTER 24

Pleasant Valley had sent her fair share of young men off to the war in Vietnam. Fortunately all of the boys came home. Some were wounded, some disabled, but all came home. The only war fatality related to Pleasant Valley was the Marine Captain husband of Abigail Appleton. There was a memorial to him at City Hall and the school had named the flag circle after him. It was called Appleton Circle; not very original, but sufficient. Many still remembered how the town had rallied around Mrs. Appleton during the days following his funeral. They embrace him as a home town hero even though he wasn't really even from the same state originally. That really didn't seem to matter. On Memorial Day, Independence Day, and Veterans' Day, the high school band and the living veterans who were able, met at Appleton Circle to start the parade. On Memorial Day it ended in the local grave yard which was ten blocks from the high school. The veterans who could still do so marched; the ones who couldn't march were pushed in wheel chairs. A few of them had their own motorized wheel chairs. The people of Pleasant Valley still lined the streets every time to honor their "boys", both living and dead.

Mark and Jay were driving slowly along Main Street. They were on their way to speak with Pastor Fogarty. The pastor had been a bit curious about the follow up. Mark had assured him that they were just trying to be sure they left no stone unturned. He explained that if they didn't find the truth this time around, they never would. When they arrived, the pastor seated them in his office. He asked his secretary to bring coffee and leave the pot. Once she had done that and left the office, Pastor Fogarty said, "Okay, I know that you have a job to do, but this is starting to feel like you suspect me." Mark replied, "Not at all, pastor. It's just that we have found some changes to the time line and we need to confirm alibis for a bit later in the afternoon. Can you remember where you were and what you were doing between three and five-thirty the day of the disappearance?" Pastor Fogarty replied, "I can look back in my appointment books. I have kept them for all of the years of my pastoral ministry. I will tell you that I had nothing to do with what happened to them, though." Mark smiled and said, "I believe you, Pastor. There is one other thing, though. Jay here is a human lie detector and he detected some hesitancy to answer some questions that I asked you in the original statement." Pastor Fogarty understandably seemed a bit defensive and asked, "Which questions specifically?" Mark replied, "When I asked you if you had good relationships with your female congregants you seemed to hedge. How do you explain that?" "It's complicated," he replied. "As you know, when I originally came to Pleasant Valley I was single. I was in my early twenties but had been so busy getting my education that I didn't date. I met my wife after the untimely death of her Marine Captain husband. He was killed in 1967, as I am sure you know. I had a small part in his local funeral and I met her then. Sometime after the funeral she showed up for services one Sunday morning. That was sometime during late 1967. She came intermittently for about a year. After the fall of 1968, she started coming regularly. Since she professed faith and had been baptized as a young girl, when she petitioned to join the church, the board had no objection. That was when she made the name change to Cheryl instead of Abigail. She had asked me to call her Cheryl from the beginning of our relationship, but she made it official when she joined the church. We started seeing one another socially, dating I suppose, during the fall of 1968. One thing led to another and we soon found ourselves to have slipped the constraints of celibacy. We married as soon as was gracefully possible to avoid any scandal. I guess the fact that she was a widow and had been sexually active and was desirous to be so again and I was inexperienced but willing to bring comfort into our lonely lives exacerbated the situation. Anyway, you can see why I would rather not talk about these things if it can be avoided." Mark smiled, maybe a bit too much, "Pastor, "he said, "Your secret is safe with me. Jay, do you think that answers our questions?" Jay grinned and replied, "I detected nothing but **sin**cerity today." Mark thanked the pastor and they said their good byes. In the car on the way home Mark looked over at Jay with a glint of amusement in his eyes. "Did I detect an over emphasis on the sin part of sincerity?" Jay burst out laughing, "You caught me! I couldn't believe what I was hearing. The preacher was getting it on with the merry widow." "He may not have been the first," said Mark. Jay gave him a sideways look and asked, "What do you know that you aren't sharing?" "I have nothing that has any bearing on the case at this point in time." "C'mon, give!" demanded Jay. Mark just grinned but said nothing. Jay gave him a disgusted look, "Like a sphinx!" he said.

CHAPTER 25

Once again all of their efforts to generate and then run down new leads were fruitless. The team sat around their conference table with little to say. They were reviewing what they had been able generate in terms of new material. Nothing pointed to anything or rather everything pointed to nothing. They were freshly out of new leads and frustrated. Mark spoke up, "Jay, have you listened to all of the statement tapes?" "Well," Jay replied, "I didn't listen to the ones of people that are deceased. Do you think that I should?" Mark thought for a moment, "I think so. We can't afford at this point to allow any point of evidence to go unexamined. I'm going to ask everyone else to look over the transcripts of all of the statements looking for anything that might contradict the statements or alibis of anyone involved in this case. We simply have to shake something loose. I don't know where else to look. The answers have to be in the file; we are just blind to them. Pass the statements around and talk among yourselves. There has to the something that we are missing." They all looked at Mark with weary but respectful eyes. Vic said quietly, "That is a really good idea to look for holes in statements in the transcripts of other statements. You might have something there." Mark nodded, "We'll see."

Mark paged Tex and Victor to come to his office. They walked in and looked at him expectantly. "What's up, Boss?" Tex asked. Mark smiled at him and replied, "The three of us are going to put on some coveralls and gloves and we are going to examine every square inch of that Mustang. We simply must find something. Nobody can pass through this world without leaving any trace. Whatever happened to those girls, and I'm leaning toward murder, the perpetrator or perpetrators left something behind. We have got to find it. Ready?" "You bet!" they replied in unison. "Let's go then," Mark said and away they went.

When they arrived at the garage where the Mustang was being stored Mark said, "We are really going to look at every square inch of this thing. Take it apart. Remove the seats, the carpets, the door panels and look at everything. We will tear the trunk down to the metal and jack it up so that we can look at everything under the hood. Let's see what we find." They went to work. As they worked, they photographed every step in the process. When they found something, they photographed it before removing it. Apart from the expected pennies, nickels and dimes, they found a few odds and ends of junk including head bands, hair doodads, and a few plastic toys which were probably Billy's. They did find a number of hairs which they bagged and tagged. There were also a couple of silver charms from a charm bracelet. Since all three of the girls wore charm bracelets, it did not seem out of place. Their charm bracelets told the story of their accomplishments. They had silver charms for academic honors, cheerleading, 4-H wins, music, church, and about everything one could think of to make and sell. They found a music symbol and a '69, which was the for the year of graduation. The music symbol was a small silver treble cleft. They were optional. For music excellence the guys got a pin and the girls an option of a pin or a charm. All in all the day spent tearing the car apart did not render anything that looked promising. There were several evidence bags that they logged. Mark told them to send the hairs for analysis and catalogue the rest of the stuff. He then sat down and held his head in his hands. It just did not look like this was going anywhere.

As they were about to leave, Tex was looking in the trunk. He called Mark and Victor over and said, "Look at this. It looks like a scrape of some kind of blue paint. It is very faded, but looks like somebody scraped something on the inside of the trunk lid. Do the inspection notes mention anything about it?" Mark replied, "I don't think that they do. Do you remember anything about that, Victor?" Victor thought for a minute and replied, "I'm pretty sure that the notes do not say anything about blue paint. Let's take a sample of it and have it analyzed." "Good idea," replied Mark. Tex got a small evidence bag and scraped a small about of the blue paint into it and tagged it. "I think we're done here," said Mark. "That was a good catch, Tex. You have a good eye. I didn't notice it." He replied, "I wouldn't have either if my flash light had not stopped squarely on it for a moment. I hope it proves to be something worthwhile." "Me too," replied Mark. "Me three," said Vic with a grin using an old line from the Three Stooges.

At around four-thirty, Willie and Jay walked into the office. They came right in and sat down in Mark's office. Mark grinned at them and said, "Come right in and have a seat!" They all laughed. Willie said, "We thought that you would like an update sooner rather than later." "I would, indeed," replied Mark. "How did it go?" "Well, let's cut to the chase and work backward from there. Is that alright with you?" asked Jay. "I like the way you think," replied Mark. Jay looked at him and said, "I could not detect any indicators that she covering anything up. She was candid about everything and I don't believe she knows anything. We asked her about her relationship with her husband before they were married. She admitted that they were active and that they needed to get married to protect his church work. Like I said, she was relaxed and forthright." Mark responded, "Do you agree, Willie?" When she affirmed that she agreed, Mark continued, "I'm not surprised. I expected as much." Willie smiled a bright smile and said, "She did say that she wished you had come to take her statement. She remembers you well from the old days. You never told us you were a musician. That was a surprise and you never told us that you were a song writer. She told us some of the songs you wrote. That was a major surprise. There's a lot to you that the world does not see, isn't there? We have been working with a rock and roll celebrity and didn't even know it" Mark dropped his head, "Not so much anymore. The disappearance of our friends, girlfriends, and classmates took the music right out of us." Jay regarded him for a long moment and replied, "Wow! That is the most personal information I have ever heard you share." Mark gave him a sardonic half grin and said, "Well, don't get used to it; there'll not be a steady diet of it." They laughed together and the meeting broke up.

Jay asked Willie as they stepped into the hall, "Did you see the expression on Mark's face when he talked about losing those kids?" "Yeah," replied Willie, "he looked positivly haunted." Jay nodded in agreement. "Good word for it; haunted."

CHAPTER 26

Mark was parked at his desk when he realized that they had not visited the scene where the car was found. He did not want to visit the marsh so much as the access to the lake. He wanted to figure out how fast the car would have had to be going to land at the point where they found it. He asked the team whether any of them knew a good engineer that might be able to help. None of them had a name on the top of their heads so Mark picked up the phone and called Mack. The phone rang twice and he heard Mack's voice, "Sheriff Mack," he barked into the phone. "Hey, Mack, this is Mark. I have a question for you." "Ask away," replied Mack. "I'm in a generous mood today. What'll it be?" Mark replied, "I was wondering who you would recommend as an engineer that could help us determine how fast the car would have had to be going to fly that far into the lake." "That is a good idea!" said Mack. "Well," Mark said, "I should have thought of it sooner, but such is life." Mack chuckled, "I would have never thought of it. It is so non-typical to the investigations that we do. Right here in Pleasant Valley there's a well-respected engineering firm that should be able to help. They are Bronson and Sherman or B&S so you know what they get called when people are not happy with them. Anyway, I think that they could help." Mark thanked him and then Mack went on. "I suppose this means that you are still digging, right?" Mark sighed, "That would be an affirmative, Mack. Sorry." He replied, "You guys are very thorough. I would have bet that there was nothing new that you would be able to find to do, but I would have lost my money." "Mack, on top of just not being a giving up kind of team, this is personal for me and I don't plan on quitting until I have answers or am sure there are none." Mack replied, "I sincerely wish you good luck. It could be theraputic for people to know what happened to those kids." "Thanks, Mack. That means a lot from you," said Mark and they hung up the phones.

Mark found the number for the engineering firm and called them. They said they thought they could help. They had an engineer available that same afternoon so they made an appointment. After getting off the phone and before going to lunch, Mark called to check on the analysis of the paint smudge they had found on the inside of the trunk lid of the Mustang. So far, they had not matched it to anything. They were still checking, but there were so many possibilities and the smudge was so old that they were having some difficulty. They didn't sound very hopeful that they would find the answer, but Mark asked them to keep checking.

After lunch, Mark drove over to the offices of Bronson & Sherman. Mike Sherman had cleared his schedule to go with them and inspect the scene of the crime. As they drove out there, he asked Mark what he wanted. Mark replied, "Let's talk about that when we get there. Basically I want to know how fast the car would have had to be going in order to land where it did in the lake. There may be other things, as well." Mike grunted and they rode on in silence. The lake was about five miles from town so it didn't take long to get out there.

There was a two-track access road that led to a spot on the north side of the lake where people went for picnics and couples went to park to pledge their eternal love and so forth. The parking/picnic spot was on a bluff overlooking the lake. It was a lovely spot. On a dark night, the stars would seem so close you could reach out and pick them. From the top of the bluff Mark and Mike could see the spot where the car had been dug out of the bottom of the marsh. Mike started by taking a bunch of photos and measurements. He then set up his transom and started shooting elevations. Getting an accurate measurement from the grave of the car to the base of the bluff turned out to be one of the most challenging tasks. Because of the underbrush and overgrowth, it was difficult to get through. They solved the problem by using a one hundred foot tape and taking turns crawling through the brush and over the downed trees and overgrowth until they had a fairly accurate measure. It turned out that it was only one hundred eighty nine feet from the edge of the lake and another fifteen feet to the base of the bluff. Mark didn't know what to make of the fact that the car had landed on one of the deepest parts of the marsh. The lake itself was deeper, but the marsh was around four feet in most spots. This spot was deeper than the rest of the marsh and most inaccessible. He wondered if the person who put the car there knew that or just lucked out. He figured it was a little of both. This was either one of the best planned murders ever or the luckiest perpetrator in history.

Mike did some quick calculations and said to Mark, "Unofficially, the car would have to have been travelling over fifty miles per hour to get this far into the marsh. There is a small rise right at the edge of the bluff that would have pitched the car into the air. That would have helped, but it needed speed to carry it forward into the marsh. Whoever did this, knew something about mathematics." Mark regarded the engineer for a long moment and said, "How in the world could someone do this without killing or injuring themselves?" "Well," replied Mike, "It's possible that they tied the steering wheel so that the front wheels would stay straight and jammed the accelerator so that it would gain as much speed as possible and left the rest to luck." Mark stood looking at the two-track leading to the bluff. He said, "The Mustang did have an automatic transmission. As we used to say, that was the only thing wrong with it. If someone could jam the accelerator and drop it into drive and dive out before it really got going, I guess it would have been possible to do it. But there are so many random circumstances that have to fall just right for that to happen. What are the chances?" "Pretty slim," Mike replied, "But it only had to happen once. Note that there is enough road for the Mustang to reach or exceed the speed required to reach the spot where it was found in the marsh. That was one smart cookie that pulled that off or just plain lucky. I wonder which. It was probably some of both." He was mumbling now with that engineer look on his face.

Mark called him back from his musings for a moment, "When you do your report, please give us as accurate a probable speed as possible. Okay?" "Sure thing, Mark and thanks for calling us. This is a really interesting case. We don't get something this interesting very often." "Also, please send me your invoice for services. I want to get you paid while we still have some money," said Mark. Mike responded, "The little birdie tells me that you are working for a third of your regular fee while getting your people full pay. Is that true?" Mark gave him a disgusted look and replied, "That was no bird, that was a smelly old fish by the name of Mackerel, but he did not lie to you." Mike laughed and said, "He didn't talk out of school. I'm on the county commission and he had to report the budget to us. I'm going to do you one better. Our services are free on this one. We all want this put to bed. We're delighted that you are thinking outside the box. Here's hoping we find out who did this and that they are still alive to pay." Mark saluted him and replied, "From your mouth to God's ears. Thanks a lot for your input."

Mark dropped him off at his office and returned to his own. When he walked in the team was all curious. He gave them a quick rundown of what had been discussed. "So," Jay said, "It was possible to get the car into the lake from the bluff. Is it not curious to you that it had to be someone, at the very least, who knew about the lake, bluff, and the marsh?" The rest of the team nodded. "That is for sure and certain," Replied Tex. "The chances of getting the car into that spot deep enough to cover it are so slim and they got it on their first and only try so it had to be somebody smart enough to figure out at least roughly how fast the car would have to be going to clear the edge of the lake and land in the marsh," mused Victor. "One thing for sure is that they were very lucky. They only got one shot at it and got it right the first and only time they did it," said Willie. "It is uncanny how many things had to work just right for this to happen like it did. Yet they did and it has been covered up for fifty years," Gina added. Mark, who was staring down at this desk, looked up and said, "But we still have no idea who it was." "This does narrow it down, though, Mark," replied Willie. "How do you figure?" grunted Mark. "Well," continued Willie, "We know it was somebody who knew about the lake, the bluff, and the marsh, right?" "That is true," replied Mark. "I had thought about that, but did not want to go down that road. I was more comfortable thinking it was an outsider. We're back to looking closer to home. This has been a tough week. Let's get back after it on Monday. We really have made progress because we have a much smaller suspect pool than we did this morning. That doesn't necessarily mean it was a home towner, but it had to be somebody who had been around the area."

CHAPTER 27

On Monday another bombshell struck but, again, nobody knew how significant it was, if at all. Mark had been in the office for a couple of hours when a couple walked in. They looked to be in their mid-fifties to early-sixties. Gina met them and greeted them. They told her that they were Jim and Kendra Williams and they wanted to speak with Mark Bellingham. Gena buzzed Mark to see if he had time to speak with them and he told her to bring them in.

As Jim and Kendra Williams entered his office, Mark greeted them with a handshake and warm smile. "Mr. and Mrs. Williams," he said, "Please come in and sit down. Gina, would you bring coffee for our guests, please?" When they were settled into their seats Mark asked, "What brings you to my office, this morning?" Jim Williams replied, "I am Jimmy Williams and I grew up here in Pleasant Valley. I no longer live here, but heard that you were looking for any kids who might have seen something the day the three girls disappeared." Mark felt a sense of excitement and replied, "Yes, we were hoping someone would come forward." "Well," replied Jimmy, "Here I am." Just then Gina came in with the coffee so they took a few minutes to prepare the various cups and then settled back. Mark asked, "Do you mind if I have a colleague join us while we talk?" "I don't mind," replied Jim, "How about you, Dear?",he asked his wife. She replied, "It's fine with me." Mark called Jay to join them and made the introductions.

"How vivid are your memories after fifty years?" asked Mark. "I have very clear memories of that day," replied Jim. Mark's brow knitted and he asked, "Why didn't you say something before?" "I tried," said Jim, "My parents thought I was just trying to draw attention to myself and told me to shut up. They said it was none of my business and I should mind my own business." Mark smiled, "Well, under normal circumstances, that is pretty good advice, but in this case the information might have been helpful. So tell me, what did you see?" Jim said, "I was riding my bicycle and I remember that it was just before supper because my Mom told me to be back in a half hour for supper. We lived just a couple of blocks from the school, you know. I rode down our block to the stop sign and turned left which would take me past the high school. I saw Cassie's Mustang ahead of me going away from me. I tried my best to catch up with her because she wasn't going real fast. I couldn't see anyone in the car because the trunk lid was up. There was a blue bicycle in the trunk so it wouldn't close. It was probably between five-thirty and six o'clock in the afternoon. We usually ate supper at six when dad got home from work. That's why I remember the general time frame. I just couldn't see who was in the car because as I gained on them, they suddenly accelerated away from me. When the Mustang stopped at the stop sign on Main Street, it turned right and went north. I don't remember anything else."

Mark stared at Jim for a few seconds, "Did you not ever tell anyone what you saw?" he asked. Jim replied, "No, my dad told me to shut up and mind my own business and just forget about it. After a few years, I actually did forget about it. It wasn't until a friend of Kendra's told her that the investigation had been reopened because Billy had found the car in the marsh that my memory was jogged. It was when we heard that you were looking for any tidbits of information that you could find that I thought I should tell you, so we took a few days off and came home for a short visit." Mark said to them, "That is what we hoped would happen, but you never know. Usually those appeals are fruitless because there just isn't anyone left who remembers anything. Thank you for coming forward. I wonder why it is you remember that it was a blue bicycle?" "Oh," Jimmy replied, "Cassie had left her blue bicycle at the school when she got the new Mustang. It had been there for a long time and nobody had bothered it. I went down by the school where the bike parking place is and it was gone. The really weird thing is that it was back the next day. I never figured that out." Mark asked with an intrigued look on his face, "Do you have any idea what happened to that bicycle afterward?" "No idea," replied Jim Williams, "It could have disappeared into thin air for all I know. A lot of that was going around back then." Mark thanked them for coming in and then asked if he could buy them lunch. They declined as they had family to visit while they were in and they took their leave.

After the Williams left, Mark looked at Jay and asked, "What do you make of that?" "He was telling the truth as far as I could tell," replied Jay. "The thing about the bicycle was interesting. A bicycle makes more sense than a wheel chair." "One-hundred percent," agreed Mark. "Now, to find out what happened to that bicycle." "How are we going to do that?" asked Jay. "I'm sure that somebody, somewhere, saw it whether they remember or not. That also explains the blue paint on the trunk lid of the Mustang." "It does at that," replied Jay.

After Jay left his office, Mark picked up the phone and called Sheriff Mack. Mack's answer was a terse, "Sheriff!" Mark chuckled and asked "Mack? I see you are your usual jovial self today." Mark could almost hear the Sheriff relaxing, then he heard a chuckle. "Sorry, Mark," he said, "It's almost lunch time and I think I may be a bit hangry, as they say." "Well," said Mark, "That is exactly why I called. Lunch is on me, if you have the time." Mack chuckled a little more enthusiastically and replied, "I'll make time for a free lunch. Do you know the back room of the Brass Spittoon Saloon?" "In about a half hour?" asked Mark. "See you there." said Mack and hung-up without so much as a goodbye or adios.

CHAPTER 28

Mark was seated, waiting for Sheriff Mack when he arrived. "Am I late?" he asked. Mark said, "No, you're right on schedule. I was a couple of minutes early and they had a table ready for us so I sat," replied Mark. "They always have a table for me. I very seldom miss lunch here. It was Jennie's favorite place and since she passed, I'm here nearly every day," said the Sheriff. "Why did you want to see me?" Mark said, "Let's order; I'm hungry. Then we can talk." "Fine with me," Mack replied and waved for a server. A smiling young lady came over to the table and took their order. When she left, Mark started, "Mack, we have uncovered some information that changes our focus once again." "What's that?" Mack inquired. "Well, for one thing, we found out that the object that the truck driver thought was a wheel chair was actually a bicycle," said Mark. "How do you know that?" asked Mack with an incredulous look on his face. Mark said, "Do you remember little Jimmy Williams that lived a few blocks from the school?" Mack cocked his head and replied, "Sure I remember him. I used to have to chase him home after dark because he'd be out riding his bicycle half the night. It didn't seem like his parents kept very good track of him. He never got into trouble to speak of, though," said Mack. "Well," Mark told him, "he responded to our appeal for information that was never mentioned before. He said that he had seen the Mustang just as it was leaving the school. He chased it down the street trying to catch up, but couldn't. He did get a good look in the trunk and saw that it was a blue bicycle. He thought it was Cassie's bike, although that is unconfirmed," said Mark. "Well, I'll be dipped in shii…ugarplums!" ejaculated the Sheriff. "Did he see who was driving?" Mark answered, "No, he was not able to get close enough to see the driver. Since the trunk lid was open, it obstructed his view." They both sat with their own thoughts for a few minutes and then their food arrived and they were busy for a few minutes.

Mack gave Mark an appraising look and asked, "Was there something else you wanted to share?" "Yes," replied Mark, "We have also come to the conclusion that whoever put that car in the marsh knew the area and understood how fast they would have to go to get into water that was deep enough to hide it. They had to know the area pretty well because they had to take the car over a hump that would flip it up into the air and give them the trajectory they would need to land the car where it was found. This was a really intelligent person who knew some complicated mathematical computations." Mack sat a moment and then said, "That's why they pay you FBI guys the big bucks. I don't think I would have thought of that in a thousand years. That's brilliant." "Mack, don't sell yourself short. You guys did an excellent investigation. We have had to really get creative to even find anything that you missed and you didn't really miss them; they're just things that we have started looking for in the past few years," Mark stated. "The truth is that I'm not sure that we are any closer to solving this than you guys were fifty years ago. The only reason this is reopened is because the car was found. So far, it has not yielded any significant evidence or if it has, we don't know what to do with it." Mack shook he head sympathetically and said as he took his leave, "I think you guys are going to crack it, but it might be something off the wall and so unexpected that finally flips the switch. Keep at it; all of us need to put this one to bed for good and all." Mark gave the Sheriff a wry grin. "Mack," he said, "Quitting is something that I never learned to do and I think it's too late to start now. I'll be at it until I figure it out or you call me off." They shook hands and headed to their separate offices.

CHAPTER 29:

Mark spent the next three days reviewing the file again. He went through it step by step and was left with the original impression. There was just nothing to see. They did not know whether the girls were dead or alive. It was Mark's opinion that the conclusion that they ran away, was as much from a denial that they could be dead, as anything else. There was no evidence one way or the other. There did not seem to be any way those three young girls would have run. It was just too painful to think of them as dead somewhere in unmarked graves. That picture was still hard to imagine all these years later.

What really amazed Mark as he went over the file was that when they closed the file, the evidence that they had led to nobody. Reviewing the file even with the new information, he was loathe to acknowledge that the evidence still led to nobody. Somebody had done something to those girls! Every instinct in Mark screamed that he was looking right at it, but just couldn't see it.

One thing that was missing was motive. What motive could somebody have to kill three young, innocent, high school girls? It could not be greed because they ditched the only thing of value that they had; that being the car. If the motive were jealousy, what did the three of them have in common that would be motive for murder? Again, nothing popped. If it were a crime of opportunity, how could things just fall into place to make it so impossible to unravel? It did not make sense. It was so confusing. It seemed to Mark and his team the harder they looked at the file and studied on the possible solutions, the less they saw. Everything that Mark saw spoke of premeditation. It spoke of high intelligence. It spoke of careful planning. He tried to pinpoint a person in their shared past that would fit that description, but came up with nothing. He was getting a headache. Mark hadn't touched alcoholic beverages in years, but was sorely tempted to just go get drunk. He wouldn't and he didn't, but it made about as much sense as anything else going on in this case. It was the kind of case that could literally break a caring, conscientious investigator. All the people on the team were like that. They cared and they cared especially about this case.

Mark discussed the idea of a profiler with the team. They finally decided to put the idea on hold. This crime was so non-typical that a profile might drive them further off the track, if that were possible. Besides, it would be extra difficult to profile a criminal from fifty years ago. The more they talked about it the worse the idea sounded to them. They all had the idea that when they figured it out, the answer was going to surprise them.

Motive was going to have to be established. Motive would help to narrow down the suspect pool. Then there was opportunity. Who had opportunity to make the girls disappear without a trace? Mark still had a hard time believing one person could pull it off.

There almost had to be a team. He thought about a man and woman team. Often people who were predators were also serial killers. There had been no other killings there. They had checked even nation-wide to see if there were similar crimes before or after and there were none that matched the M.O. The original investigation had thought about the concept of a killing team. They had checked everyone they could find including transients. Everyone that they identified alibied out.

Mark asked himself how one person could logistically commit this crime. He kept coming back to the fact that it was nearly impossible. Killing three people, moving the bodies, cleaning up the crime scene so that it was never even located, were monumental undertakings. It just didn't seem possible. To commit this crime would have been so complicated. It was astounding that it was done without leaving even a tendril of physical evidence. It was truly a marvel. But…, there was always a but, there had to be something somewhere. Most investigations were made or broken on one small piece of evidence. They just had to uncover that piece of evidence. The answer was always the same, keep digging.

Suddenly a thought hit Mark like a flash of light. He picked up the phone and called the families of the three girls. He had an idea. They all agreed to meet him in the office and bring the girls' jewelry boxes. They said they would be right in so Mark waited. They arrived within fifteen minutes of one another. Billy Patterson showed up first, followed by Esperanza's younger sister, with Kerry Franklin Smith bringing up the rear. They all greeted each other and then Kerry, who had appointed herself spokesperson for the group asked, "Mark, why did you want to see the girls' jewelry boxes?" "Good question!" Mark replied. "We found some charms in the Mustang and I'd like to see the girls' charm bracelets to see which one of them lost the charms." She replied, "Good idea; do you think that would help?" Mark said, "It might; let's see." They opened the boxes that looked like they had not been touched in years. Mark examined all three of the charm bracelets. He looked up with a thoughtful look on his face. Billy asked intently, "Mark? What is it?" Mark looked at Billy and the others and replied, "We found charms from these bracelets in the car when we examined it, but these three bracelets are all intact. The charms are all here. There was someone else in that car; someone who also had a charm bracelet!"

CHAPTER 30

Mark thought over the weekend about the new twist. On Monday, he called Sheriff Mack and told him the news. Mack let out a long breath and said, "Wow! There's no way we could have known that in 1968, is there?" Mark replied, "Absolutely not, Mack. That evidence has been buried for almost fifty years. There's no way anybody could have known about it. The good news is that there is a trail to follow. I'm not sure it will lead us to a killer or another dead end, but it is a trail. I just don't know how we can examine all of the charm bracelets. In fact, many of them are probably lost or in storage and long forgotten. All we really know is somebody besides one of the three girls was in that car and lost a couple of charms off their bracelet. Apart from that, we know little more than we did before."

In their team meeting that Monday morning, Mark's team went over the evidence in the car yet again. There were no finger prints left after so much time submerged in water and mud. The car was remarkably well preserved and intact. The loss of finger prints was a critical loss to the investigation. The forensic team was trying everything that they could think of to find even one finger print. So far there was nothing useful.

Mark and Tex went over to the Wascally Wabbit for lunch at around twelve-thirty. They were seated at their table when Willy and Jack walked in. They joined Mark and Tex without an invitation or if you please! Tex had become acquainted with the town folk over the weeks and really liked Mark's old friends. Tex said, "So you three were the old First String from back in the day?" Willy replied, "You are right. We did have another part time member. Cassie's older brother Peter, but he never wanted to be a full time musician. It was us. The townsfolk used to call us The Three Musketeers, The Three Stooges, or The Three Blind Mice, depending on what they were blaming us for at any given moment." They all cracked up at the memory and Tex just laughed because it sounded so crazy. "Are you for real?" he asked. Jack interjected, "He absolutely is telling you the truth. We were together almost every day of our lives from kindergarten until the disappearance of the girls. Something happened to us that summer. It marked us forever." Nobody said anything for a few minutes as they all sat with their own thoughts.

Mark broke the spell by asking them, "Do you guys remember the haberdashery?" Jack grinned and replied, "Oh, Man! I hadn't thought of that place in years." "Me neither," added Willy. "Did you guys ever tell anyone about that place?" "I didn't," Mark stated. "Me neither," said Jack. "It's amazing that we kept that place a secret all those years. I wonder if anybody else has been down there." "Who knows," replied Willy. "It was a dark, ugly place. We just loved it because it was our place."

The boys had discovered the spot one day when the sixth, seventh, and eighth grade classes were tasked with planting trees around the new building. It had been finished the summer before their sixth grade year. The three of them had been sent to find some more shovels, rakes, and hoes. They went into the furnace room where they were told they would find the tools. While going down the stairs into the furnace room, they saw an access door in the wall. Mark, who had learned to pick locks, was curious about where such a door would lead so he picked the lock and opened the door. What they found was like a cave of wonders to three sixth grade boys. It was a passageway that ran under the hallway to a huge crawl space under the new gymnasium. It was positively delicious. They decided to come back after school and check the place out and then went about their work of planting trees with purpose.

The boys met after school and snuck into the utility room. Willie had thought to bring a flash light. Neither Jack nor Mark had even thought of a light. They jimmied the door open again and stepped into the passageway. It was really just a crawl space. They left the door open so they could find their way out and headed to their left. Walking very carefully they made their way down the passageway and emerged into a large area. They were just able to walk standing at full height. They looked around them in wonder. They figured that they must have been under the new gymnasium. Willy flashed his light around revealing nothing but dirt. They felt like explorers. Forget that the construction workers had left the crawl space. It felt like they were seeing something that nobody before them had ever seen. They poked around for about an hour and then headed back to the access door. When they were back inside the school building they just stood and stared at each other for a few seconds. Jack spoke up and said, "We have got to keep this place a secret!" "Yeah!" said Willie, "What should we call it? We need a code name; something better than a crawl space." Mark had been reading some English literature and had come across the word "haberdashery". He knew that it meant hat store, but was pretty sure that other sixth graders would not. "Let's call it the 'haberdashery'," he suggested. Willie looked at him with a confused look on his face. "A haberwhat?" he asked. "Haberdashery," Mark said, "It is an old word for a hat store and is used mainly in old English literature. That way we can talk about it and nobody will know what we're talking about." Although it was very naïve, they were sixth graders in the early '60s. It was to be expected. "Hey!" interjected Willie, "My dad was looking at some of the township plat books and we found out that originally there had been a street planned to run right through where the new school was built. It had 'extension of 13th Street', which ends about a half mile north of the school. Let's call it the '13th Street Haberdashery'!" "Done!" shouted Willie and Mark together. They had their secret and they vowed that they would never tell anyone about it.

Mark, Willy, and Jack looked at each other across the table and, as in years past, it was like they were thinking the same thing at the same time. They raised their glasses and then looked at Tex. Tex gave them a funny look and then raised his glass as well. "To the 13th Street Haberdashery!", said Willy. "The haberdashery!" responded the other three. Mark looked at Tex and said, "To my knowledge you are the only person other than the three of us who even knows about that place."

Just then a trembling voice said, "Excuse me?" They turned and looked at Billy Patterson. "Billy!" Mark greeted him with pleasure, "what brings you here?" Billy replied, "What was that word you said, haber..what?" Mark looked at Billy and said, "Haberdashery?" Billy replied excitedly, "Yeah, that's it. That's the word that I heard Cassie say in my dream! I didn't know the word so I didn't understand. I thought it was just gibberish, but that was the word!" Mark scowled and said, "I wonder what that means? She shouldn't even have known about it because we never told anybody about it." Billy was insistent, "That is the word I heard. I know it now that I have heard it."

Mark, Jack, and Willy all stared at each other. Finally Jack said, "She may have overheard us using the word, but she could not have known where it was or what it meant. She was never there. I mean, she and her friends were around many times when we were "talking code" as kids. There is no way she could have known where it was or what it meant. I never told anybody." "Me neither," Interjected Willy. Mark added, "I never breathed a word of it either. I am going to take my team out there check it out though. Please stay away from there until we have had a look. If there is evidence there, I don't want it compromised." They assured him that they would not go out there. Everyone else just looked mystified. They all wanted details on it but the three of them divulged nothing.

Mark went back to the office and told his staff, "Tomorrow wear clothes that can get dirty. We're going on a field trip and we could get dirty." They all had questions, but Mark told them that he would explain in the morning. He realized that it could all be a wild goose chase, but at this point he was willing to follow a ghost if it would give them something solid to work on.

CHAPTER 31

Bright and early the next morning, Mark and his team assembled in the conference room. As they sat around the table sipping coffee, Mark started to explain the quest of the day, "When we were in the sixth grade, the school that is now the middle school was the high school. The complex included sixth through high school, but the junior high was in the old part of the structure. The part, where the gym is, was new construction that year. The first year that it was used was the year that we, Willy, Jack, and I, were in the sixth grade. To make a long story short, we discovered that under the gym and the hallway leading to it, there was a large crawl space with an access door that was kept locked. I had learned how to pick locks and although I never used it for any criminal activity, I did use it on occasion. We found the access door one day when we were sent to do something else and I picked the lock. What we found opened a world where we could invent anything we wanted. We named it the 13th Street Haberdashery so that we could talk about it around other kids, but they would not know what we were talking about. It was all very cloak and dagger, you know." That bought a chuckle from around the table. "Its name came from the fact that I had been reading some English literature and had come across the word and really liked the sound of it. The street number came from the old city maps that showed 13th Street running right through where the school was built. So we had our own personal hideaway. I don't think any of us has been back there since our freshman or sophomore year of high school. We became way too busy and life became too real with football, music, and all that was happening in the mid to late '60s." Again there was a chuckle, but everyone was listening intently. Mark continued, "The only thing that makes this even slightly relevant is that Billy Patterson recently told me about a dream he has had. Now wait! Before you roll your eyes, hear me out. He has had this dream many times over the years where he was at a funeral back in about the time his sister and her friends disappeared. Before, he was never able to see who the deceased person was. Just since the discovery of the car, he had another recurrence of the dream and he saw his sister Cassie in the casket. She opened her eyes and spoke to him and said, 'It's dark in here.' Then she said a word he didn't understand until yesterday. When I was having lunch yesterday with Tex and two of my old friends, Jack and Willy, the haberdashery was mentioned. Billy came over to our table looking like somebody had stepped on his grave and asked, 'what was that word you said?' I repeated it and he said 'that is the word that Cassie said to me in my dream.' I'll be honest with you. I was stunned because the three of us never told anybody about that place. I have no idea how, or if, she knew about it, but I would like to know. I am asking for your help and inviting you into the most secret place of my youth and childhood. You may refuse, if you don't want to go, but I am going to search that place to see if there is something there. Clues have been precious few in this investigation. And those that we have found have so far led nowhere; how about it, Team?"

That all stared at him with various versions of stunned expressions. Finally, Willie sort of spoke for all of them, "I thought that I had heard and seen it all, but there you are! I'm in. You have piqued my interest big time, Mark. Wild horses couldn't keep me away!" They all responded with "Me, too" and "Absolutely." Mark nodded his thanks and said, "Well, then let's saddle up. I have all the tools we'll need in the back of my truck and the superintendent of schools is going to meet us there at nine o'clock. Tex, why don't you drive, too. Between the two of us, we have room for everybody. I have arranged for lunch. Shall we go?" They all headed for the door.

When the team arrived at the middle school, they were met by the superintendent of schools, a Mr. Greenbush. He explained that while he had reservations about the search, he realized that they could get a warrant and decided to save them the trouble. There was a hint of sarcasm in his attitude regarding the basis of the search. There was also more than a little bit of curiosity. Although he had not grown up in the area, Mr. Greenbush's family had owned a cottage on the river and spent summers in the area when he was young. In fact, when he came to teach at Pleasant Valley, he had converted the cottage to a full time residence, expanding it to meet the needs of his growing family. He had been at the Pleasant Valley Schools for forty-five years. He had started as a high school history teacher and football coach. He had gone back to school during the summers to earn a master's degree and then a doctorate in secondary education administration. He had moved from the classroom to the office of an under principal. Later he became principal and then five years ago, he had been promoted to superintendent of schools. It was legitimate. He had been hired after the school board had interviewed more than a dozen other candidates. That said, Mr. Greenbush felt that he had a vested interest in the story of the disappearance even though he had not been there at the time. It was part of the lore and fabric of the school's history.

They shook hands all around and then Mark handed out miners' helmets that had a light on the front. "It will be very dark in there," he told them. "You will only be able to see straight ahead of you where your light is shining. It will be important to shine a light on every square foot of the place and look at it. I'm not even sure what we are looking for so keep an open mind and eye. Look for something that seems out of place or abnormal. Are there any questions? Oh, by the way" he continued, "use the rakes rather than the shovels and hoes, at least until you're sure what you're seeing. We don't want to destroy any evidence we might find if we find any." "Oh ye of little faith," mumbled Tex. Mark chuckled and said, "Tex, I never took you for a Bible-thumper." They started their quest in a good humor and light mood.

As the team entered the crawl space there were comments about how dark it was. There was no light entering the place and no lighting in there. Mark assigned Tex and Willie to work the area under the hallway. He and the rest of the team proceeded to the large area under the gymnasium. Victor commented, "Wow, this looks so much larger from this perspective than it does in the gym." Jay responded, "And, it is so much spookier! This place gives me the creeps!" Mark chuckled and replied, "Jay, I'm surprised at you.

I thought that you were unflappable." Jay gave him a sidelong look and said, "Apparently not." That response brought a chuckle from the team. "I guess you never know how you'll feel about a situation until you are in it, huh?" he said. "I guess not," responded Gina. "You're right; it is creepy. It gives me the heebie-jeebies." Mark grinned, "I've always wondered exactly what that meant. It's hard to explain, but when you feel it, it requires no further explanation." Gina looked at him, "Isn't this creepy for you?" "No," replied Mark, "We used to play down there when we were kids. Willy, Jack, and I shared it, but we never told anybody else about it." "That's kind of cool in a creepy way," said Victor.

"Okay," Mark said, "Let's walk very slowly and close together shining our lights on every square foot of this place. If you need to stop to look at something, say so, and we'll all stop and then move on together. Remember, be careful with the rakes. Let's preserve everything we find, if we find anything, at least until we can identify it. So, bag and tag everything you find." It took them nearly an hour and a half to work a section the length of the gym and about fifteen feet wide. They made several stops to sift through the soil finding nothing but a couple of skeletons of dead rats. There were plenty of spider webs to fight through which creeped out Jay and Gina. Over all, it was not a pleasant job. By lunch time they had inspected about half of the soil beneath the gymnasium. There had been several stops on the way back. One of the "discoveries" was a bag of marbles that Jack had lost years ago and had accused everybody of stealing them. The bag was long since rotted but since it was leather, there was a residue of it. The marbles, however, were still very much intact. They bagged them and tagged them and then ate lunch out in the fresh air. Mark had picked up cold cuts with whole wheat rolls, macaroni salad, chips, pickles, and an assortment of juices, sodas, and water. Everyone dug in as though they were hungry and then relaxed. There were several comments about the overall creepiness of the job. Willie, who was one of the most pragmatic people Mark knew said, "I get the feeling that someone is watching us from the shadows." Jay looked at her and said, "I wish you hadn't said that." "Why not say it?" she asked. "Because," he replied, "saying it makes it seem real. I was thinking it but did not want to say it. The place is just creepy!" Mark looked at them incredulously, "You guys are FBI and have seen much worse than this. What is going on?" Jay moved his shoulders uncomfortably and replied, "There's something different about this place. I've been places that were supposed to be haunted. There was always a sound or movement that you could attribute to manmade phenomenon. This is dead silent, but there is something there. I don't know what it is, but it is creepy." Mark regarded him for a long moment and then asked, "Do you want out? Anybody who wants to can walk away no questions asked and no hard feelings." Jay replied, "No, I want to see it through. There's a heavy, sad feeling, but nothing menacing. I'm in to the end." Mark asked, "How about the rest of you?" Everyone agreed to continue so they trooped back to the crawl space and picked up where they left off. After two more hours they were about half way through with the remaining part of the gym but had not turned up anything significant. They found a few more treasures that the boys had lost in there over the years, but nothing that could be called evidence. Mark said, "Okay, let's knock off for the rest of the day. By the time we pack up and get back to the office, it'll be time to head home. We'll go at it again in the morning. Okay?" They all voiced their assent and headed for the exit. They left their tools as they would need them the next day.

CHAPTER 32

When Mark arrived home, he was just bushed. He and Sarah had dinner and then sat down to have a quiet evening at home. Sarah asked about his day knowing that they had started searching the crawl space under the gym. She said to Mark, "You know, it is very unusual for three boys to keep a secret so well for that many years." "I don't know about that," he replied, "but we did have our pact and we kept our word to each other over the years. After a few years I think we just forgot about it. Keeping our fishing hole a secret was harder than the haberdashery because when we stopped going there, we stopped thinking about it. The fishing hole, we kept using so we had to be more creative with that. For example, if anybody saw us fishing there, we would use bait that the fish never hit so nobody would see us hauling fish out of there." Sarah laughed out loud at him, "You devious, mischievous boys!" she exclaimed. Mark grinned, "I guess we were. We didn't think so at the time, though."

Suddenly the doorbell rang. Mark jumped up saying, "I wonder who that might be this time of the evening." He looked through the peep hole and there stood Billy Patterson. Mark opened the door and welcomed him, "Billy! Come in and have a seat. How are you doing?" Billy replied, "I'm fine, Mark." Mark noted that Billy was very stiff and uncomfortable. "Relax, Billy," he said, "you are among friends here." Billy relaxed a little bit and said, "Thanks, Mark, you have always been a good guy." "What's up, Billy?" Mark asked. Billy looked at Mark for a long moment and said, "Before I tell you, I have to tell you that I am and have been stone cold sober for several weeks. You understand that?" "Yes, Billy, I understand," replied Mark. Billy's demeanor caused Mark to take a step back and look at him. "Here's what happened." Billy said. "After I ate supper this evening, I was watching TV and fell asleep and I had the dream again. It was exactly the same until I was looking at Cassie. She said to me, 'Thank you, Billy. I saw Mark today.' What was she talking about, Mark?" "Billy," replied Mark, "we started searching under the school. I just hope it's not a wild goose chase. We'll finish tomorrow. Did you know that we were looking there?" Billy stared at Mark and said, "No, I had no idea." Mark muttered, "That is so strange." "How so?" asked Billy. "My team kept feeling like they were being watched today as we were working. They kept commenting on how creepy it felt. I didn't feel it, but they did." Mark said. Billy replied, "Maybe it was because the girls were your close friends. Maybe their presence wouldn't be creepy to you. I mean, I didn't feel creepy when Cassie talked to me from her casket in my dream. It seemed natural." Mark said, "That is thought provoking. I don't know what to think about it." All this time Sarah was listening quietly without saying a word. Finally she spoke up, "You guys are crazy! There is no such thing as ghosts." Mark said to her, "Nobody is claiming to have seen a ghost. Billy is talking about a dream he had. He didn't actually see a spirit manifestation." "But she said she saw you today! That is impossible! It's just plain weird!" Sarah nearly shouted. Mark said, "I will admit that in all my life, I have not seen anything quite like this. That doesn't make it untrue, however. It makes it unusual." Billy added, "I have never experienced anything like this either. I don't know what to do with it. I can't talk to people about it, but I don't want to dismiss it either. It might be crazy, but it also might be important. Can it be both?" His eyes were pleading for understanding. Sarah immediately grabbed him and hugged him. "I'm so sorry, Billy!" She said. "Your story just took me by surprise. Everything in my life tells me that it's impossible, yet there it is. I can't imagine what you have been through with the loss of your sister, then your wife, then your dad, and now your mother." Billy patted her shoulder and replied, "Forget it, Sarah. You guys are some of the few people that I trust. I don't understand it myself to be truthful about it. I didn't know what to do and Mark has always given me good advice." "Of course you should come here," Sarah said. "We are your people from the old days. I'm glad you came and shared and your secret is safe with us until you see fit to share it, if ever." Billy looked relieved, "Thanks. Mark, what are you going to do?" Mark looked at him and said, "First, I'm going to finish what I started. Tomorrow we'll go and finish checking out the crawl space under the gym, the haberdashery, if you please. If we don't find anything, we'll have to try to figure out where we go from here." Billy replied, "I want to be there tomorrow. I need to be there, if fact." Mark said, "Billy, you can be there, but you cannot participate in the work. You can only observe. Can you live with that?" "I can," Billy replied. "See you in the morning."

After Billy left, Sarah looked at Mark and said, "Wow! That was intense!" "It was indeed," replied Mark. "That's how it's been on this job." She asked, "Is it true that your team is creeped out by the haberdashery?" Mark said, "They really are. These are experienced agents who have seen nearly everything, but that place had them spooked. Jay said he felt like somebody was watching from the shadows. They are all uncomfortable. I gave them the option to bail if they wanted to, but they stuck." "Wow," Sarah said softly. "First time for spooky?" "Yes," Mark replied, "In my experience you watch for threats, but there is no threat, just a sense of a presence, of watchers. It is strange; I'm not going to lie." She looked at him and finally said, "You be careful tomorrow." He replied, "Always."

<h1 style="text-align:center">CHAPTER 33</h1>

The drive to the office the next morning felt long. When Mark arrived at the office, there was nobody there. That wouldn't have been remarkable except Mark was few minutes late. He started the coffee pot brewing and went into his office. He was sipping his first cup of coffee when the team started to trickle in. They were all apologetic about being late. It seemed that nobody was eager to get back to the examination of the haberdashery. Mark understood their misgivings. He had them himself. If they found nothing, he was going to look a bit silly. If they did find something, it could be quite ugly. Last of all Billy showed up about a half hour late. He said, "I drove down to the school, but you weren't there. I thought you would be working by now." Mark replied, "It seems that nobody is really excited about going back down there." Billy nodded and said, "I get it. It's an unsettling place." "Well," Mark said, "Let's get going. Whatever we find or don't find, we should know by the end of the day."

They drove back over to the school and donned their gear. The batteries for the helmet lights had been recharged overnight so they were ready to go. Today they all worked together, because Tex and

Willie had finished the area under the corridor. They moved slowly all morning stopping as they, yet again, found stuff that had been left by the boys playing in there. Mark was astonished at all the junk they found in there that he had no idea they had left behind. They broke for lunch and went back to work. They had just the last section to do. It was about the last eighth of the area under the gym. Mark was starting to feel like they had wasted their time when way over in the northeast corner they found some disturbed soil. It was hard to tell because the surface under the gym had never been graded or finished in any way. It undulated where dirt piles had been left from excavation. That was part of what made it attractive for the boys to play. There were hiding places and with a little imagination, it became a battle field or whatever it needed to be. Victor spotted shovel marks in the soil and stopped the line. Because the area was completely sheltered from any weather, the shovel marks could have been made fifty years ago or last week. As they examined the area, they discovered three places where the soil was slightly mounded up along five or six feet by around three feet. They all just stood and looked at each other for a long moment. Mark said softly, "Please be very careful here." His voice was tight.

Victor, Jay, and Tex started carefully moving the soil at one end of each of the spots that had been found. They used rakes and were very gentle. After going down between two or three feet, Jay's rake scraped on something. They all stopped as Jay dropped on his knees and began brushing the dirt back with his hands. In a short time, he was staring into the empty eye sockets of a skull. He recoiled in shock even though he more than half expected to see bones. It was a reflexive reaction. He then sat down and looked up and Mark and said, "Mark, I think we found them." His voice held a profound sadness. Mark looked over at Billy who was transfixed, staring into the grave. Mark said almost automatically, "Don't touch anything. Everybody move back. I will call the State Police forensic team and the county coroner. We will want to see if we can determine cause of death. We will also have to confirm identity. I expect that we'll find two more right here in these other two spots, but that is not our task, now. Let's get out of here and ask the county to post a guard on the door." Billy walked over and stood face to face with Mark and just looked at him for a long moment. Then he, uncharacteristically, grabbed him and embraced him. Billy's body shook with sobs as he released pent up emotions and pain that he had been carrying around for fifty years. Everyone tactfully walked away and gave them some space. When Billy stopped shaking, Mark asked him, "You going to be okay now, Billy?" Billy looked at Mark with no embarrassment and said, "I think so, Marky." Mark smiled; that's what Billy had called him when they were young. Billy had called them Paulie and Marky. That was a throwback for sure.

On the way back to the office, Mark called Sheriff Mack and told him what they had found and asked him to post a guard on the school and the entrance to the crawl space. When he arrived at the office, Mack was already there. He looked at Mark and said, "After all these years you found them! I knew that they didn't run away. I never even knew there was a crawl space under the gym. That's just crazy. They had been right there all this time." Mark replied, "I am inclined to agree with you, but let's wait until we get the forensic report, coroner's report, and whatever else we can find before we start high-fiving." Mack responded, "You are right of course, but how could it be anybody else?" "I don't know," Mark replied, "I just want to be sure before we get too much deeper into this." Mack looked a Mark and said, "All those years ago the brass just got so mad at me because I didn't go along with their explanation. I remember the old Sheriff wagging his finger under my nose and telling me that if I couldn't get on board, to at least shut up about it. That was the hard part. I saw no evidence that they had run. I made the mistake of telling the Sheriff that he was just trying to put that one to bed before he retired so he could say he closed the biggest case that he ever handled. He almost fired me then." Mack dropped his head for a few moments then said, "You know that you are going to be a legend among investigators, don't you? This is huge; finding the bodies after fifty years. I still can't figure out how you did it." Mark looked at Mack and replied, "I'll tell you about it sometime, but not today. I'm beat and emotionally strung out. Tomorrow will be a monster day with forensic teams, coroners, and questions from reporters. I'll get a lot of credit that I don't deserve, but that's the way it goes. Besides, now we have a murderer to catch and we do not have anyone that we can point to as a clear suspect. This makes it more difficult because it points us back to a suspect pool that has been examined through a microscope already. It's not productive to point back and say that you guys missed something because you didn't even know what you were looking for. Wow!"

When Mark arrived at home, Sarah had already heard. She asked no questions. She just hugged him and held him. That was what he needed.

CHAPTER 34

The next morning, after a fitful night that had not felt restful, Mark was on his way back to the office. He was about ten miles outside Pleasant Valley when his phone rang. It was the coroner and she wanted to talk. Mark called the office and told them that he would be meeting with the coroner before arriving at the office and headed for the morgue.

When he walked into the morgue, there was an entire forensic team in there and they had worked through the night. Mark saw Sally Franklin, a cousin of Pauline's, who was the county coroner. "Mark!" she exclaimed, and hugged him, "It has been forever!" "It does seem like that. I didn't see you at Billy's place the day he found the car." She replied, "I know; I wasn't there. I was out of town all day that day and it just felt overwhelming and a little bit unbelievable. I thought it would turn out to be a false alarm." "Well, it wasn't." said Mark. "I was stunned that they actually found it. Nobody ever suspected. I expect now that we have found the remains of the girls. Am I right?" Sally nodded, "You are correct. It's them. We worked all night mostly because nobody could slow down. Many of us remember the day that the girls disappeared and those that don't have heard so much about it that they feel like they remember. It is the biggest thing that ever happened in this town and now fifty years later, the story goes on. It is unbelievable, but here it is right in front of us." Mark nodded, "I know. After all these years it feels surreal to me. We were so broken and distraught back then. Maybe we would have found them if we had been able to think straight. Most of us refused to acknowledge that they were dead. We imagined them living out their lives somewhere even though we knew that it could not be true. They weren't the kind to abandon the people they loved for a selfish adventure. Once I joined the FBI and saw the outcome of so many cold cases, I came to the conclusion that something terrible happened to them back there, but had resigned myself to never knowing."

Sally suddenly changed to a more professional demeanor and said, "We have identified all three of them but DNA will confirm. We were able to identify them because they were all wearing the class rings you guys gave them." Mark felt his eyes sting a bit at that. He asked, "Were you able to confirm a cause of death?"

Sally replied, "Yes! The COD is gunshot wound. I think the slug is a .38 or maybe a .32. We've already sent it off for confirmation and ballistics. We'll find out if the gun has ever been used in a crime other than this one." "Good work!" Mark said. "Can you give me any more details?" "Yes," Sally responded, "I can. Cassie and Esperanza were shot in the back of the head. I don't think they ever saw it coming or suspected they were going to die. Pauline must have been the last one because she took off and was shot in the back of the torso from farther away. It looks like the killer caught up to her once she fell and put one more in her forehead between the eyes. The others were shot once each, but Pauline was shot five times, which indicates that the killer had a semiautomatic weapon." Mark stood in stony silence for a long moment and then softly said, "She must have been so scared. My God! How could someone be so cruel? What could possibly motivate such depraved cruelty?" Sally put her hand on Mark's arm in an instinctive gesture to calm and comfort him. She murmured, "It must have been awful; I can't even imagine." "You know," Mark said, "I always thought that you looked a bit like Pauline. Your moms, being sisters, looked a lot alike. Is your mom still living, by the way." "Yes, she is," replied Sally, "and she is going to take this news hard. She and my aunt always held hope that one day that red Mustang was going to come cruising right back into town and we'd all pick up where we left off. They were quite upset when you left town, you know." Mark looked at her a bit surprised, "What was I supposed to do with my life? Park myself on the porch and wait for fifty years? People certainly have some strange ideas. If it is any consolation to them, I never got over her and probably never will. This will help to get closure, but there are just too many loose ends. We'll never know the whole truth. Speaking of which, where in the world are we going to find a motive. That would help a lot to point us toward a killer, if the killer is still alive." Mark hugged Sally again and headed for his office.

When Mark walked in to his office, Willy and Jack were there waiting for him. They just stood for a long moment and stared at each other. Jack spoke first. "You found them!" He said. "It has just been confirmed this morning by the medical examiner. She's your cousin Sally," Mark replied. "Yeah," Jack said in almost a sigh, "She called me to let me know late last night, but I didn't tell anyone." Mark said, "That's okay. Normally she shouldn't do that but this is far from a normal situation. Pauline was your sister and Pera your girlfriend. It's both a relief and a disappointment to know for sure." Willy interjected, "It puts a cork in the bottle that many of us have left open for many years. We didn't want to make any presumptions, but many of us knew they had to be dead or detained or they would have called or come home. Really, they're better off than they would have been if sold into slavery. I mean, the things that we know now that we didn't in 1968 make me realize that there were, even then, fates worse than death." Mark asked, "Jack, what details did Sally give you?" Jack looked Mark in the eye and said, "None, because I stopped her and told her that I was not ready for details." "Good choice," said Mark. Willy asked, "What are you not telling us?" "That's a conversation for another day," replied Mark. "While I have you here, though, think carefully now, did either of you ever breath a word about the haberdashery to anybody? Somebody clearly knew about it." They both vehemently denied ever saying anything to anybody about it. "I'm glad that we all have solid alabis," Mark said, "because I just might have to arrest us otherwise." Jack asked, "Do you think that this casts suspicion back onto the custodial staff?" Mark thought for a moment, "There were a lot of people who could have known about that place in addition to the custodial staff." Willy frowned, "Like whom?" He asked. "Well, for starters the construction crew, anybody who was around during the time that the construction was being done, delivery drivers, various school faculty, and administration. Surely I'm not the only person in town who knew how to pick a lock. What this has done is reopened a suspect pool that has been pretty heavily fished. On top of that, most of them are no longer around. Most of them would be dead by now. Those that are alive may not be entirely clear in their memories of those times. This has thrown another monkey wrench into the works. I guess the upside is that we can now bury our girls," Mark said thoughtfully.

CHAPTER 36

The funeral was spectacular. The entire town turned out as well as TV crews from most of the major networks. It was a really big deal, finding the remains of the victims of a fifty year old murder. For many of the family it was like tearing the scab off a cut that they thought had healed.

Pastor Fogarty, who had been pastor of the church where two of the girls had attended, returned from a couple of towns over to officiate. Not to be left in the shadows, the current pastor insisted on having part in the service even though he never knew any of the girls and none of their families continued to attend there. Abigail Cheryl Jenson Appleton Fogarty led the choir and music program. It was wonderful; everyone said so. Pastor Fogarty was mercifully brief in his comments as there were a number of eulogies for each of the girls. Following the service, Esperanza was taken to the Catholic Church for a private mass and burial in their cemetery. The other two girls were interred in the Pleasant Valley Municipal Memorial Gardens.

Poor Billy Patterson nearly lost his mind trying to deal with the TV people wanting to talk with him since he was the one who found the car and got this whole ball rolling again. He was very glad that his older brother Pete had come home for the services. Peter was more experienced in dealing with the world so he handled the media and kept them off Billy's back. Peter was devastated. He, along with his mother, had always held out hope that Cassie would one day come home. That was now proven to be impossible. Well, in a sense they had come home, but not the way in which he had hoped. He had imagined a return in grandeur that would be as spectacular as their disappearance. Peter and Billy both agreed that it was a relief that their mother was gone before they found the remains because the shock and loss of hope would probably have killed her anyway. At least, that's what they thought.

Mark was a hot commodity in the eyes of the reporters. He was the retired FBI guy who had made his FBI reputation solving cold cases that others had given up on. Now he had found the remains of three girls murdered fifty years ago. The disappearance was sensational at the time and it seemed to insist on remaining sensational. Mark did not say so, but in his heart of hearts, he held the belief that some cases had a life and destiny of their own and nobody controlled them; they just happened. This seemed like one of that kind of case. He endured six different interviews and then disappeared. When they couldn't find Mark, they descended on Mack and started in on him. He was glad to tell them that he had never accepted the explanation that the previous Sheriff had given for closing his case, but there was just no proof of anything. He was lavish in his praise of Mark and his team and told the press that Mark was working for less than half of his normal fee. That impressed the news people and they wanted Mark again, but he was gone. Some of them parked outside his house and others outside his office, but he was done talking with them. He had work to do. His team had wisely disappeared immediately after the services. Victor and Willie, who were Catholic, went over to the Catholic Church for the services for Esperanza. Her family really appreciated that gesture. Their explanation was that after working so many weeks on the case and reading so much about the girls, they felt like they knew them. They did not mention the presence they felt in the crawl space while looking for the remains. They just wanted to put the girls to rest and hoped that this would do it.

The funerals were on Friday; by Monday, most of the media hordes had moved on to other stories. There were just a few reporters and photographers who stayed in the area hoping to be on hand when the murderer was caught. They made pests of themselves for a week or so. When they realized that the perpetrator was not going to just walk out and say, "I did it!" they began leaving town one by one until Pleasant Valley was finally free of the outside press. By the time they left, most of the town's people were ready to run them out of town. They did spend a lot of money while there, though. The restaurants were happy they were around. There were several features done with the Wascally Wabbit in the middle. They were thankful for the free advertisement, but even they were glad to see the pests leave. One old regular was heard to grumble, "I thought we were going to have to call an exterminator to get rid of those vultures." The best defense against a nosey reporter however, is nothing to report. That's what finally sent them packing. Other than a few locals who fancied themselves celebrities heretofore undiscovered, the locals were glad they were gone. Mark and his team were already settled back into a routine.

CHAPTER 37

Mark and his team were sitting around the conference table in their offices. They were studying the coroner's report. Tex finally spoke up. "Damn!" he said, "the first two girls probably never saw it coming, but Pauline was running. She must have been so scared. It makes a Texas boy mad enough to chew nails and spit carpet tacks!" They all nodded or gave some sign of assent. Victor added, "Amen to that, Buddy. The shooter had to be somewhat experienced. Pauline was a moving target; she was taken down on the run. That is no mean feat, especially in the limited light. The shots were in her right side which means it was broadside shooting. That is harder than straight away or toward the shooter." "Anything else?" Mark asked. Willie looked up, 'It looks like they were laid out in their graves by somebody who cared about them. They weren't just thrown in; they were laid out with their hands folded in a typical pose one would see from a funeral director. I wonder why?" Jay added, "It doesn't appear that anything was missing. Their money was still in their purses and their jewelry was still on their remains. The motive clearly was not robbery." Gina spoke up, "The bullets are.32 caliber which points to a hand gun. Anybody have any idea how we would find out who owns or owned a.32 caliber hand gun?"

Mark looked at them with no particular expression on his face. His words were not encouraging, "There is nothing in this report that points to a motive or a suspect. We are still right where we were before we started except we now know where and how they died. What we need to know is why and at whose hand. How are we going to dig that out of the dirt? Are there any ideas, People?"

Tex spoke as though he were thinking out loud, "The likelihood of that gun being registered back in 1968 is very slim. We could check with known gun collectors and enthusiasts. There may have been one sold or traded after the murder. I mean, would you hold onto the piece if you had killed three girls with it? We could ask anyone who has a.32 caliber weapon to surrender it for ballistics testing. It's a shot in the dark, but better than nothing. What do you think?" Mark nodded, "It is definitely a place to start. Anybody else have an idea? I want any new ideas brought to me immediately. This is still far from over. I also want to thank you for your hard work to date. Let's get back on the horse now."

When Mark got back to his desk, his first call was to Sheriff Mack. "Mack," he said, "I'd like to come by your office if you have a few minutes." Mack replied, "I'll stop by yours; I'm just a couple of blocks away anyway. Just give me a few minutes and I'll be there." "Okay," Mark replied and hung up the phone.

Mack walked into Mark's office about twenty minutes later. Mark had a copy of the coroner's report for him. As he read the report, Sheriff Mack grunted and spit out a couple of "Damns". Finally he looked at Mark and couldn't even speak for a long moment. Finally he swallowed and said, "This is what I always expected, but hoped to be wrong about. Who in God's name would do such a thing?" Mark shook his head, "Mack, I wish I knew. We can't even imagine a motive for such an atrocity. Do you have any thoughts?" Mack looked at Mark and said, "How does somebody so completely control three healthy young girls, get them to go down to that place, and then kill them all by himself? It seems like it has to be a team. Don't you think so?" "I do think so, but I don't want to get so focused on one thing that I miss something that is shouting at me for notice," replied Mark. "Do you know anybody with a.32 caliber firearm?" "I have one," said Mack, "but I bought it brand new about ten years back. What are you thinking?" Mark said, "Tex suggested that the killer may have sold or traded the gun after the murder and it may be setting in somebody's collection with the owner none the wiser. Is there any way we can entice people to voluntarily bring their.32 caliber firearms in to be tested to see if we can find the murder weapon?" Mack made a face and said, "I don't know. People around here really want the killer found, but they are also very private. I'll see what I can do. I'll talk to a few of the leaders of the gun collectors to see if they would lend a hand. If they are on board, it would be much easier." "Mack, we would really appreciate any help that you can give. This case has turned into the most unpredictable one I can remember," said Mark. "Mark," replied Mack, as he got up to leave, "you guys have done an unbelievable job. I always thought in my deputy and now sheriff heart that you guys were overrated. That is not the case. If anything, you are underrated. What you guys have done with this case is astounding. I thought we did a good investigation, but we really missed something!" Mark replied, "Thanks, Mack, but don't beat yourself up. We started with a lucky break when Billy found the car. And for the record, the original investigation was one of the best I have ever seen. I would use it as a prototype to teach new investigators good methods and thorough investigative procedures. You can't see what isn't there." Mark dropped his head replying, "Thanks, Mark, that's kind of you to say." Mark grinned at Mack and replied, " If you ask people who know me, when it comes to work, I don't do kind. If you screw up, I say so. You did not screw up. It was solid police work. You can trust me on that." They shook hands and waved goodbye to one another.

Mark sat down at his desk and wondered to himself if they would ever figure out who killed those girls and why. Mark realized that, had they not had a rock solid alibi, the three members of the First String would have been in the crosshairs of the investigation and rightfully so. It made him wonder how many times the wrong guy had gone down for a crime he did not commit because he was so perfect for it and didn't have a solid alibi. That was a scary thought.

CHAPTER 38

Mark looked at his team as they sat in their conference room. "Look at it this way," he said. "We are starting now where most murder investigations start except we have already eliminated every suspect that we could see and we are fifty years after the fact. Now that we have said that, we now have to generate a new pool of suspects. Anybody have any suggestions as to where we should start?" Willie spoke up saying, "I don't have a clue where to go next. I'm pretty sure that there were people back fifty years ago that slipped through the cracks. There's no way that we can figure out at this point, who they were and if they are still alive, but we should try all the same." Tex added, "It could be absolutely anybody. I think we need to start with motive. If we can figure out why it would help point toward the killer." Jay suggested, "We also need to see if we can figure out who is missing from the previous investigation and why. Sometimes what is not there is as important as what is there." Victor said, "That was pretty damned good shooting to get all three of those girls. Maybe we're looking for a veteran or a cop. Does that make anyone else as uncomfortable as it does me?" Gina had been listening without comment, in fact, almost without movement except to breath. She finally said, "I think we should do another deep dive into the file by each one of us separately and take notes and then compare our notes and see what each of us notices without any outside influences. What do you think?" Mark replied, "The answers have to be available. I think the file is the right place to start. Be aware of what is in the file and what is missing. Maybe if we take note of what is missing, we can fill in the gaps. While we're doing that, let's keep in mind all of the other recommendations, as well. If a new angle presents itself to one of you, don't hesitate to toss it out for consideration. We are in uncharted territory. Anything could be important."

It was quiet around the office for several days while each of the investigators reviewed the file section by section, sheet by sheet. After spending most of the week looking at the file, they reconvened in the conference room for a recap. They all looked tired. Mark asked, "Is everyone about blind by now?" They were too weary to laugh at him. They just grunted and looked at him. "Let's take the weekend to digest what we have noted and each of us will summarize our notes and then we'll compare them on Monday to see what, if anything, we have found. Is that acceptable to you?" They all nodded their assent. "It's eleven AM and it's Friday. Let's knock off for the rest of the day and I'll see you Monday," said Mark. It took about two minutes for everyone to be gone. Mark sat back in his chair to rest his back and eyes.

The phone awakened him and he jumped, not realizing that he had fallen asleep. He answered to find Sheriff Mack calling. "Mack!" he said, "How are you, old friend?" Mack grunted, "Don't rub it in," which caused Mark to laugh. "What's up, Mack?" Mark asked. He replied, "We have been canvassing gun collectors and have sixteen .32 caliber guns to test. I just thought you would like to know. I'm going to take them down and fire them and collect the slugs this afternoon."

Mark asked, "Do you mind if I tag along?" Mack replied, "No, glad for the company. I'll drop by your office after lunch. See you then." Since Mark had brought a brown bag lunch, he sat at his desk and ate while quietly pondering nothing in particular and everything that crossed his mind. It suddenly occurred to him that they should try to find out where the bicycle came from and what happened to it. It was a long shot, but could be important. He made a mental note to start trying to chase it down. He had just the guy to do it, too. When he finished his lunch, he punched Victor's number into his phone and waited for him to answer. "Vic," Mark said, "I have an assignment for you." "What would that be?" Victor asked. "We need to try to figure out who owned the bicycle and what happened to it," Mark said. "What do we know about it?" responded Victor. "We know that it was blue which would have made it most likely a girls bicycle fifty years ago. Mostly boys' bikes were red and girls' were blue. There were exceptions, but that was the norm. The color of blue paint that I saw probably came from a girl's bike. See if you can find it." Victor replied, "Will do; is there any time restrictions on this?" "Not really," replied Mark, "it's been fifty years, but the sooner the better." "Roger that!" barked Victor. Mark grinned as he could almost see Victor's salute. As an ex-Marine, he had a very snappy salute. Not that there was any such thing as an ex-Marine.

Mack was walking in the door just as Mark and Victor finished their conversation. Mack asked, "What's new, Mark?" "Nothing really," said Mark, "we're just starting to run down loose ends on some of the new evidence. For example, I have asked Victor to find out what he can about the bicycle that was seen in the trunk of the Mustang as it was driving out of town. It might be meaningless; on the other hand, it could crack the case. You just never know." "That is so very true," responded Mack. "I have seen the smallest detail be the crack that let enough light into a case to break it wide open. That's why we investigators have to notice the details that other people don't even think about." Mark nodded and said, "Yeah, and that is why bad cops are the hardest criminals to catch. They know about the details. An experienced detective that goes south is probably the hardest of all to catch." Mack gave Mark a long look and said, "What if somebody has committed the perfect crime by purely dumb luck?" "If that is the case, and it may be," replied Mark, "then we are going to need purely dumb luck to catch the killer. That worries me because I don't believe in luck." Mack chucked, "Neither do I, but somehow this one has eluded us, me especially, for fifty years. Mark, a day has not gone by in those fifty years that I have not thought about this case. I am glad that I'm still Sheriff. I was planning on retiring this year anyway, but now maybe I can put this one to bed and then retire." Mark nodded, "I sincerely hope so, Mack. It has been hanging around way too long." They both lapsed into a moody silence.

When they arrived at the lab, they met with the lab techs and explained what they were doing. The guns were all tagged with the owner's name and the identification information on the piece. The manufacturer was listed, the model number, the caliber, and the serial number. One of them did not have a serial number. It had been burned off with acid. There were modern techniques available that would often restore enough of the number to read it. They would try doing that if the outcome of the test warranted it, but there was no use going to the expense until there was a reason for it. The technicians said they would have the results in a couple of days so Mack and Mark drove back to the office. They were strangely quiet. When they were almost at Mark's office, Mack asked him, "Mark, do you think you could show me that old bass hole you guys found years ago? I'd love to do some bass fishing this weekend." Mark looked at Mack and replied with a smirk, "If I show you, I'd have to kill you." After a mutual chuckle he replied, "Sure, Mack, I'd be happy to do that. You know that it must remain a secret, though, right?" "Yeah, I know," replied Mack. "When can you show me?" "You got a boat?" asked Mark. "Of course, I have one down at the launch. I keep it there," replied Mack. "Well, how about right now? You game for a trip up the river?" said Mark. "You bet," replied Mack, "I was born game."

Mark turned right on Main Street, heading toward the river rather than left toward Mark's office. When they arrived at the boat landing, the Sheriff had him pull up to the boathouse and he unlocked the door. Inside was a beautiful, sleek bass boat with all the bells and whistles. Mark looked with appreciation at the boat. "Very pretty," he said with a grin, "but can it find bass?" Mack laughed at the obvious movie reference. He said, "You're borrowing from Donald Sutherland in the "Dirty Dozen" in that scene where he is pretending to be a general." "Very astute of you Sheriff; you give me hope that we might solve this case after all. Now, however, let's head up the river." Mack fired up the big outboard motor and they were soon flying up the river. It was a beautiful day and a great place to be. About two and a half miles up the river, Mark told the Sheriff to slow the boat. There was a sharp bend in the river and above the bend there was an outcropping of rocks. Mark said, "This is it." Mack said, "I have fished here many times and I have never caught the monster bass you guys used to catch out of here." Mark replied, "You have to fish it right, Mack." "Oh, you mean like I have to hold my mouth right?" Mack asked. "No, nothing like that; most people fish the bend and they always catch fish. You need to fish the down-river side of the rock outcropping. The big bass lay in there. You have to cast a little bit above the rocks and let the current take your lure under the rocks. That's where they are. You'll only get one or two per trip, but they are in there." Mack stared at Mark, "People followed you and watched you and never saw any of you fish that spot. Everyone tried to figure out where you guys caught those big bass." Mark laughed, "Mack, we knew people were following us. We never fished that spot when there were other people around. Try it! I'll run the boat for you." Mark maneuvered the boat above the rocks and floated on the current. Mack tossed his lure into the current and the current took it down under the rocks. There was a light tug on his line and Mack set the hook. He grunted as soon as he felt the power on the line. "Whoa! He didn't hit all that hard!" he said. Mark grinned, "The big ones never do, Mack. Bring the big boy home, now!" Mark moved the boat into the middle of the river to give Mack room to work the fish. Finally, after several minutes of running, the fish came to the side of the boat. It was about a six-pound small mouth bass. Mack was ecstatic. "Wow! That is the biggest one I ever caught out here. They are so much stronger in the river than in the lakes!" Mark nodded, "I agree. Nice job bringing him in. Now you know. There's almost always a big one lying in there. We usually hit that hole going up river and then coming back down." Mack said, "I need to get back to my office, but I owe you big time. I have searched for that spot for years." Mark replied, "Well, now you know. We found it by accident ourselves when we were just kids. We were probably eleven years old when we found it. We kept it secret because we could, I guess. We never even told our own dads where it was." Mack laughed, "That's funny! How did they react to that?" "I really don't remember," said Mark. "I guess they learned to live with it. For my part, when my dad would question me about it I'd say, 'what secret hole?' I didn't want to lie to him, but neither did I want to tell him. He would have told his buddies and the next thing you knew, there'd be a boat parked on our spot every day of fishing season." "You are right about that," said Mack. "I mean," said Mark, "we found that spot by pure accident." Mack shook his head and said, "I saw how you guys fished when you were kids. You were thorough and meticulous. You fished slowly and thoroughly, giving the fish every opportunity to bite. It was almost inevitable that you would eventually hit on that spot. It's the same way you work your cases. That's why it is inevitable that you will eventually find the killer. It's just the way you work. You are working this case just like you used to fish the river, giving the killer every opportunity to show himself." Mark looked at Mack appreciatively. "Thanks, Mack," he said, "those are kind words coming from you. I know how much this case means to you." Mack chuckled, "I just calls 'em like I sees 'em," he stated with his best baseball umpire impression.

CHAPTER 39

Mark drove home with his mind full of the complexities of the case. He was feeling a bit overwhelmed and needed to remind himself of the progress they were making because it felt like they were getting nowhere. They found new roads but they all led to nothing. It was enough to give a guy a headache.

After dinner, Sarah sat down to watch TV and Mark wandered into the den and broke out his Stratocaster. It had been awhile since he had played it and it really felt good. Even though he was a little rusty, the notes of some of his old favorites began to fill the room. There was something quite therapeutic for Mark in playing those old, familiar tunes. He started playing some of the songs that the First String used to play. After what seemed like just a few minutes, Mark saw Sarah standing in the doorway watching him. He stopped playing and she strolled into the room. "I love to hear you play that thing," she said. "It always takes me back to happier times." "Yeah, me too," replied Mark. "Play 'Gone on You', please," she said. Mark started the song and something seemed to take him over. He played it like he did back when the band was together. When he was done, they both felt it. They sat there in silence for a long moment. Then Sarah whispered, "That was magical! You should have kept playing. Your gift should have been shared with the world." Mark replied sadly, "I have wished that we had kept playing, but at the time, we were broken and could not go on. It didn't seem like it would be right. Maybe it was a mistake, but it's of no consequence now." Sarah touched Mark's arm, "You have done really good work in your life and you are presently doing something that is important to many people. It might be the roll of the dice of fate, but I prefer to believe that God has brought you back to here to finish something that started a long time ago. There is a feeling that this was destined to end this way. I don't know, but I do know that I believe in you and what you are doing. Who knows, maybe with this is over, the music will come back. It's not too late." Mark gave Sarah a gentle, loving look and replied, "I promised the other guys that, if we solve this case, I would break out this old guitar and we'd play together again." Sarah replied, "I would love that!" "Me too," Mark said.

Mark awakened on Monday morning with the feeling that he had not slept so well in months, maybe years. He felt so rested. He wasn't sure why, but was pleased nonetheless. As he drove in to the office, he was listening to a CD of the First String which was something he had not done in a very long time. He just felt optimistic for some reason. Even if it was just a false positive, it felt good.

He sat down at his desk and his phone rang almost immediately. It Mack and he was excited. "Mark!" he barked into the phone. "We have a match! We found the weapon!" Mark felt the old surge of adrenaline that came with a major break in a case. "Mack," he said as calmly has he could muster, "that is great news. Can you bring the piece over or do you want me to come by there?" "I'll bring it. In fact, I'm almost there, now." Mack said. "Excellent!" replied Mark. "See you in a few minutes." Mark waited and did not tell his team the news. He wanted Mack there for the reveal. He tried to go back to work, but his mind was not having it. He was about the burst with the news. Mack walked in just in time to save him from spilling the beans.

They shook hands like two seasoned professionals who could take great news like it was the weather report. Inside, though, they were jumping up and down. The news was that good. They were a major step closer to finding the killer of the three girls so many years ago. Mack sat down and passed the ballistics report to Mark. As he looked it over, Mark started to nod his head. It was a positive match to a .32 caliber Browning owned by one Felix Fenton, who was a collector. Mack had the piece with him and he handed it over to Mark, as well. It was clean and well maintained. Mark looked down at it with a certain amount of loathing. This little semiautomatic pistol had taken the lives of three people that he had dearly loved. It was hard not to hate the gun, but it was clearly not at fault. Mark said to his friend, "I want to call my team together and tell them all at the same time." Mack agreed, "Good idea; they deserve to know first."

Mark called an impromptu team meeting and they gathered slowly around the conference table. Once all were assembled, Mark said, "Mack has something to share with us this morning…Mack?" Mack looked surprised and then stepped up, "I am pleased and honored to be the one to advise this team that we have had a major break in the case. We have identified the murder weapon." He had to pause for applause and high-fives before going on. "We have confirmed that this.32 caliber Browning is, without doubt, the weapon that took the lives of the three young ladies back fifty years ago. I am so proud to be a part of this investigation. I don't mean to gush, but I have dreamed of moments like this for fifty years. I'm just glad to be around to see this. I will now give the floor back to Mark." Mark stood up and said to his team, "This afternoon we will drive out to speak with the owner of the murder weapon. It would be too easy if he were the killer. I doubt that it will be that simple, but it is a step closer to the goal. Are there any questions?" There were none. The entire team knew the process very well; they knew that they were probably still a long way from solving the case, but were elated at the news. Having the murder weapon was huge.

As Mark and Mack drove out to the Fenton place, Mark said, "I don't remember any Fentons living around here when we were young. Have they been here long?" Mack replied, "Marge Fenton is the daughter of Harley and Hazel Smith. She and Felix married and settled down here around '71 or '72."

"So he wasn't even here when the girls disappeared, right?" Mark said. "That's right," Mack responded, "he is originally from Oklahoma. They met in Tulsa when Marge went to school out there," replied Mack. "I think he inherited Old Man Smith's gun collection. Smith didn't have any sons. I expect that he has added to it. He had quite a collection; I think that you will appreciate it." When they arrived at the Fenton place, Marge answered the door. Felix was seated at the dining room table drinking a cup of coffee.

Marge insisted on coffee and cookies all around before she would seat herself. She finally did sit down next to her husband. Mr. Fenton asked quietly, "What is the nature of your visit? I suspect it has something to do with the gun that you took for testing; am I right?" Mack replied, "You are correct, Mr. Fenton." Felix Fenton protested, "Mack! We have always been on a first name basis. I don't remember the last time you called me Mr. Fenton, but it was probably the first time we met." Mack looked a bit embarrassed, "You're right. This is just really difficult for me. Felix, we found that the handgun from your collection matches the murder weapon." Felix nodded, "I suspected as much when you showed up this morning. You don't think I had anything to do with that murder do you?" "Of course not," Mack replied, "I remember when you and Marge married. In fact, I was at the wedding. You didn't even live here when the girls were murdered. What I would like to know is when you acquired the piece. Could you help us with that?" Mr. Fenton looked very relieved and replied, "Absolutely! I keep detailed records on all of the weapons that I purchase. I can tell you the date, the price, the seller, and the condition in just a couple of minutes." Mr. Fenton went into his den and came back out after a few minutes with a file. According to the file, the Browning had been purchased in 1975 from Pastor Fogarty. Mark and Mack both looked stunned. Mark was the first to speak, "Did Pastor Fogarty tell you anything about the gun?" Felix replied, "All he said was that he came across it in the church when he was getting ready to move. He had asked the church people if they knew whether anyone had left it there and nobody claimed it or confessed to knowing anything about it. He had called the police, but they had not received any reports of a lost or stolen hand gun. They told him to hang onto it for a while to see if anyone was looking for it. If nobody came looking for it, he could keep it. He told me that he had held it, but didn't want to keep it so he sold it to me for two hundred dollars." Mark said, "Thank you, Felix. You have been most helpful. We will need to hold onto the weapon for the time being as it is now evidence in a homicide." He said, "I understand, it is not a problem."

The drive back to the office, where Mack had left his car, was a quiet one. Both Mark and Mack could sense that they were on a trail. Nothing in this case could be construed to be a hot lead, but this was about as close as they were going to get. They were a couple of old law dogs who now had a distinct scent and they were going to follow it out. When they arrived and as they were parting, Mark asked Mack, "Mack, are you going to check on Felix's story that Pastor Fogarty reported finding the gun to the police? It would check a box for us." Mack answered, "Yes, I am, but I don't doubt that it is true. Nothing in this case has been easy. Why would it start now?" Mark added, "Do you want to go with me when I ask Pastor Fogarty about the murder weapon?" "I was hoping you'd ask," responded Mack. "I would very much like to be there." Mark nodded, "For sure; I'll call you."

<h1 style="text-align:center">CHAPTER 40</h1>

When Mark walked into the office, Victor was waiting for him. "Victor! What's up?" Mark asked. "I have some word on the bicycle that might interest you," replied Victor. "Fire away!" Mark said. Victor started, "To begin with, I found that a blue Schwinn bicycle was left at the school for a long time. The bike belonged to Cassie Patterson and she just left it at the school when her dad bought her that Mustang." Mark looked at him expectantly, "That's interesting, but there has to be more." "Indeed," responded Victor, "there is more. It seems that many people made use of the bicycle and just brought it back. It was there for several months and nobody stole it. They just used it like a community bicycle. The phrase that I heard from most of the people who knew about it was, and I quote, 'everybody knew it was there and anybody who needed it for something used it.'" Mark gave Victor a long look and then asked, "Where does that leave us?" Victor replied, "I'm not sure. I need to keep at it. I'm going to try to see if anybody saw who used the bike immediately following the disappearance. Maybe that would give us a glimmer of light." Mark put his hand on Victor's shoulder and said, "Vic, that is good work, so far. Keep on it until you find something or are sure that you won't be able to find anything, okay?" Vic grinned, "You bet; I'm all over it."

Mark sat at his desk and outlined the questions that he wanted to ask Pastor Fogarty. He was pretty sure that the pastor was telling the truth about the gun, but he wanted details. After an hour or so of forming questions and rewording them, he thought that he had his interview outline about right. He then picked up the phone and called Pastor Fogarty. They made an appointment for the next morning and he hung up the phone. Mark then called Mack and informed him of the interview. He asked Mack to drive himself over to the church since it was closer to Mark's house and he was going to do the interview before coming to the office.

That done, Mark sat and went over what they knew and what they did not know. They now knew what had happened, where it had happened, how it was done, and very close to when it happened. What they did not have was the big question. WHY had someone killed those three innocents? Mark decided to go over what they had in common to see if he could find something.

They were all going into their senior year of high school

They had been classmates since kindergarten

They were all church girls, although they didn't attend the same church

They were all athletic, sharing: softball, basketball and volleyball

They were all varsity cheerleaders

They were all honor students

They were all going to top notch colleges

They were all members of 4-H, Girl Scouts, choir

It suddenly occurred to Mark that they also had First String in common. For the first time Mark wondered if the motive had something to do with the band. It was hard for him to even consider it, but he knew that he had to think about it and find an answer to the question. Who could have wanted to hurt First String so badly that they would kill three beautiful, innocent girls to accomplish their ends? It just seemed preposterous to even think it. There was nobody that Mark could remember that had any animosity toward the band. There were some studio people and promoters that were pushing them to forget college, high school, and their girlfriends, and commit fully to the rock and roll life style. None of the guys were really willing to do that. Mark doubted, however, that any of them would have resorted to murder to get their desired result. It just didn't make sense. The world had changed since 1968, but back then stuff like this just didn't happen.

Mark started writing down the names of everyone that he could remember from the music business fifty years ago. The list was short mostly because he just didn't remember most of them. He did remember that one of the fellows pushed the guys really hard to take high school on the road, forget their girlfriends, and hit the music scene full time. His name was Faron Stewart. He was a promoter who had brought several bands to moderate success. He was looking, at the time, for a group to take him to the top. Of course his pitch was that he would take them to the top. Mark had long since figured out that guys like Faron were passengers on other peoples' trains, who pushed themselves into a front line position to live off the success of others. He was basically a parasite who sold himself as a necessary go-between insuring the success of his "clients". In fact, he was trying to generate his own success. He needed a band that would propel themselves and him into the winner's circle. Mark wondered if Faron Stewart had been around the weekend that the girls disappeared. He was the only person that even had a remote motive as far as Mark could see. Mark called Victor into his office.

"Victor," Mark said, when Vic had flopped into a chair across the desk from him, "I have another project for you." "Name it," replied Victor. "There is a name that I would like for you to run down." "Who is it?" asked Victor. Mark responded, "The name is Faron Stewart. He was a promoter and hustler in the rock and roll business back in 1968 when we were on the rise." Victor cocked his head, "Were you guys that good?" Mark gave him a wry look, "I don't know. Some people thought that we were. Our record company was pushing for a long term contract. F-stew, as we used to call him, was pushing us to allow him to manage us to stardom, his words not mine." "Wow!" said Victor with an appraising gaze, "I never knew that about you. You could have been one of the beautiful people and you just walked away. That is fascinating!" "I wrote a few songs that were big. That's a long way from the success that he had envisioned for us. After the girls disappeared, the song just went out of me for many years." Victor nodded and then said, "That is really too bad. It's kind of sad really. So what do you want me to do?" Mark replied, "See if you can chase Stewart down. Find out if he is still alive and where he was the weekend that the girls disappeared. He left our tour on Thursday of that week and I think he said he was flying to LA to look at a band out there. See if you can find out if he was out there. If he is still alive, he would be around seventy to seventy-five. He was in his early-twenties back then. Let me know what you find out." "Will do," Victor replied. "By the way, I think that Cassie's dad eventually came into town and took her bicycle home. Maybe it is still there." Mark thanked him and Victor left.

Once Victor left his office, Mark placed a call to Billy Patterson. Billy answered after the third ring, "This is Bill Patterson," he said. "Hi, Billy," Mark said, "I wonder if you still have Cassie's old bicycle out there at the farm?" Billy paused a long moment, "I think so; why do you ask?" "It may have become material evidence in the investigation. Could I come out and take a look at it?" Billy answered, "Sure can; I think it's out in the shed. Dad put all of Cassie's stuff upstairs in the shed. I'll bet it's still there. I haven't been up there in years. I'll see if I can find it. When are you coming out?" Mark replied, "I thought that I'd come out this afternoon, if that's alright with you." Billy replied, "Absolutely! Come on out. How's the investigation going?" Mark said, "We'll talk about it when I see you. Is that okay with you?" "Yeah, that's fine. See you later," replied Billy and he just hung up. He never had been really big on social graces. Why change now?

CHAPTER 41

Mark arrived at the Patterson place. Billy still lived in the old farmhouse that his parents had lived in. It had been built by his grandfather just after World War I. It was a large, two story house with a high peaked roof that made room for a big attic. There were windows in the attic and it could have been a third floor of the house, but was never finished as such. It was, however, finished more completely than most attics. He had been up there many times over the years with Jack. Mark admired the beauty and grace of the old house as he approached. He noted that Billy kept his property up better than he did himself.

Billy was on the porch and came out to meet Mark. They shook hands warmly. "What's going on, Mark?" Billy asked. Mark responded, "I want to look at Cassie's bike to see if it has some red paint from the Mustang's trunk on it." "Why would it?" asked Billy. "Billy," replied Mark, "a witness puts the bicycle in the trunk of the Mustang just before the car disappeared, but it was not in there when the car was taken out of the marsh." Billy replied, "No, it's here. I checked after we talked. I'll show you."

As Mark and Billy walked out to the shed, Mark was noticing the flowers in the yard and the overall loveliness of the place. "Billy," he said, "you are really taking great care of the place. It looks beautiful around here." Billy chuckled with some apparent embarrassment. He said, "Peter pays a gardener to take care of the flowers. I mow the lawn and maintain the buildings. I could never make flowers grow like this. I love them, but I do not have a green thumb." Mark laughed, "Well," he said, "A man should know his limitations." With that they both chuckled and arrived at the shed.

As they entered the shed, Billy said, "It's upstairs. I found it, but I didn't touch it. I don't know if there would be any evidence on it or not. As far as I know, the last person to touch it was my dad when he brought it up here. I'm not sure he ever even came up here again after that day." Mark put gloves on and began to look the bike over. He examined it front, back, and both sides, snapping pictures as he inspected it. "Billy!" he exclaimed. "Look at this rear fender." Sure enough there was a scrape of red paint just above the reflector. The tires were flat, but that was to be expected after fifty years. Mark gave Billy a solemn look and said, "I'm going to have to put this in evidence. There may be finger prints on it, but unless there is a match in the system, it won't do us much good. I will try, though." Billy nodded. "It's okay," he said. "It's not doing anybody any good here anyway. Maybe it can help you find out what happened to my sister."

In order to change the subject, Mark asked Billy, "How often does Pete come home to visit?" Billy smiled at that and replied, "He comes about two or three times per year." "Have you ever gone to California to visit him?" asked Mark. Billy gave Mark a rueful look and replied, "I went out there just once. That is a strange place. I just didn't fit in. Pete didn't prepare me for anything. I guess he is so used to it that it doesn't seem strange to him. I couldn't stand it. It made me crazy. I wondered for a while if everyone in California is crazy. I'm still not completely convinced that they are not." Mark was laughing by the time Billy finished. "That is so funny," he replied. "The sad fact is that I am not sure that you are wrong about that. I have worked some in California. It's a great place to visit, if you can afford it. The lifestyle just is not for me either." Billy nodded wisely, "Smart man," he said.

Mark loaded the bicycle into the back of his pick up and waved goodbye to Billy. Billy looked like that forlorn kid that he had seen so many times after the loss of the three girls. Mark realized that Billy was one who had never really recovered from the loss. His life was permanently marked by a tragic loss fifty years ago. He had never really gotten past it. He shook his head as he thought about Billy, Cassie, and the others. So much pain…

After placing the bike with the evidence, he called the lab to come and get it for analysis. They might get some finger prints. From the information that Victor had generated, a few finger prints on it would not mean much since it had been so available for anybody who wanted to ride it. Bits and pieces of evidence, however, would weave a tapestry that could very well show them a picture of a killer.

As Mark sat at his desk, his mind wandered back to the motive problem. He knew that until he had some kind of motive he would probably never nail the killer except by sheer luck. There was one angle of motive they, or at least he, had not considered seriously. That was jealousy. Could somebody have been so jealous of those three girls that they wanted them dead? The idea seemed preposterous, but it was time to go beyond the previous limits of their thinking. He typed out a quick email to his team members asking them to consider jealousy as a motive and look for any angle in which they could make a viable case for it. He was thinking of some of the recent cases of cheerleader and dance moms who went to ridiculous extremes to put their daughters in advantageous places. Maybe crazy moms weren't such a recent thing after all.

CHAPTER 42

After the team meeting the next morning, Mark asked Willie into his office for a chat. "Willie," Mark began, "what was your general impression of Cheryl Fogarty when you interviewed her?" "Well," replied Willie, "she seemed to be very straightforward in her responses. It appeared to me that she was heartbroken after the loss of the girls. I had the impression that she is a genuinely sweet, kind, and thoughtful person. Do you think I'm wrong?" Mark smiled and replied, "No, that is the Abigail Appleton that I remember, as well. I'm just trying to get a handle on anything. The only advantage we have with the Pastor and Cheryl is that we have personal impressions from the interview. With the others, we only have the tapes and transcripts. It would have been helpful if they had filmed the interviews, but they weren't doing that back in 1968." "Yeah, no doubt," replied Willie. Mark, returning to the immediate subject said, "So…there is nothing in her statement or her demeanor that would cause you to doubt that she is telling the truth?" Willie looked Mark in the eye and replied, "Nothing. What is this all about anyway?" Mark replied, "I'm looking for motive. I have begun asking myself if jealousy could be a motive." Willie looked at Mark like he was losing it and replied, "How or why would a teacher be so jealous of three of her students? I mean, one of them I can understand, but all three? It just doesn't track." "You're right," Mark replied. "I guess I'm just reaching and grasping at straws. I am not accustomed to not seeing a motive. This is really frustrating to me." Willie nodded, "To all of us," she replied. "We'll figure it out." "Do you really think so?" asked Mark. "Yes, I do," she replied. "We have made way too much progress to have this die on the vine. Besides, there is something working behind the scenes here that wants this truth revealed." Mark replied, "I hope you are right. Thanks for your input. It has been very helpful." "Just here to serve," she said with a bright smile and a snappy salute. "Ah," said Mark, "you have been taking saluting lessons from Victor!" Willie left his office laughing.

Mark walked out and grabbed Victor. "Victor," he said, "let's go for a drive." "Okay, boss!" Victor replied. "Where are we headed?" Mark replied, "We're going to take advantage of the nice weather and do a little outside work." "Sounds like fun," Victor said. They got into Mark's truck and headed out. "Where are we going?" asked Victor. "We're going out to the lake," replied Mark. "Hmm.." was Victor's eloquent reply.

It was about a ten minute drive out to Patterson Lake where the car had been found. Mark stopped the truck as soon as they turned off into the lane leading to the north side of the lake. Mark reached into the back of his truck and pulled out two metal detectors. He looked at Victor and said, "We are going treasure hunting!" Victor looked at Mark with huge question marks in his eyes. He asked, "What are we looking for out here?" Well," Mark said, "there were a couple of charms from a charm bracelet found in Cassie's car, but no broken bracelet. If it's not in the car, it has to be somewhere. I'm betting that it's still out here in this field somewhere. What do you think?" Victor looked at him like he had lost his mind, "Talk about your needle in a haystack," he muttered under his breath. "You'll forgive me if I'm a bit skeptical, won't you?" "Of course," replied Mark, "but it has to be somewhere. Out here is a good first place to start looking. We are also going back to the crawl space to look for brass from the gun. We probably won't get to that today, though. We'll start here." "Okay by me," replied Victor. "Let's get 'er done."

"I think we need to try to determine the line that the car would have had to take and then go back to the ditch and crisscross the line with the metal detectors until we run out of dirt or find something. Starting right here," said Mark. They started crossing the drive line and covering about fifteen yards on each side. They were careful that their lines overlapped so that they didn't miss any spots. The item that they were looking for was so small it could easily be missed. They were about twenty yards from the ditch when Victor suddenly stopped and called for a stop. He dropped to his knees to start digging. He carefully pulled the grass back and dug into the soil. After a short minute, he pulled a broken silver chain out of the soil. Victor looked at Mark and said, "I would have never believed it possible. After all these years it's still here." Mark looked at him and replied, "It had to be somewhere. If nobody came looking for it, it would wait until someone did." Victor was quite effusive in his praise for his boss, "How in the world did you think to come out here looking for this? That is just amazing!" "It occurred to me last night that finding the broken charms in the Mustang should lead me to ask questions. I checked the girls' charm bracelets, so we know that they didn't lose charms from their bracelets. Now, I know that there are a lot of them out there, but they are not all broken. Somebody is missing a charm bracelet. If we can figure out who it is, we have a good idea where to look for our killer." Victor gave him a wry look, "Smart!" he said, "Really smart." "Well," replied Mark, "before we start dancing a jig, I'd like to see if it leads us anywhere." "Roger that," replied Victor. "By the way, we have time to stop by the school and look for that brass today, if you want." Mark thought for a moment and replied, "I think that I'd like to get this to the lab and have the techs have a go with it. Let's save that for another day."

Driving back to the office was a quiet drive. Victor kept mumbling to himself, but Mark did not ask him to repeat whatever he was going on about. They stopped for a quick lunch and then headed to the office. Mark logged the new evidence in and asked Gina to send it to the lab. Victor asked, before Mark settled down in his office, "If you don't mind I'd like to go look for that brass this afternoon. It seems like the trail is heating up and I'd like to see if there is something there." "It's fine with me. I've just had about as much adventure as I can handle for the day. Go for it and Godspeed." Victor grinned, "Thanks, Mark."

CHAPTER 43

Mark was rethinking the motive question. The discovery of the bracelet out at the site where the car had gone into the marsh changed the scenario he had in his mind. He had been thinking a team of outsiders, but now he realized that he was looking for an insider or a team of insiders. Could it possibly be so insidious as to involve the necessary premeditation required by a team of local people? How could they keep it secret for so long? It was either a single operator, or a dominant personality had coerced and then eliminated a subservient personality.

Mark called Mack and asked if there had been any other unexplained disappearances of a person or persons soon after the girls had disappeared. He replied that he did not think so, but would make an official check. Mark also told Mack about finding the charm bracelet out in the area where the car had gone into the marsh. Mack replied, "Do you think that it could have belonged to the killer?" Mark replied, "It is possible, but not conclusive. We have shied away from the idea that a lone woman could have done all of this without help. Are you still committed to that point of view?" Mack replied, "I don't know. I don't see how a woman could have done all that was done. Killing three active, young girls alone would have been difficult. Burying them was difficult, as well, but disposing of the car? I can't imagine how a woman could do that without help. Given that we probably need to start thinking beyond the limits of our expectations and consider the possibility that what we believe to be impossible, actually happened." "I agree," replied Mark, "as unlikely as it seems, we need to start trying to figure out that, if the impossible did happen, how did it happen? I doubt that any DNA on the bracelet will be useful after years out in the elements. We'll see what the lab says, but it's almost a slam dunk." Mack asked, "Can you think of anyone who would have a jealously motive?" Mark replied, "I have gone over it and over it in my mind. I can't think of anyone. There may have been a girl who tried out for cheerleading and didn't get picked who was disappointed, but enough to kill all three of them and dispose of the car? That level of sophistication belies a student. It had to be someone with a more mature thinking ability who could anticipate what would be necessary to make it look like a disappearance. It would also have to be someone who could compute the necessary speed and just the right launch point to put the car into the marsh. This was not a crime of passion. This was premeditated, cold-blooded murder and a well-orchestrated cover up." Mack nodded, "I agree, but who in the world could be so cold-blooded?" Mark shared his short lived theory about a recording exec, but it just did not check the boxes. Mack nodded and finally said, "Mark, once again, you have surprised me. Who would have thought to look for the bracelet out there?" Mark replied, "You would have, Mack. We found part of it in the car. The rest of it had to be somewhere. It was logical that it was broken in the effort to bury the car, so it was probably somewhere between the starting point and the launching point. It was just logic. I will admit that we always look smarter when our hunches pan out though." Mack chuckled and replied, "True dat, for sure!"

Just before five o'clock PM, Victor came bursting through the door with a grin on his face. "You were right, Boss. We found two shell casings from a.32. Good call!" Mark grinned too, it was infectious. He replied, "That is great news. It seems like today is a big step or two forward. Did you send them to the lab?" "Thought maybe you'd like to do the honors," replied Victor. "No," replied Mark, "you found them; you go ahead. Be sure you tag that with your own name as the finder." He said, "C'mon, Boss, I would have never looked if you hadn't started it." Mark smiled, "Take the win, Victor. I appreciate your initiative in getting out there and looking once the idea was presented." "Okay, Boss, whatever," replied Victor.

Two days later they had lab results back. There was no usable DNA on the bracelet. That was no surprise. There were fingerprints on the shell casings, but there were no matches found. That was not a surprise either. Working this case was like crawling up an icy slope. Just about the time you think you have a grip, you slip and slide all the way back to the bottom.

CHAPTER 44

Mark had a headache. For two and a half days he had been going around in circles in his mind trying to settle on a motive. Maybe there was no motive. Maybe it was just a random act of insanity that happened without motive or further explanation. Maybe they would never know. Never in his life had a case so tormented his mind. Come to think of it, he had never wanted to solve a case more fervently than he did this one. It had gone from an investigation to an obsession. He knew that wasn't good and he didn't think it was showing on the outside. He also knew that it would not be long before people began to see. Sarah was already showing signs that she knew something wasn't right with him. He had been sitting at this desk without moving for over an hour when he came to himself. He needed to take action. This sitting and thinking was going to destroy him.

Looking at his watch, Mark noted that it was past lunch time. He grabbed his keys and drove over to the Wascally Wabbit. As he walked in, he saw Willy and Jack in the back. "Do you guys eat lunch wherever you think I'm going to show up or what?" asked Mark. They chuckled and denied any culpability. Mark sat down and they asked about the progress on the case. He gave them a measured look and sighed, "I guess there is no harm in discussing the case even though it is ongoing. We have hit a wall. It is the same one we have hit over and over again. According to Mack, they hit the same wall back then, during the original investigation." Willy and Jack sat and waited expectantly. Finally Jack said, "And what, pray tell, is that wall?" "Oh, yeah," Mark said, "It's motive. We can't find solid motive for killing the girls. Without motive, it is almost impossible to focus on a suspect. Without motive it will be sheer luck if we ever locate a suspect. We have the what, when, where, and how. What we don't have is the why. Without the why, the who remains hidden in the shadows." Willy said, "You sound so discouraged." Mark replied, "I guess the harsh reality of the probability is getting me down a bit. It seems that we won't find the killer without a motive or a sudden confession after fifty years. What are the odds of that?" Jack replied, "Not ones that I'd like to bet on." Mark looked at his two old friends until they became a bit uncomfortable. Finally, he asked them, "Can either one of you think of a reason someone might have wanted to kill even one of them, let alone all three of them?" Jack asked thoughtfully, "Could it be that someone hated one of them with such passion that they would kill all three to get the one?" "Could be," replied Mark, "but, who… and why?" "I don't know," Jack replied. "I guess I was just fishing," Mark looked at him with a lopsided grin and continued, "We were always pretty good at that so maybe that's how we'll break this. Work it like a trip down the river. Remember how we would fish a hole and if nothing bit, we'd change baits and keep at it until we figured out what the fish were biting that day?" They both grinned and Willy said, "We should do that again; it has been way too long." "Well," said Mark, "in the meantime let's work this problem like we used to work the river. The killer or killers, if they are still alive, are probably out there. We need to figure out how to draw them out." "What do you want us to do?" Jack and Willy said together. They looked at each other with surprise then they all laughed. Mark replied with a grin, "For starters, I would like for you to brainstorm with some of our old friends and see if anybody anywhere, for any reason, had a grudge against any of the girls. In addition, do you think anyone could have hated First String enough to go after them to hurt us?" "Are you for real?" Willy asked. "Everybody loved us back then." "I know that's what we thought, but there were undoubtedly people who did not love us and others who were jealous or just hateful. Let's not leave any stone unturned. It's time to get down to cases. There is an answer and we need to find it." "We'll see what shakes out," Jack replied. "Ditto that," said Willy.

On the way back to the office, Mark called Mack to see if there was a good time that they could meet. Mack said he was just leaving the saloon after eating lunch and he would meet Mark at his office.

CHAPTER 45

Mark arrived at his office and had returned a couple of phone calls when Mack Becker walked in. Mark quickly finished the call that he was on and hung up the phone.

"Hi, Mack," Mark said. "It's good to see you again. How are you doing?" Mack replied, "Remarkably well for an old geezer, if you know what I mean." Mark grinned and replied, "I have no idea what you are talking about and don't know why you would think that I would." They both chuckled at that. Mack asked, "What's up, Mark?" "I have been puzzling over the motive question for several days almost nonstop. It is about to drive me crazy. I want to take a hard look at the jealousy issue as a motive for killing. To be really honest, it is hard for me to imagine anyone who would hold such animosity for all three of them. I have wondered if one of them was the target and the other two were collateral damage. If that is the case, we are dealing with a particularly cold-blooded soul." Mack looked at Mark for a few moments and replied, "That doesn't seem possible. Can you think of any reason someone might have been jealous of all three of them?" Mark shook his head, "No, Mack, I can't. I have been over everything that I can remember about people that were around back then, but nothing pops for me. We are even trying to run down any of the old record company producers and promoters from back then. There were a couple of those guys that thought that the First String was going to be their meal ticket. Some of them kept telling us we should ditch our girlfriends, sports, college, and everything else in our lives in order to pursue music. None of us wanted to do that." Mack looked thoughtful, "Do you think any of them would have done that?" Mark replied, "The only guy that I can remember that was very sleazy was in Los Angeles that weekend. He had been on tour with us until Wednesday or Thursday of that last week. He hopped a plane to LA to look at another group out there. We haven't been able to find him, but I have no reason to suspect that he was anywhere but LA. The only reason that I even thought of him was because I never really trusted him. He seemed too cut-throat for my taste." Mack nodded thoughtfully and said, "You were pretty sharp even as a kid. It is interesting that you would pick up on that given the fact that he was probably spewing exactly what he thought you wanted to hear." Mark replied, "That's the thing, I didn't want him blowing smoke you know where. I had always dealt with people who said what they meant and meant what they said. He just did not seem genuine to me."

Mack put his hands on his knees and asked, "What would you like me to do?" Mark said, "Please give the jealousy angle some thought. Maybe you came across somebody who reacted strongly to one of the victims. Usually when that happens, it is memorable. Think on it and see what comes to mind, if you would." Mack responded, "For sure, I will give it some thought and check around with people I know who might have some such memories. Those girls were involved in everything and good at everything they did. That kind of success does sometimes breed envy and jealousy in others. We'll see what we find out." Mark thanked the Sheriff for coming by and for the cooperation. Mack laughed and said, "Are you kidding; you're working for me. I better cooperate if I want to get my money's worth." Mark nodded and laughed, as well. He had the thought that it was too bad that Mack was retiring. He was a good cop and a good man.

CHAPTER 46

Sunday morning found Mark and Sarah in church again. It had been a number of years since they had regularly attended services. It wasn't that Pastor Fogarty was such an outstanding preacher because he was not. It seemed like being in church had a calming effect and helped put their lives into perspective. As the service proceeded Mark pondered that the gospel and the Bible didn't really offer a life with no problems, but promised that one didn't have to walk alone through the dark hours that life sometimes brought. That was a comforting thought.

Following the dismissal, as they were working their way out of the church, the pastor's wife approached them and asked if they had lunch plans. Discovering that they did not have any specific plans she invited them to have Sunday dinner at the parsonage with her and the pastor. Having no reason why they should not, they accepted.

As the pastor's residence was next to the church, they left their car parked in the lot and walked over to the house with the Cheryl/Abigail. It seemed strange to Mark to think of her as Cheryl. He still thought of her as Mrs. Appleton or Miss Abigail. He was trying to get accustomed to the name change. It was something that he would like to discuss with her, but today was probably not the time for such a discussion.

Mark was seated in the living room, with the ladies in the kitchen, when the pastor came in. He had to greet everyone as was the custom. He took his suit jacket off and flopped into a chair. "I'm always glad to get through Sunday morning," he said with a sigh. "Is it quite stressful to preach?" Mark asked. "It's not that it is so stressful as it is a relief to get the message off my mind. It is with me for several days and I can't get it off my mind until I preach it. Then I can clear my mind and relax for a while." Mark replied, "I guess I never thought of it that way. Of course, I have never preached so how would I know?" Pastor Fogarty nodded and said, "I guess it is a unique vocation. It's really more of a calling than a vocation. At least, that is true in my case." Mark looked thoughtful, "What do you mean by a calling?" "Well," replied the pastor, "I guess it's like a conviction that it is what one must do. It's rather hard to explain unless one has experienced it." "Maybe it's a bit like trying to describe to somebody the fragrance of a rose," responded Mark. "The only way to really understand is to smell a rose. Then you know and no explanation is necessary. Until you know the fragrance of a rose, no explanation will do it justice. Plus, there is no way one would recognize the fragrance of a rose from a description. It must be experienced." Pastor Fogarty responded, "That is an excellent parallel of what I was trying to say. I think you get it."

Just then the ladies called them into the dining room for lunch. As they ate there was a warm, friendly atmosphere around the table. Both Mark and Sarah had known Cheryl before she was Mrs. Fogarty. They had lots of old times to talk about. Pastor Fogarty had been pastor of the church in Pleasant Valley during many of those years so he, too, was conversant in their history. He especially remembered the football team making the playoffs. It turned out that he was quite the football fan and had also played in high school. There was just a good feeling around the table as they enjoyed lunch.

After lunch Elliot, as he insisted they call him, and Mark went into the den while the ladies cleared up from lunch. Elliot asked Mark how the investigation was going. Mark looked at him for a long moment and said, "It's a bit funny really, because we have learned so much to know so little." Elliot looked at him with a knitted brow and said, "What does that mean?" Mark smiled and answered, "We have the car, we found the bodies, we have shell casings with finger prints that we can't match, we have the weapon, and we found a charm bracelet in the field where the car was taken before being driven into the marsh, but still have no idea who the killer was/is. That is why I say that we have learned so much to know so little. In fact, we don't even have a clear motive." Elliot regarded Mark and asked, "So, what are you going to do?" Mark replied, "I only know one way and that is to keep digging. Quitting is not an option. In fact, at this point, if they pulled our funding, I would keep working. I may lose my team, but I'd stay on the case until I figured it out. It is the most intriguing case I have ever investigated." "What is the most baffling thing about it?" asked the pastor. "That's a good question," said Mark. "I think the luck factor is most interesting." "Luck factor, what is that?" replied Elliot. "Crime takes a lot of planning and preparation to be successful and even the best, most seasoned of criminals makes mistakes. It takes lots of preparation and a bit of luck to get away with a crime for five to ten years. Eventually though, with persistent investigation, the truth comes out and the plan unravels. The luck factor in this case is off the charts." Elliot looked at Mark inquisitively and asked, "How so?" Mark replied, "The disposal of the car is a perfect example. Normally a seasoned criminal would have to take a dry run to see if they could do what was obviously done. That car had to be hitting close to fifty miles per hour to get that far into the marsh, but we found only one car, so clearly they did not do a dry run. That means that a one-time shot had to go perfectly the first and only time it was tried. It should not have happened like that, but it did. That is an off the charts luck factor. In a matter of hours, the killer made three healthy young girls disappear, disposed of their car, and did so without even being noticed or identified. There is not even a sniff of who did this even though we have almost every piece of the puzzle. I call that extremely good luck." Elliot responded, "I see what you mean. It should not have happened like that, right?" "Exactly," replied Mark.

Mark turned to see the ladies standing just inside the doorway of the den. "I'm sorry," he said, "We should not be discussing such unpleasant business on such a fine day. I apologize!" Elliot interjected, "You should ask Cheryl about the odds of getting the car out into the marsh with one shot. She is really good with math. In fact, she had a double major in music and math and once aspired to be a math teacher. She just found her love for music was more compelling." Mark looked at Cheryl and said, "That's a surprise. That is something I never knew about you." Cheryl smiled and replied, "There was never any reason to mention it, I guess. It was no secret that I did math tutoring to help students that were struggling with the concepts. It was never a subject of conversation, I guess." "Well," replied Mark, "I am impressed, none the less."

They spent another hour in pleasant conversation and then parted company. When they were leaving, Pastor Fogarty took Mark aside and asked Mark if he and Sarah were interested in joining the church. Mark said, "I can't speak for Sarah, but it is something that I never even considered for myself until this moment. I'd like to think about it and we should probably talk about it." "That's fine," replied Elliot, "think it over and let me know." They said their goodbyes and Mark and Sarah walked to their car and headed home.

As they were driving Mark asked Sarah, "Did you know Mrs. Appleton, I mean Cheryl, was a math major?" "No," she said, "that was the first I heard of that, as well. It's funny how layered people can be." "Sometimes I wonder whether you can really know somebody," mused Mark. Sarah looked at him with a scowl and asked, "What do you mean by that?" "Well," he replied, "I'll bet there are things about you that I don't know. There may even be things that you don't want me to know. There are probably things that I don't even need to know. Am I right?" "I guess so," replied Sarah. Mark went on, "Do you think there are things about you that would surprise me if I knew about them?" "Maybe, but where is this going?" Sarah asked. "It's not going anywhere, because you have a right to your privacy. BUT, how well do I really know you?" he asked. She smiled and replied, "Surely better than anyone else in the world and that's a fact." "It is indeed," he replied, "and that's good enough for me. Do you get the point, though?" She gave him a sweet smile and said, "You have made your point, Counselor." They both laughed at that.

As they were pulling into the drive way Mark mentioned to Sarah, "Oh, by the way, Elliot asked me if we are interested in joining the church." Sarah asked, "How did you respond?" Mark said, "I told him that I personally had not even thought about it and that we, meaning you and I, should talk about it." Sarah gave him an appreciative look and said, "Thank you for that. What do you think?" Mark shook his head, "I'm not really ready to give anything that serious much thought while I'm in the middle of this investigation. It is really devouring my head and maybe part of my soul. It is really heavy. Can we put if off until this is over?" "Absolutely!" Sarah responded. "I'll say no more. Truthfully, I had not thought about it either."

CHAPTER 47

Something was nagging at the back of Mark's mind or memory. He knew there was something that he should be seeing, but couldn't figure out what it was. It had been there for a couple of weeks and he just couldn't shake it. Neither could he put his finger on what it was. It was really frustrating. He felt like he was missing something obvious. Even while examining the evidence that they had, he constantly had the nagging feeling that the next thing that he looked at would uncover the missing piece. It made him restless and it was starting to show. His team was noticing his restlessness. It wasn't that he was irritable, because he wasn't. He was just quieter than usual. He was always the first one in the office and he looked like he wasn't sleeping very well. The truth was that he wasn't sleeping well.

It was frustrating knowing that there was something in front of you that you that was invisible to you. That was not a good feeling. This was Mark's area of expertise. Seeing what others missed had built his reputation in the bureau. Yet here he was in the same boat with everyone else.

Mark looked at his team on Monday morning through weary eyes. He asked them, "Does anybody have any new ideas this morning?" Nobody offered anything. "Okay," Mark said, "I have asked Sheriff Mack to join us this morning, if any of you noticed that he is here and wondered why. Here is what I want for us to do, this week. Let's go back to the evidence once again. This time, let's select the six least likely candidates for suspicion and investigate them as though they were our number one suspect. Try to build a case against them." He had the team's attention now. They were staring at him like he had lost his marbles. "What is the point?" asked Tex. Mark grinned and responded, "I am glad you asked that question. The working theory is that none of the obvious suspects from the original investigation panned out. None of the ideas that we have had, so far, has produced squat. So let's branch out into the wild unknown. We will select one suspect each and try to make a case. Let's see what happens."

Mack was looking at Mark with an appraising gaze. He finally said, "Is this a strategy or a Hail Mary?" There were appreciative grunts around the table which were both eloquently in support of the question and yet noncommittal. Mark replied, "I am going to be brutally honest. I have no idea where to go next and I am tired of chasing my tail. If this doesn't produce a viable theory, I have no idea where to go next. I have never given up on an investigation, but I don't know what else to do. If you have any ideas, I'm listening." Finally Gina spoke up, "This is really not a bad idea; it is just so unorthodox. It's bass-ackwards from the way we are taught to investigate. It just might work." Willie mused, "Wouldn't that be something; cracking the biggest case of our lives with a trick play.

I'm in! If nothing else, it'll be a ride to remember. Let's do it!" The others all chimed in and went back to the files. Mark reminded them, "Don't be limited to previously investigated persons, but don't shy away from them either."

CHAPTER 48

After another exhaustive review of the file, the team along with Sheriff Mack sat in the conference room of their headquarters. Mark said to them, "We are going to be operating on the theory that the perpetrator of this murder had to have incredibly good luck in order to pull it off. We are going to try to reverse that luck by invoking it for ourselves. What we have done is written down names of people that seem unlikely to have committed the crime of murder. There are about twenty eight names. In this hat, all of the names are written on a slip of paper. Each of us will draw a name. We will then try to make a case against the person we have drawn. When it is clear that we cannot make the case, we will draw another name until we have exhausted the names." The team looked at Mark with more than a little surprise. Finally, Victor spoke up saying, "That seems like a lot of punching at shadows now that we actually start trying to do it. I feel a bit ridiculous taking a name with no evidence and trying to make a case against them." Mark nodded, "I feel the same way and am open to suggestions. If none are forthcoming, it seems like the only play we have at this time." Mack, looking every bit a grumpy old man said, "Let's get on with it!"

The first of the seven names drawn was Robert Barns, who had been the football coach back in the '60s. He left after the playoff year and went to a bigger program, eventually coaching in college. The second was Homer Gladding. He was the owner and manager of the Wascally Wabbit back in the '60s. He had sold out in the early '70s and moved to a nearby town. He and his wife had divorced and his life fell apart. The third was Orville Wonk. Orville was a handy man who was good at almost everything so he kept very busy fixing things for people. He could fix almost anything mechanical, electrical, or structural. He knew everybody and everybody knew him. He had a good reputation as an honest business man, but he drank a bit. He was retired now and lived on the edge of town. He still ran a little "fix it" business just to keep his hands occupied. The fourth was Jim Bronson. He ran a used car lot in town and had for years. In fact, he still ran it. He was new in business in the early '60s and was always seen about town promoting his business. He seemed harmless and that is probably how he landed on the list. The fifth person drawn was Pastor Fogarty. Mark was a little taken aback at that, but each person needed to be thoroughly investigated. It struck Mark a bit odd that he had drawn the Pastor's name, especially since they were beginning to develop a relationship. Well, he would do his job. The sixth name drawn was Janice Milford. Janice had been the home economics teacher at the high school. Over the years, she had been in and out of therapy for mental issues. Her instability made her a bit of a pathetic figure, but a perfect candidate for the "good luck" theory. The last person drawn was Emily Jansen. She was the mother of one of the girls who always seemed to be a rival of one or another of the three missing girls. Her daughter wanted to be head cheerleader, the soloist, lead actress in the school play, the homecoming queen, the first at something, really anything. One of the three dead girls was always coming in ahead of her. That one went to Willie. Mark looked at them and said, "You all have your assignments. Use whatever means you can to either nail them or eliminate them. Let's see where this goes." He knew that they were going to stir up a hornets' nest when they started working this angle. They would just have to ride it out and let it happen as it happened.

Mark started by reviewing every shred of evidence even remotely connected with Pastor Fogarty from the original investigation and then reviewed the materials gleaned from any recent follow up. He saw no gaps in the pastor's story. The only thing that remained heretofore unaddressed was the fact that the girls' car had been seen as late as five o'clock PM on the day of the disappearance. Mark called the pastor and asked him over the phone, "Pastor, I have some follow up questions regarding the day the girls disappeared." The pastor asked a bit quickly, "Am I a suspect, now?" Mark replied, "Not really, Pastor. We just came up with some new information and we're contacting people who alibied out back in 1968 because we discovered that we had the timeline wrong." "How do you mean?" asked Pastor Fogarty. Mark replied, "We found a witness who saw the car leaving the school as late as five-thirty to six o'clock PM on that Friday afternoon. Can you remember where you were at that time?" Mark heard the pastor relax and let out a long breath. He replied, "Yes, I can. I went out to visit with Jason Black and his family. After visiting with them for a while, I went outside and started playing basketball with his boys. We played for a couple of hours until Millie Black said supper was ready. I told them that it was time for me to leave, but they would have no part of that. They insisted that I stay and eat with them, so I did. I probably headed back home at around seven-thirty. The Mustang was gone by then." Mark asked, "Elliot, do you think any of them could confirm your alibi?" The pastor replied, "I'm sure the boys, well they're men now, would be able to confirm it. Everyone remembers what they were doing on that Friday." Mark replied, "Thanks, Elliot, I'll follow up with them. I hope you don't take offense, but we need to tie up loose ends in order to find out where the ones are that we can't tie up." He chuckled and replied, "No offense taken. I meant it when I told you that we appreciate your efforts to bring this to a final conclusion. Already you have brought more closure than any of us expected to have." They finished their conversation and ended the call. Mark made a quick call to Jason Black, Jr., and confirmed what the pastor had told him. He clearly remembered that day. His statement was, "I didn't believe that any preacher was born that could beat me one-on-one, but he did it. Oh, yes! I remember." Mark thanked him and sat back in his chair.

He sat at his desk and reviewed everything the file contained on Elliot Fogarty and determined that he had officially eliminated him as a suspect. He walked out and placed the file back in the file room and left the office. He got into this truck and drove down by the school. On a whim, he drove from the school out to Patterson Lake where the car had been found. He sat there in the old "lovers' lane" and pondered how such a thing could even happen. He had been over it hundreds of times, but he knew that the tape would continue to play until he had the answer or he was dead. He noted that it took about eight or nine minutes to drive out there. He figured it would take nearly a half-hour to ride a bicycle back to town from there. That was something to think about. He was still convinced that he would need uncommonly good luck to crack this one even with all of the data they had.

While Mark was there, another car pulled in. He saw that it was Cheryl Fogarty. He got out of his car and walked over to hers. She rolled down her window and smiled at Mark. "I love this place," she said to him. "I always have." Mark asked her, "Do you come here often?" Mrs. Fogarty replied, "From time to time I drive out here because it is so peaceful." Mark said, "It's a long drive from your home, now." She said, "Yes, it is. I wanted to come out here since hearing about finding the car. I hadn't been out here, yet. It is so amazing that the car was found. Who would have thought this old marsh would ever dry up?" Mark replied, "Indeed it is unusual. How have you been over the years?" She replied, "Life has been good to me. I have a fine husband. I do miss the old days and I miss you boys and your band. Those were really good days for me. After the death of my husband and the disappearance of the girls, things changed, though. We never recaptured the magic, did we?" "No, I guess not," said Mark, "It was just never the same. It was like someone turned the music off in me. My mind would not make melody and lyrics for so very long." She looked at Mark sympathetically and said, "I know. We tried to turn it back on, but it just fell apart. I was so sad to see the changes in you guys. I never dreamed something like that would happen." Mark nodded and said sadly, "Who could imagine such a thing?" She asked him, "Do you ever think about those times?" "Yes, of course I do," replied Mark. "The past is the past, though. We can't go back and undo what is done." "Clearly we can't, but some things back there may be recaptured. It's possible." Cheryl replied. Mark had the distinct impression that she was flirting with him. He said, "It was nice seeing you. I really need to be going. You take care and I'll probably see you in church." She smiled brightly and said, "Bye."

CHAPTER 49

Mark knew that he had reached a dead end with Pastor Fogarty. His alibi checked out. It could not have been him. That would just be too easy. Most of the others had eliminated the person they were investigating as a suspect, as well. They were waiting on Victor and Jay to finish before starting round two.

There was a feeling lurking around the office like they really weren't going to crack the case. Nobody had said anything, but there were those looks that passed between coworkers. It was a familiar look. It basically said, "We're wasting our time here." or, "We're just beating our heads against a wall." Mark felt like he needed to do something to renew hope, but had no idea what it might be.

As he was driving to the office he pondered the next step. Frankly, he had nothing. They had exhausted every bright idea that he had and so far, there was nothing to show for it. The good news was that they had enough names for two more rounds then it was "back to the drawing board".

When Mark walked into the conference room, everyone was already there including Mack who had been hanging around more and more. "Am I late?" Mark instantly asked. "No, you're not late," said Willie, "I guess it wouldn't matter if you were. You are the boss, you know?" Mark grinned at them and asked, "What's up?" One of them responded, "Doc!" Mark wasn't sure which one said it, but it brought a chuckle.

Victor said, "Jay and I have officially cleared our names. We are back to having no suspects." Mark looked at the team and replied after a moment, "Okay, do you want to draw names again today or give it a day and do other stuff?" Gina replied, "What other stuff? As far as I can see these names are what we have. There's nothing else to do." Mark asked them, "Has any of you come up with even the slightest wisp of suspicion? Anything at all shake loose while you were working?" Nobody said anything. They just sat with their heads down. "Okay then," said Mark, "let's pass the hat."

As the hat went around and the names drawn, it seemed like such long odds. Mark, who knew all of the people represented by the names, felt like it was a waste of time. They were now looking at classmates, retired teachers, store keepers, soda jerks, and just about anybody that was breathing. When Mark looked at the name he drew, he was taken aback. It was Mrs. Fogarty. He mused, "What are the odds of me drawing the husband and then the wife? Mark had seen a path where a man might have committed the crime, but a woman alone? It seemed preposterous. Besides, Mark had never known a person less likely to hurt anybody than Abigail Appleton. That is how he still thought of her. He chuckled inwardly. "This shouldn't take long" he thought.

He said aloud, "Everyone has their new assignment. Let's see if we can turn these people into suspects." Jay gave Mark a sidelong, appraising look and said, "You don't sound very convincing or rather unconvinced that we will accomplish that." Mark gave him a mock disgusted look and said, "You and your human lie detector nose! The truth is, I'm beginning to feel like we'll never get to the bottom of this one. I know I should not say that, but you guys have worked way too hard for me to blow smoke." Mack looked at him and said, "That is an all too familiar feeling relative to this case. We felt that way many times on the original investigation and I have felt that way many times over the years. I happen to believe that you, this team, is going to crack this case wide open. In all of my fifty-plus years in law enforcement, I have never seen a finer, more dedicated, and tenacious team. You are going to take this one home. I just know it!" They all expressed their thanks. Gina said to the Sheriff, "Sheriff Mack, I have been looking at investigative files for more than thirty years. You guys did the most exhaustive and in-depth investigation that I have ever reviewed. Seeing the quality of your work and knowing your dedication to this case makes your statement all the more encouraging and helpful to us. For my part, I am going to do everything that I can to make your prophecy come true." Again they all chimed in with their support. Mark looked thoughtfully at Gina and interjected, "That was well said, Gina. I'm going to let your statement stand for the group. Let's find ourselves a killer!" There was a round of spontaneous applause and they broke up and went about their business.

CHAPTER 50

Mark sat at his desk thinking. He was the one who had asked that they investigate the least suspicious people that they could find so he had nobody to blame but himself that he was stuck with trying to make a case against one of the people from his past whom he admired most. Mrs. Appleton had given so much to him and his friends when they were young. She had asked nothing in return except the joy of watching them grow musically. She had been so sad when they stopped playing and had urged them to try to play to honor their friends, but it just never felt right to him and the others, or so he thought anyway. He decided that he would talk with the Jack and Willy as a springboard into this phase of his work. He picked up the phone and found that they were both available for lunch. They agreed to meet at the saloon and he went back to work.

The first thing that Mark did when the three of them met for lunch was to swear them to secrecy. He knew he could trust their discretion from long years of experience. Then he told them what was going on with the investigation and how they had decided to investigate the least likely persons in town to see what, if anything, they could dig up. They both said almost in unison, "Are we suspected?" Mark chuckled and responded, "If I didn't know you better, I'd think you had guilty feelings, but I was with you and I know exactly where you were and even who you were with and what you were doing. Not that I'll ever tell." They all laughed at that. "We are drawing names out of a hat and I drew Miss Abby's name." said Mark. They looked at him in shock and Willy asked, "You don't suspect her do you?" He had the most incredulous look on his face. Jack added, "There's no way she could do such an evil thing as that!" Mark responded gently, "It's not that I suspect her either. The strategy we are working is to treat each person we investigate as guilty until we prove that they could not have done it. We have already cleared one round of names. I had to investigate her husband, the pastor, the first round. Now I have her; what are the odds? Anyway, I need to try to remember everything about her and dig up anything that we didn't know about her back in the day until I prove she could not have done it. I can't eliminate her on my opinion of her. I, personally, would have never put her name in the pot. Somebody else did that; I just drew it out. In fact, I didn't know her name was in there until I drew it out."

Their waitress brought their lunch about then so they were otherwise occupied for a few minutes. When Mark was about halfway through his grilled fish, he asked the other two, "Okay, so I want to try to recall everything we can about Abby whether it's good, bad, or indifferent. Any seemingly casual bit of information could be important coupled with something else, so don't leave anything out. The favor I'd like to ask of you is to write down or video tape all of the memories you have of her. I'll have my team go over the pages or tapes, whichever is the case, and we'll see if there are any anomalies in her life. Please, don't leave anything out. Can I depend on you guys?" They both dropped their heads and then looked up with an almost furtive glance and responded to the affirmative. Mark thanked them and then said, "Oh, by the way, lunch is on me today. I'll be looking forward to seeing your responses. Don't put it off too long."

Jack asked him, "Have you thought any more about playing?" "To tell you the truth, I had Miss P out a couple of Sundays ago in the evening," said Mark. "It felt really good. I mean it felt GOOD, like it used to feel. I'd love to play again, but I need to get this case out of my head first. Comprende?" "Yeah, we get it," replied Willy, "It's the same for us, but I'm feeling better about it, too. Hopefully we can do it soon." "I hope so, too," said Mark. Jack chimed in, "Me three." In true Three Stooges fashion. They said their goodbyes and headed out.

CHAPTER 51

When Jack arrived at the office, Gina was the only person there. He said to her, "Gina, I have a favor to ask of you." She smiled brightly and responded, "Ask away, me lord." Mark laughed at her and said, "I'd like to know if there were any reports of suspicious vehicles, abandoned vehicles, or citations for illegal parking or police mandated towing on that Friday 13th, 1968. Could you check with the Sheriffs Department? It may take some time to dig out the reports if there are any." "I'll get right on it," Gina replied. "Thanks," Mark said and went into his office.

Mark made a call to the pastor and explained what they were doing. He was somewhat familiar because Mark had just interviewed him the previous week. Elliot Fogarty told Mark he could come right over that afternoon if he wanted, so they set it up. Upon arrival at the parsonage, both the pastor and his wife were there which was really better in Mark's opinion. In fact, Mark asked the pastor to set in on the interview. Cheryl Fogarty was a bit reluctant saying, "Are you certain that this in necessary? I told the Sheriff back when this happened everything that I knew. What more can I say?" Mark smiled reassuringly, he hoped, and said,

"Just answer the questions to the best of your ability. If you don't remember or you don't know, it's okay to say so. There are no right or wrong answers. I am not looking to trip you up. There are no "gotcha" questions. Are you ready to start?" "I guess so," she said. Mark turned on the recorder and started, "This is Mark Bellingham and I am interviewing Abigail Cheryl Fogarty. Mrs. Fogarty is the former Miss Jensen and Mrs. Appleton…" The interview wound on for about an hour. Mark went over everything that he could think of. He asked her about her alibi and she said that she had gone to her grandparents' home for the weekend. He asked her what she drove and she replied her green Plymouth Lancer. He asked her if she stayed there the entire weekend and she said that she did. He asked her if she left for any reason during the weekend and she said she did. When pressed, she said that she went to buy some items that she needed for her house. When she was asked when she came home, she replied it was the next Tuesday, the day that the girls' disappearance was noticed. They ended the interview. Mark thanked them for their time and he headed back to the office.

When Mark arrived back at the office, Jay happened to be there. He asked Jay into his office and played the tape for him. Jay listened and stopped the tape where Abigail was talking about her trip to her grandparents. He said, "There is something about the question, 'What did you drive?' that bothered her." As the tape went on, he stopped it again. "She is lying about when she came back," he said. Mark replied, "I wonder why she would do that?" Jay looked thoughtful, "She said that she went to buy some stuff for her home. I wonder if she went to get furniture. If so, it most likely would not have fit in her car. She would have needed a pickup truck or a trailer." Mark was disgusted with himself, "I should have thought of that while we were doing the interview! I should have asked her what she bought and how she got it home. I guess I'll just have to do a follow up. Thanks Jay; you are worth your weight in gold. At least you are today." They both chuckled and Jay left Mark's office.

Mark picked up the phone and called Cheryl. She answered the phone. Mark said, "Hi, Miss Abby." He could hear the smile in her voice. "I haven't been called that for years. It sounds so good! What do you need, Mark?" He replied, "I just have a couple of follow up questions." She replied, "You could stop by the house. My husband is not home. We could have a nice chat." There was something inviting and suggestive in her voice. Mark replied, "I'm sure that would be fun, but I'm back at the office so it's out of the question today." "Oh, well," she said, 'Maybe another time. What was your question?" He said, "You said that you did some shopping. What did you buy?" "Oh, my" she responded, "that has been such a long time ago, but as it happens I do remember. I bought three items; a chest of drawers, an easy chair, and a table lamp. I had been waiting for a sale at a furniture store over where my grandparents live. They called me and told me that a sale was coming up so I planned to be there for it." Mark smiled at her enthusiasm and said, "Did the store deliver the items?" "No," she replied, "I had to pick them up. It was too far to Pleasant Valley for delivery." "How did you get them into your car?" asked Mark. "Oh! I didn't use my car. I used my grandfather's pickup truck." Mark asked, "Did you take them home or to your grandparents' farm?" She said, "No, I took them home to my place and then went back to my grandparents' farm."

"So you were in Pleasant Valley on Friday the 13th in August of 1968?" She paused for a long moment, cleared her throat and said, "Well, yes, but just for a short while." "What time did you head back for your grandparents' place?" Mark asked. She replied, "I'm not exactly sure of the time to be quite honest." "Was it on Friday or on Saturday?" Mark pressed. She expelled her breath in an exasperated way and said, "Do you thing I killed those girls!?" Mark replied, "No I don't, but your alibi is starting to fall apart. I am just trying to totally eliminate you as a suspect. This is just routine stuff." Again she paused for a moment and then said, "It may be routine for you, but it is anything but for me, I'll have you know!" "I understand," replied Mark. "Getting back to the point, do you remember when you left for your grandparents' farm after unloading your new furniture?" "I do remember that I had nobody to help me so I had to unload that stuff all by myself. That was no easy task, let me tell you." Mark paused for a thoughtful moment. She was obviously much stronger then she looked back in the day. She continued, "I'm not sure what time I left, but I know that I arrived at their house in time to sleep awhile before breakfast. That's all that I can tell you for certain. It was a long time ago." "Yes, it was," responded Mark.

Mark changed the direction of the conversation for a moment asking, "Where were you living back in August of 1968?" She responded, "I had a small house over on Vanderman Street, don't you remember?" Mark let the question hang in the air and asked her another question, "Did you ever use Cassie's bicycle?" That question seemed to take her by surprise. Mark heard a small gasp, but she responded quite calmly so maybe he was mistaken. She said,

"Everybody used her bike from time to time. It just stayed there at the school after she got her car. Her Dad finally took it home after she was gone." That all fit with what Mark had already learned. He did follow up, "So to be clear, you did use the bike from time to time? Correct?" She replied, "Yes, that is true." Mark said, "How fast do you think Cassie's Mustang would have had to travel in order to land where it did in the marsh?" She replied, "Oh, I have no earthly idea. I would have to sit down with measurements, a slide rule…. Well, I guess I could do it on a computer now, but I'm old school. I'd do it the way I was trained." Mark was quiet for a moment and then said, "So you could make those calculations?" "Oh, yes!" She replied. "It would take me awhile since I haven't done it for such a long time, but I could still use it, I think." Mark asked her, "Have you ever owned a gun?" Her reply was emphatic, "Absolutely not! After all the grief guns have caused me, I would not have one in my house!" Mark said comfortingly, he hoped, "Sorry to upset you. These are some things I just need to know. That's all I need for now. Thank you for you cooperation." She responded sweetly, "You can call me anytime, Mark. Feel free to stop by anytime. Even if Elliot is not home, we have so much to talk about." They said their goodbyes and ended the conversation. That invitation sounded a bit weird, but Mark shook it off.

Mark sat back in his chair and rubbed his eyes. For the first time, they had found somebody with holes in their alibi. The problem he now faced is that even though Abby was in town during the time of the murder, he still had no evident motive. He could neither put her at the scene nor anywhere near any part of the crime. It was hard to imagine that she could have done what it took to commit the crime. She had opportunity, but means and motive were not in evidence. Still, under the rules of the investigation which he had established, he had to keep digging. So where should he look next?

CHAPTER 52

Mark and Sarah were watching a TV series episode which centered around the FBI and crime solving. He was both amused and disturbed with the way the FBI people were portrayed. It seemed like there had to be one perfect, by the book agent who was usually head of the team. Then there was the maverick of the group who was trying to defy conventions in some way or another in each episode. The rest of the cast sort of complemented the first two, and their roles in some way or another, supported the conflict between the two. The agents were over romanticized, very unrealistic, and had a one-hundred percent solve rate. Mark yawned and said, "Hooray for our side! TV does more to distort the truth than to shed light on it. I wish they would quit trying to portray the FBI. They are worse at it than we are!" Sarah laughed right out loud at his comment. "That is so funny!" she replied. "But sadly true," Mark continued. "Nobody has hurt the reputation of the FBI quite as much as the FBI. I'm afraid that our operation will not stand the scrutiny of the bright light of truth in some of our dark corners." Sarah sighed, "Is that why you retired?" He replied, "Nah! I was ready for a change of pace." "Looks to me like you are right back at it," Sarah stated. "Well, it does look that way with this case, but I hope that this is an anomaly. Mack thinks if we crack this one, we'll get calls from all around the country, maybe around the world to work old cold cases. I'm not sure I would even want that," replied Mark.

"That reminds me; I wanted to talk with you about something," Mark said. "I have been tasked with investigating my old music teacher." Sarah looked shocked, "Cheryl Fogarty? What would be the point; I thought she had a rock solid alibi." Mark gave her a crooked grin and replied, "I did too, but it appears that there may be a couple of cracks in her alibi." Sarah looked skeptical, "How so?" Mark, nodding his head started, "To summarize, it's like this… She was out of town. She drove to her grandparents place on Thursday because there was a furniture store over there putting on a sale and there were a couple of things that she had been planning on buying for the house. On Friday, she borrowed her grandfather's pickup truck and bought the furniture which she brought back to her house here in Pleasant Valley. She unloaded the stuff she bought and then spent the night in Pleasant Valley, or at least part of it. She is not sure what time she left, but said that she arrived at her grandparents' place in time to sleep a couple of hours before breakfast." Sarah scowled at him asking, "So what's the point?" Mark, continuing to nod his head said, "The point is that she was here when the murders were committed. She had opportunity. Nobody has reported seeing her that night so she has no alibi for the time of the murder. On the other hand, I can find no motive or means." "What do you mean by means?" Sarah asked. "By that, I mean the physical strength and skill to pull off all that the killer had to do to bury this crime for fifty years." Mark replied. Sarah asked, "Do you consider her a suspect?" He replied, "The funny thing is that I do not suspect her even a little bit. That, however, does not matter at this point. The present strategy under which we are working is taking the least likely suspects and investigating them as though they are guilty until we are forced to eliminate them." Sarah looked at Mark with a confused look on her face and asked, "Who came up with that idea and how does it work?" Mark grinned at her and replied, "It was my idea. I was studying the case one day and thought 'since we can't find any likely suspects, let's take the least likely people we can find in the file and investigate them as though we know that are guilty until we are forced by the evidence to eliminate them.' We all reviewed the file and jotted down names. We then threw them into a hat and drew names. My first was Elliot whom I eliminated quite quickly. Now I am working on Cheryl. Other people have other names." Sarah thought for a moment and stated emphatically, "That is either a stroke of genius or an exercise in idiocy. I'm not sure which." Mark gave her a rueful look and said, "I guess we'll find out. I have a great team and nothing to lose but time, so why not?"

Sarah asked softly, "So why tell me all of this?" Mark gave her a tender look and said, "First of all, I don't want you to feel like my work is more important than you are. If you're not interested, I'll stop sharing. Secondly, you might have some insight or pick up on something I miss. If so, I'd like to hear about it. There is nothing too small or unimportant at this point. How do you feel about that?" "Well," she said and settled down into her seat, "I'm flattered that you thing I might be able to help. I'm not so confident. I don't like the idea of spying on our friends, but they really aren't friends, are they? So, I'm in as long as I don't have to attend any meetings." "Deal!" said Mark.

The next morning when he walked into the office, Jay was waiting for him. "Mark," he said, "there is nothing more to look at on this guy. He could not have done it." Mark replied, "Okay, do you want to pick up another or give me a hand on Mrs. Fogarty?" Jay's eyes brightened, "Getting a nibble?" he asked. "Well," replied Mark, "let's just say that I can't eliminate her, yet. I have found that her alibi does not hold. Still can't find means or motive, though. It's getting interesting, though. What do you think?" Jay said, "I'm in like Flynn! I never was quite sure what that meant, but have said it for years. What do you want me to do?" "For starters," replied Mark, "I want you to review all of the voice statements taken from her, including transcripts of any phone calls, to include my most recent with her. I would like all of your impressions, please. Look for anything that smells even slightly off. Okay?" "Roger that!" Jay replied with a salute. Mark snapped a salute back at him and said, "Thanks, my friend."

When Mark sat down at his desk, he called Victor and asked him to come in to his office. When Victor was parked opposite Mark, he asked, "What's up, Markus?" Mark responded, "I have a big job for you." Victor gave him a look of relief and said, "Good! I am so tired of investigating the innocent." Mark said, "Here's what I want you to do. Do a deep dive, and I mean deep, on Abigail Cheryl Jensen Appleton Fogarty. I want to know absolutely everything about her from her birth to the present day. I want to know where she went to school, who her friends were, what clubs she joined, what awards she won, what sports she played, who she ate with, who she slept with, and what drove her then, and what drives her now. Think you can handle that?" Victor looked at Mark and said, "You know I can handle it. This is what I do; it is my specialty, but why her?" Mark nodded, "Good question. I found a hole in her alibi. She was in town the night of the murders. Even though I really don't suspect her, she did have opportunity. I see no motive or means. It took an enormous effort on the part of somebody to do what was done. I can't see her being able to pull that off. That being said, our job is to eliminate her as a suspect. Since her alibi fell apart, I want to see if there could have been a motive, or opportunity, or both. I would take two out of three." "Boss," Victor said, "I have always known you were thorough, but this takes it to a new level. If there is anything to find, I will find it and thanks for finding some real work for me." Mark replied, "You bet'cha. I like to see you doing what you do best. See ya later."

Mark gave Mack a call to meet for lunch. It happened that Mack was going to the saloon where he always ate so Mark met him there. When they sat down, Willy and Jack showed up and just sat down as though they just belonged there. Mack chuckled, "The Three Stooges all together again. I would have never wished or dreamed such a thing upon our fair village." They all laughed and chatted as the waitress took their orders. Mack then sat back and asked Mark, "Why did you want to see me?" Mark replied, "I thought it time to bring you up to date. We're taking a new approach to the investigation." Mack interjected, "Yeah, I have heard about that. Explain to me how that works; it sounds all wrong." Mark smiled and replied, "It does sound all wrong. You were in the meeting when we started it. The initial group that we investigated came up clear. So far, the only one that shows any promise is he dropped his voice and looked around, 'Mrs. Appleton.'" Mack looked at Mark with an incredulous expression. He sputtered, "You can't suspect that sweet lady! Why it's almost un-American!" The entire table burst into laughter and everyone in the place was looking at them. Mark said to them, "I found out that there are holes in her alibi." Mack looked aghast and exploded, "How in the world did you do that!?" "Well," Mark replied softly, "I interviewed her again and she told me that she had gone to her grandparents' place because she had been watching for a sale on furniture at a store near their place where she liked to shop. I asked her if she bought anything and she said yes, so asked her what. As it turned out the things that she bought would not fit in her little car, so I asked her how she got them home and she told me she borrowed her grandfather's pickup truck. Then I asked her when she brought them home and she told me it was Friday afternoon. She did not leave for her grandparents' place until the early morning hours, so she was in town when the murders took place." Willy asked with a mystified look on his face, "Do you suspect her?" Mark shook his head, "Not really," he said, "but we need to eliminate her. Since her alibi had blown up, we need to eliminate her on the grounds of no motive or means to do the crime." Mack shook his head, "I don't know how that little lady could have done all that without raising one eyebrow in the whole town. In fact, the shooter had to be highly skilled and I just don't see it." "Neither do I, Mack, but I'm going to do my job," stated Mark. "The motive gives me more problems than the means. Why would our music teacher do such a thing? It is inconceivable!" Mark noted that Jack and Willy shared a glance when he said that, and he made a mental note to follow up on that sometime in the future.

CHAPTER 53

All of the other team members cleared their subjects and picked up another name to continue on. Mark continued studying the possibility that Mrs. Abigail Cheryl Jensen Appleton Fogarty could have done the deed. In the pursuit of an answer, he asked Victor what progress he was making on the deep dive into her. He reported that the more recent stuff was not incriminating. He advised that he had pretty much covered everything from her college graduation until the present and found nothing of interest. He did say that unless there was something in her childhood or adolescence, they would have nothing that provided motive or means. Mark was getting frustrated again. It seemed all too common these days.

Once again he was reviewing reports, statement transcripts, and file notes to see if he had missed anything. Jay came into his office and sat himself down. Mark looked up and said, "Howdy, Jay. Have a seat." Jay laughed and said, "I guess it was a bit presumptive of me to just walk in and sit down." Mark shook his head and said, "Not at all, I was just joking with you. My door is open and I want you guys to feel free to come in and chat. Maybe by doing so, we'll shake something loose." Jay nodded and said to him, "That is exactly why I came in here. I have gone over the tapes of Mrs. Fogarty more than a dozen times. There was something that was nagging at the back of my brain, but I couldn't lasso it until today. I was just listening to them again and I got it." Mark waited while Jay paused and finally asked, "Got what?" "Oh, yeah," replied Jay, "I heard it right for the first time today. When she lies about her alibi, although we didn't know it for years, she used the identical voice inflection that she did when she talked about never owning a gun and not knowing how to shoot." Mark sat back in his chair and looked at Jay for a long moment. He then asked, "Are you sure?" Jay replied, "I am positive. I did not want to waste your time so I listened to it over again three times. I heard it every time once I knew what to listen for. I don't know what this means exactly, but she had been lying for fifty years. It could be huge for us." Mark nodded in agreement. He said, "I don't even want to think it, but we have to pursue this to the end. This is outstanding work, Jay. Thank you. I'd appreciated it if you would keep it to yourself for a bit. Can you do that?" "You got it, Boss," he replied.

Mark picked up the phone and called Mrs. Fogarty. When she answered, he said, "Mrs. Fogarty, I need to see you." He heard the light laugh of Miss Abby from years gone by as she responded, "You were ever the formal one. You were always calling me Miss Abigail or Mrs. Appleton. You would never call me by my name." He replied, "I didn't think it was appropriate. My mother pounded into me that I should always address people properly. I couldn't help it." He heard that same light laugh as she said, "I'll be home all afternoon; you are more than welcome to stop by." He replied,

"I'll do that and thank you. See you soon." They said their goodbyes and ended the conversation.

Mark drove over to the church complex after lunch. He told Gina that he would quite likely not be back until the next day. He wasn't sure how long it would take to get his business done with Mrs. Fogarty. He arrived at their home at around 2:15 PM. When Mrs. Fogarty answered the door, Mark noted that she was dressed in what looked like a kimono. It was flowing and silky. From the way her body moved under the material he didn't think she was wearing anything underneath it. He began to think coming out here was a mistake. He asked, "Will you ask your husband to join us, please?" She replied, giving him a sidelong glance, "He isn't here and won't be back until after dinner today." He thought that she sounded way too happy about that. Mrs. Fogarty seated Mark on the sofa and took a seat opposite him in another chair. Mark couldn't help but notice that when she sat down, she was very careless with her hemline. He was now certain that she was wearing nothing under her dress. That was disturbing. She smelled freshly bathed so it didn't appear to be an accident.

"Mark, what was it that you wanted to talk about or did you just want to see me?" she asked with a certain coyness. He was careful to keep his eyes on her face. "I wanted to follow up on a couple of points in your statement, if that's agreeable to you," he said. She responded, "Of course we can do that or anything you want to do." She was wriggling and moving around on her seat and Mark carefully kept his eyes above her neck line. He could see in his peripheral vision that she was making every effort to distract him. He was starting to react and he did not want to do that. "My questions have to do with your answers when you were asked about whether or not you were proficient in shooting a gun and whether or not you had ever owned a gun. Jay thinks you are either lying about that or hiding something. What do you say?" Mark asked. Cheryl Fogarty replied, "Mark, you know me better than that!" He looked at her bright smile and innocent eyes and was nearly convinced, but he knew Jay to be the consummate professional. She continued, "I told you before that I hate guns because they have taken so much from me." Mark replied, "I remember that, but how about before all that happened?" Mark had to refuse to allow his eyes to stray because her display was quite blatant at this point. She said, "I grew up on a farm where there were guns for hunting and I did participate some, but I would never call myself a marksman." Mark pressed the issue with her, "Have you ever owned a gun?" Her response was an emphatic,"No, never!" "Okay," replied Mark, "I appreciate your time." So saying, he stood to leave. When Mrs. Fogarty realized that he was leaving she ran to him and threw her arms around him, pressing her body into his. She immediately realized that she was effecting him with her antics. She gave him a coy look and an alluring smile. "Oh, I see that you didn't miss my little effort to pique your interest, did you?" she said. "No, I didn't miss it. You are very alluring Miss Abby. I never mix work and pleasure plus I am one very married man. I can't help the reaction, but it goes no further," he said. She made big eyes at him and asked, slowly grinding herself against him, "Are you quite sure, Mark? I always wanted you, too. In fact, I wanted you most of all." Mark pulled himself away from her and looked at her mystified. "What are you talking about?" he asked. "Oh, never mind. I've said too much," and with that she pushed him out the door as though she suddenly could not wait to be rid of him.

Since it was late in the afternoon, Mark decided to go home. He felt like he needed a shower and a quiet evening at home with his wife. He was curious about her comment regarding wanting him, too. That piqued his curiosity. Later that evening, he called Willy and asked him to meet him in the office tomorrow morning and then went to bed.

CHAPTER 54:

At breakfast the next morning, after an almost sleepless night, Mark told Sarah about what had happened at his meeting with the pastor's wife. At first she thought that he was joking and started to laugh at the absurdity of the story, but she stopped, realizing that he was very serious. "She really did all that?" she asked incredulously. "She did indeed," replied Mark, "it was really bizarre behavior." "It was more than bizarre," replied Sarah. "It was unhinged. What could she mean by saying that she had wanted you, too?" Mark shook his head and replied, "I don't know, but I intend to find out. I slept very little last night puzzling over that very question and the uncharacteristic behavior by Mrs. Fogarty. I have asked Willy to meet me at the office this morning to see if he has any memories that either I don't have or I have forgotten." Sarah asked, "Aren't you going to have Jack there, too?" "No," replied Mark, "I want to talk with them separately. Sometimes I think the two of them have something hidden that I don't know about. I didn't think there was anything about those two that I didn't know. Just goes to show you." His coffee was gone so he gave Sarah a peck on the cheek and started out the door when she grabbed him in a big hug. He embraced her and she said, "Thank you, my husband, for telling me about that. You are a good man." Mark gave her one of his crooked grins and said, "I hope to be, if I can." With that, he was out the door and on his way.

It was around ten o'clock AM when Willy walked in. He was very relaxed as one is only with old friends. He sat down in Marks office and asked, "Is this an official visit; should I have an attorney?" He said it with a laugh, but there was an underlying question there. Mark responded, "You don't need an attorney with me, Willy. I would never interview you if it were as a suspect. I would have to have somebody else do it because of our history. This is not that kind of interview. You were at lunch the other day when Mack and I were talking about the investigation. Do you remember that conversation?" Willy replied, "I do remember it quite well. What does this have to do with that?" "It's like this," answered Mark. "We are still trying to eliminate people by proving them innocent. We are presuming guilt until we prove they could not have done it. I know that it is backward from our American Justice System, but it is only for investigative purposes." "Yeah, I get that," replied Willy. Mark continued, "You have to keep this conversation one-hundred percent between the two of us. Can you do that?" Willy grinned, "You know that I can keep a secret. I give you my word." Mark nodded, "Your word is good enough for me. So here's the deal. When I went to interview Mrs. Fogarty I discovered that she does not have an alibi. The alibi that she gave fifty years ago was false. She did go to her grandparents' home on Thursday the 12th of August, 1968, but she came back Friday to bring some furniture that she had bought to her house here in town. Do you remember where she lived, Willy?" Willy gave Mark a sharp look and answered, "Yes, I remember where she lived. Why do you ask?" "Just curious," Mark said. "So, to make a long story short, she doesn't have an alibi, but you already knew that because of the lunch time conversation the other day. I drove out to the pastor's house yesterday afternoon to meet with Mrs. Fogarty. It is hard for me to call her that. I remember her as Mrs. Appleton or Miss Abigail." Willy laughed, "Yeah, we knew her in such a different context than a pastor's wife" "Exactly," replied Mark. "So to get to the point, I wanted to ask you if you remember anything about those days that either I did not know or have forgotten." Willy gave Mark a blank stare and said, "Like what?" "Well," Mark began, "Mrs. Fogarty made a sexual innuendo that went back to our high school days and implied that she was having sex with somebody, but had wanted me, too. Do you know anything about that?"

Willy looked at Mark with a look that Mark had seen a few times in his career. It was the look of a cornered man looking for the best way out of a bad situation. Mark said, "Willy, just tell me what happened. Tell me the truth. I have to know; it may go to the motive behind the murders." Willy looked at Mark with a shocked expression, "You don't think she did it, do you?" "Willy, I just don't know," said Mark. "I don't see how one lone woman could pull off what was done, but stranger things have happened. I have to gather the facts so that I can put the pieces of this puzzle together. So, help me out here, Willy." Willy dropped his head, "She seduced me our junior year of high school. It was actually during the summer before our junior year. It was wild. I guess it started when I was mowing her lawn one day. Once it started, it was like a snowball; it just got bigger and bigger and harder to control.

She was really jealous when Cassie and I started dating. I had to really work at keeping both of them happy. I swore that I would never tell anybody about it. I was so ashamed at first, but then I got used to it. I can't believe that I let her comfort me after Cassie was gone. That's downright ghoulish." Mark said, "We're not sure of anything, but you have just provide a very important missing piece of the puzzle." "What's that?" Willy asked. "Motive" Mark said. "That is the major missing link. We still don't have enough to charge anybody, but for the first time in fifty years, we have a suspect. I'm still having trouble with the means. How could one lone girl do all this and not be detected?"

Willy got up to leave. They shook hands and Willy took his leave. Mark sat at his desk in wonderment. How could that have been going on without him knowing it? It really was a crazy world. He picked up the phone and called Jack to see if they could meet. He said he'd stop by that afternoon, too.

When Jack arrived, the conversation went much the same except that Jack avoided talking about Mrs. Appleton. He cleverly diverted the conversation every time they got close to her. Finally, after several diversions, Mark looked at Jack and said, "I know about it." Jack looked at Mark with feigned innocence. Mark could tell he was lying because he overplayed it. It was a textbook ploy of a nonprofessional liar trying to cover. Mark said, "I know that Miss Abigail seduced both you and Willy. "Him, too?" was Jack's immediate response. Then he realized that he had tipped his hand and sort of slumped in his seat. "I promised her that nobody would ever know about it. I have kept that promise for years." Mark asked, "How did she feel when you started seeing Esperanza?" "She never actually said anything, but she was jealous. She hated that she didn't have me to herself anymore. She kept asking me if we were having sex. I told her no, but I don't think she believed me," blurted out Jack. "Hope was a virgin and she wanted to remain that way until she got married. I respected that." Mark nodded, "I know." Jack looked shocked, "How could you know that?" he almost shouted. "Don't worry," Mark said, "it is not common knowledge. I read her diary as part of the investigation. It felt intrusive, but we were looking for anything that might have put us on the trail of the killer." Jack gave Mark a serious look and said, "Do you think Miss Abby killed those girls?" Mark shook his head and replied, "She is a person of interest, but I don't see how she could have done it. It is logistically unlikely that one person could have pulled this off as it happened. It would have taken an incredible amount of luck along with some skills that I don't know that she possessed. We are a long way from locking this down. I do admit, though, she is the only thing that we have had that even looks like a suspect in fifty years."

CHAPTER 55:

When Mark arrived at home that evening, he really unloaded on Sarah. He told her what he had learned, what he suspected, and shared his frustration of not being able to prove anything beyond a reasonable doubt. Miss Abigail was the only suspect, but there were big holes in the narrative and he wasn't sure that he would ever be able to prove it.

After several minutes of him nearly raving about the case, Sarah stopped him and said incredulously, "Do you mean to tell me that Mrs. Appleton, Cheryl Fogarty, was having sex with both Willy and Jack and wanted to seduce you, too!?" "That is what they said," replied Mark. "That is a stunner!" she said. "I agree," said Mark. "In addition, I have no idea what to do next." Sarah looked at Mark aghast, "You have to confront her with the fact that you know about her past!" Mark nodded and said, "I will when the time is right. Right now, though, it is their word against hers and the statute of limitations has run out on statutory rape, child endangerment, or contributing to the delinquency of a minor." She looked at Mark with a funny expression on her face and asked, "What does that have to do with it?" Mark shrugged and said, "That is all that we could charge her with based on their testimony. The fact that she had sex with them does not prove murder. It only provides us with a basis for a motive. We're a long ways from locking this down. There are still just too many missing pieces." She sat quietly for a few minutes letting the reality of the situation sink in and then asked, "What are you going to do then?" He was staring out through the window so long that she didn't think he'd heard her, then he turned and looked at her and said, "Just keep on doing what we have been doing. We turn over every rock; we dig around until we find something that has been buried for fifty years just like Cassie's car. Winning or losing depends on the quality of the police work we do. A little good luck wouldn't hurt our chances either." Sarah smiled, "It appears to me that you have already had some good luck. The discovery of the car seems to be incredibly good luck." Mark, too, smiled and replied, "You are right. It does seem like good luck, but I wonder sometimes." Sarah said, "You're talking about the girls again. You think they are causing this?" Mark replied, "It seems too crazy to say but something is going on here that is not normal. The commission and cover up of this crime took planning, but it also had to rely on outrageously good luck. I think we are going to need every bit of that luck to untangle it as the perpetrator had in doing it in the first place. If the spirits of the girls want to pitch in, I would not say to them nay. We need all the help we can get."

After several more minutes of silence, Sarah asked, "Do you think Cheryl did it?" Mark again paused a long time before responding and then said, "I don't know, Honey. What I do know is this, if she did it she is the coldest-hearted person I have ever known. I just don't get that from her. Do you get that kind of vibe from her?" "No, I don't." replied Sarah. "But if she did this, she has to be a psychopath. If so, none of the rules of behavior and motivation apply to her." Mark replied, "That is an interesting point of view. We have been looking for someone with typical motivation. Maybe we have been looking at it wrong. A psychopath has underlying layers of anger, resentment, etc. that are well concealed from everyone else and sometimes even from themselves, until something triggers them. We need to look for some trauma in the past life of Abigail Jensen Appleton Fogarty to see if there may be a hidden trigger. It may not be proof, but it may get us closer to the truth. Thank you for that insight, my dear, you have been most helpful!" She smiled with true pleasure and then said jokingly, "I am honored that the great Mark Bellingham would take notice of my humble contribution." Mark laughed at her and then said, most affectionately, "Put a cork in it."

CHAPTER 56

The next morning found Mark sitting with his team, bringing them up to date. Sheriff Mack was there as well. For all practical purposes, he was an ex officio member of the team. They listened as Mark outlined the idea that came out of the conversation with his wife and the two conversations with Jack and Willy. He had sworn them to secrecy which they already knew was required. Gina quipped that they should have Sarah join the team, which brought a chuckle around the table. Mark made sure that he made the point that they could trust her discretion. There was a good feeling around the table that morning.

After Mark had outlined what he had learned, Mack spoke up and said, "So we have our killer. Let's go arrest her!" Mark replied, "Whoa! Slow down, Cowboy. We don't have enough evidence for a conviction. We still need to establish means. What we have, so far, is the first viable suspect in fifty years. We do not, however, want to let this get out and spook her. I would like to have another conversation with her without her feeling threatened. If we let it out, even that we have a suspect, she may smell a rat and run from us or disappear inside herself. If she did it, she has had fifty years to build hiding places inside her mind where we can't reach her. Let's not chase her away. OK?" "Mark, you're right and you know it; what's more, I know it, too," said Mack. "Mum is the word."

Willie and Tex spoke in unison, "What do we do next?" Everybody laughed again. Part of the laughter was the exuberance of the hunt. They finally had a suspect and they were getting excited after months of having to grind it out. Mark said to the team, "I am thinking that we should drop the other people that we are looking at and go full-court press and all hands on deck for Mrs. Fogarty. Vic is already doing a deep dive into her so I am going to ask him to coordinate this. Get your assignments from him. As you complete one thing report the results back to him and get another assignment. Let's uncover everything in the lady's life, if a lady she is after all. We have to know everything about her. Everything!"

When everyone else was gone with their new assignments, Mack and Mark sat down in Mark's office. Mack asked, "What do you want me to do? I noticed that I didn't get a job from Vic so I presume that you have something for me." Mark nodded, "You are right. You and I are going to partner up for a bit. We're going to work a part of this that I haven't mentioned to anybody else." Mack looked at Mark expectantly and said, "Don't keep me waiting, spill!" Mark smiled and said, "We are going to pursue two things. Number one, we are going to do a deep dive into her past to see what kind of shooting experience she may have had." Mack looked surprised, "Are you kidding me?" Mark said, "Not even a little bit." Mack asked, "What is the other thing?" Mark replied, "We need to find out if she ever owned or had a gun in the house." Mack asked, "How are we going to do that?" "We are going back into her life and talking to people who knew her. We are going to check old records of groups like 4-H, rod and gun clubs, country clubs, and see what we can find." Mack said in a grumpy voice, "It sounds like a wild goose chase to me." "It might be," replied Mark, "but I have a hunch and it just won't go away. I think there is something back there." Mack nodded because he understood hunches, "Okay, when do we start?" "How's today sound?" asked Mark. "Good!" said Mack.

Mark said to Mack, "According to the file, Abigail Cheryl Jensen grew up in Lofton which is about an hour from here. It is a fair-sized town. She attended all of her school years in their school system and graduated from Lofton High School with honors. I think we should visit the school and look at all of the clubs and organizations that she was part of. We should look at old year books, especially from her senior year. We should ask her if she still has the yearbook from her senior year. Seniors write things to each other and nick names are often used that drop off as time goes on. We should find out if she has attended class reunions and who from that class is still around and what they remember." Mack stopped him, "Mark! Don't you think that's enough for starters? Wow! I will say it again, you are thorough, if nothing else." "I intend to be at this point, especially. We can't afford to miss anything," replied Mark. "Okay!" Mack said, "I'm in, but I doubt we'll find anything useful." "Famous last words," replied Mark dryly.

Mark started by calling and asking Cheryl Fogarty for her old high school yearbooks, especially the one from her senior year. She said he could pick them up that afternoon, if he wanted to do so. Mark declined but said he'd ask Sheriff Mack to pick them up, which he did. Mack said he would get them that same afternoon. Mark wondered if Mack, too, had been bitten by the music teacher's love bug way back when. He shook his head to clear it. That wasn't an image that he wanted stuck in his brain.

CHAPTER 57

Mack came storming into Mark's office the next morning acting furious. "Why didn't you warn me about her?" he almost shouted. "Would you have believed me?" Mark asked calmly. Mack grinned, "Probably not, but you could have tried," Mack groused. Then he started chuckling. "I guess nothing you could have said would have prepared me for what she sprang on me. Good night! She was hot to trot and wanted me to go along for the ride. She's still a mighty fine looking lady for her age." Mark replied with an arching look, "I don't know whether or not I'd use the term lady, but she doesn't look bad, I'll admit." The Sheriff grinned, "So you, too, have had your exposure to the flame?" Mark nodded, "Indeed. I'll not be going out there alone again." Then the both laughed. Mark said, "Show me what you got." Mack reached into his brief case and drew out some books and papers. "Good work!" Mark said.

The next hour or two were pretty much crowned with silence as the two old law dogs went over the yearbooks and school memories. It was surprising how much stuff Cheryl Fogarty had saved from her high school days. There were several interesting comments from friends that knew her when she was a student. One stood out from the others. The person who wrote it was one "Howie" Howe. Looking at the yearbook, they located a Howard Howe. He looked like a likely candidate to be identified as the signer of the entry that read, "Best to you, Deadeye. May you always reach your goals and hit what you shoot at." It was signed Howie. Mack sat back, "I wonder if this Howard Howe is still around?" Mark responded, "I think that there is a Howe's Pharmacy in her home town. We should call and see if he is related.

Mark grabbed his computer mouse and quickly did a check for a phone number to Howe's Pharmacy. They picked up on the second ring. The voice on the other end was a male voice saying, "Howe's." Mark quickly asked, "Is this Mr. Howard Howe?" The voice replied, "Which one? I am Howard Howe, Junior. My dad is Howie Howe. Did you want to speak to him or to me?" Mark replied, "I really need to speak with him, if I may." The voice on the phone replied, "Sure thing, let me get him for you." After a substantial pause, another voice which sounded older, came on, "This is Howie Howe, how can I help you?" The voice had a smile in it. Mark chuckled and replied, "I'll bet you get great pleasure out of saying that to people, don't you?" Mr. Howe chuckled, "You caught me. I have been saying that since I was in high school. You'd be surprised how few people even comment on it any more." "Funny," replied Mark, "I wonder if we could get together sometime soon. I am Mark Bellingham and I, along with a team of investigators, am re-investigating the case of the three lost girls from Pleasant Valley back fifty years ago." Howie replied, "Yes, Sir. I heard about that. It was and is a terrible thing. We heard that you're making progress though. Is that true?" Mark replied, "Well, yes, it's true. That is why I want to talk with you." "Meee!? Howie said, with his voice starting high and sliding lower at the finished. "Why do you want to talk with me? Am I suspected of something?" Mark replied as reassuringly as he could, "No, Mr. Howe; you are not suspected on anything at all. You might have some information that is pertinent to our investigation." He replied in an astonished voice, "What could I possibly know that would be of help to you?" "Mr. Howe," Mark said, "I really would rather speak with you in person and in private if we could make that happen." Mr. Howe relied, "When can you come over?" Mark responded, "I can be there in an hour and a half. Would you allow me to buy you lunch?" Mr. Howe relaxed. Mark could feel it over the phone. Howie said, "Free lunch is one of my specialties. You've got a date." Mark said, "Name the time and place and I'll be there." Mr. Howe gave them the name of the restaurant and the address and they hung up the phone.

Mark looked at Mack and asked, "Got time for lunch?" Mack said, "If I didn't, I'd clear my schedule for this, but it happens that I do." Mark said, "Well, then let's hit the road so we don't have to hurry." Just as they were leaving, Howie Howe called back and asked them to meet him at his home. He decided that he'd rather not make the meeting quite so public. Mark agreed and secured the address.

Mark and Mack arrived at the home of Howard Howe about ten minutes before the appointed time. They sat in the car for a moment looking at each other. Mack finally spoke up. "Do you think this is worth the drive over here, Mark?" "I don't know," replied Mark, "But I do know that we have to follow every lead until there is nothing more to learn. That's the only way I know to do this job." Mack nodded, "Me, too," he replied, "That's the only way you get to the truth, but sometimes the truth isn't what you want to hear." Mark was quiet for a few minutes then said, "I try to approach an interview without expectations. Too many times detectives have talked people into confessions in order to close a file only to find that it was a false confession. The worst part about that is that the detective will fight tooth and nail for a conviction based on a false confession just to save his reputation with little or no apparent sympathy for the victim. It's important to remember that we don't find justice for a victim by incarcerating the wrong person due to pressure interrogation. It becomes a crime with two victims." Mack replied, "Yeah, I hate it when that happens. It is worse than an unsolved crime really, but it doesn't feel like it. There is something satisfying about locking up a convicted felon. When it is shown that the perpetrator was wrongly convicted, it still feels wrong to let them go. I'm not sure why." Mark said, "Maybe because it messes with the closure we feel when we finish one." Mack nodded, "Could be. Shall we go in?" "Yes, let's do that," replied Mark.

When they met Howard Howe, he insisted that they call him Howie. He said, "Everybody calls me Howie. When someone calls me Howard, I think they're mad at me for something." He chuckled at his statement. Mark and Mack smiled and nodded. Mark started, "Thanks for meeting with us today, Howie. I'm sure that you are curious that we wanted to meet with you." He replied, "As a matter of fact, I am curious." Mark said, "Here's the scenario. We have reopened the case of the three young ladies that disappeared from Pleasant Valley so many years ago." "Yes," Howie replied, "the fifty-year anniversary of that event is coming soon is it not?" "Yes, it is," replied Mack. Mark went on, "Without going into a long explanation, we have re-investigated everyone that was originally cleared thinking that we may find something that was missed so long ago. As part of that investigation, we are looking into Mrs. Cheryl Fogarty." Howie scowled at them and said, "I don't know anyone by that name." Mark nodded, "I know that already. You do know, however, an Abigail Cheryl Jensen Appleton. You signed her yearbook the year she graduated high school. In fact, it appears that you were in the same class. Isn't that true?" "As a matter of fact, it is," replied Howie. "She and I were friends. I heard that her Marine Captain husband was killed. In fact, I attended his funeral. I have to confess that we lost touch after that, though. I haven't seen her in years." Mark nodded and replied, "That's the way it goes. What I wanted to talk to you about was how she was as a young person. How was she in school? Was she a good student, athlete, friend, etc?" "Oh, I get it," Howie replied, "you're doing background." Mack nodded and said, "Exactly." "Well, let me see." Howie mused, "Abby was a lot of fun. She worked hard and was, therefore, a very good student. She played hard and was a good athlete. She played basketball and softball. She played in the band and sang in the choir. She was also a varsity cheerleader. I always had the impression that she thought that she should be the best at everything. She really pushed herself." Mark asked, "Did she have any boyfriends?" Howie dropped his head, "I always wanted to date her but was afraid to ask. She dated Hoss Wilcox. His name was really Francis, but he didn't like Frank and hated his name, so he insisted that people call him Hoss. He loved Hoss Cartwright on Bonanza so he wanted to be him. He grew into a pretty big guy so it worked for him." "What happened with Hoss," asked Mark. "He broke up with her their senior year after prom. He said she was too controlling and he didn't want a girl bossing him around all his life. I guess she was bossy. I know she always thought her way was the best way and didn't give much place for another point of view." "Okay," replied Mark, "tell me about the name Deadeye. Why did you call her that?" Howie started laughing and said, "She was the best shot around with any kind of bow and arrow, sling shot, or fire arm. She could outshoot all of her brothers, her dad and uncles, and anybody else that came along. I heard that the only person to ever beat her in a one-on-one competition was the Captain. Some say that she let him win, but I doubt that. I knew her too well." Mack jumped in, "Did she just shoot standing targets or moving targets, too?" Howie replied, "That girl could out shoot anybody I ever saw. We could all shoot six out of ten apples off a tree by cutting the stem at twenty-five yards. She could consistently hit nine out of ten. The truth is that it was better than that. It was more like ninety-seven percent. Hell, you could throw four apples up in the air and she could shoot them with a pistol before they hit the ground. She was good!" Mark and Mack sat back in their chairs and were silent for a few minutes. Mark followed up with another question. He said, "Howie, did she ever enter any competitions where there might be records we could look at?" He replied, "Oh sure, there is a display at the public library of the trophies and citations that she won over the years. Her father was, and her brothers still are, members of the local hunting club. She won every competition they had for several years. I think they were glad to see her move on to college. They were tired of being beaten by a girl, I think." He was chuckling at the memories. "Why all the interest in her shooting?" he asked. Mack jumped in again, "We're just trying to get as complete a picture as possible of every person.

About that time, Mrs. Howard showed up with fresh strawberry pie and coffee. She served it up and sat down with them. She said, "I couldn't help but overhear your conversation. You don't think that Abby killed those girls do you?" Mack said to her, "We aren't thinking along those lines, yet. We just need to get as much data as we can accumulate so we know what could have happened. It's hard for me to imagine that the lady that I know as Cheryl Fogarty could have done such a thing." "Me, too," said Mrs. Howard, "it's interesting that she is using her middle name. I wonder why she started doing that?" Howie chimed in, "That is a strange thing, her starting to use her middle name. It's like she was trying to change her identity." After finishing their coffee and pie, Mark and Mack left.

On the drive back to Pleasant Valley both of them were quiet for a long time. Finally, Mack blew out a long breath and said, "What do you make of that, Mark?" Mark hesitated so long that Mack turned and looked at him as if maybe he hadn't heard him. Mark said, "I heard you, Mack. I just don't know what to make of it. Nothing I heard today did anything to indicate that we should remove Abigail from the suspect category. I was frankly shocked to hear about her shooting expertise. I wonder why nobody ever knew about it over in our neck of the woods." Mack just shook his head and said, "It was apparently something that she did not want to continue doing. Maybe it was the death of her husband or maybe it was something else. We need to try to find out if she owned that.32 caliber handgun that was the murder weapon. How are we going to do that?" Mark replied, "I have been thinking about that. Some of her brothers are still alive. Maybe we can talk with them and see if they could or would supply any information. Also, we could check with the library to see if they have any records of weapons used during matches. We could also see if the hunting club has any records of matches and weapons used. We could check the range and see if she ever fired a .32 caliber piece. We have some options before we throw in the towel. So far, we don't have evidence enough to convict after fifty years. We will need an ironclad case or it won't stick." "I agree," replied Mack. "That, however, will be a tall order, my friend." "Right," agreed Mark. They arrived at Mark's office and the Sheriff took off on his own errands.

Mark sat down at his desk. Everyone else was out of the office. It was about time to go home anyway. He allowed his mind to go where he had not before permitted it to wander. Could Abigail Appleton Fogarty be guilty of such a horrendous act? It really seemed unthinkable. It was easy to slip into denial because Mark had known her back then and she was such a kind, gentle soul. He had to force himself to accept the fact that the evidence was starting to pile up and it was pointing in her direction. Besides, she was the only suspect that they had. He noted that he had just thought of her as a suspect. He had not done that prior to today. But now he had half of the means. There was still no evident motive, but that was not as important now that they had both means and opportunity. His head was starting to ache. He got up, locked his office and went home.

CHAPTER 58

Sarah had a wonderful dinner of oven roasted chicken and mashed potatoes, along with a salad and green beans. Mark was really hungry so he ate well, then sat back with a comfortable grunt and looked at his wife. "That was a great dinner," he said. "I'm so glad to come home after a day of hard work. Thank you for a great dinner." Sarah smiled and replied, "I wonder when we're going to get back to being retired. It's almost like it was when you were working for the bureau." Mark made a pained face and replied, "I know; I had no idea that we would be at it this long and this hard. I am so sorry, but this investigation has taken on a life of its own. I feel like I have to see it to the end, now." Sarah replied, "Oh, I agree. You do need to see it to the end, but I just regret that we don't have the time together like we did before. I miss those times." Mark put his arm around his wife, "Me, too," he said. "We'll get our life back soon, I believe." Sarah gave Mark a look. She asked, "Do you really think you've found something?" He replied, "I don't want to believe what I am finding, but the short answer is yes." When he told her what he had found out regarding Cheryl Fogarty's past as a competitive shooter, she was as shocked as he had been. "Wow!" She said, "Do you think she did it? I mean that is wild! I just can't believe it! What are you going to do?" Mark started laughing and said, "Slow down there girl. We have a lot of work to do before we can prove anything. What we have is means and opportunity. What we don't have is motive. Why would she do such a horrible thing?" "But," sputtered Sarah, "how can you even suspect her? She is and always has been such a sweet person. She is so kind and thoughtful. How can you even think that about her?" "Honey," Mark said softly, "at the end of the day, I have to follow the evidence. It's not like we have a suspect pool from which to choose. This evidence has taken us down one road and it has been in very short supply, by the way. I mean I have never seen a case so stingy with leads in all of my career." Sarah stared at him for a long time and then asked, "Are you going to arrest her?" Mark smiled gently, "No, we don't have nearly enough evidence to make a case. I don't like this any better than you do. Believe me. Mack is more blown away than I am. He is just in a fog over this. I think that he is mad at himself for not cracking Abigail's alibi back fifty years ago, but he shouldn't be. They could have found out what we now know if they had suspected her, but they didn't. The investigator's suspicions determine the way they question people. That's just the way it is. If you don't ask the right questions, you don't get the answers that you need. The problem that investigators encounter is that they have preconceived notions, too. The presumption of innocence can be just as damaging to an investigation as the presumption of guilt. I give Mack a pass. He was just a year off his rookie year when this happened. Some of the others might be to blame, but they've been dead for years. This is not the time to figure out what they did wrong, if anything. It is time to finish this. I'm a little apprehensive as to where it is going to take us, but I'm moving forward anyway."

Mark continued, "What I don't understand is what motive she might have had to kill three beautiful young girls just as their young lives were beginning to blossom. Even with the means and opportunity nailed down, why would anybody do that? What kind of darkness would have to lie hidden in a person's psyche to inspire such evil? I just can't imagine what it might be." Sarah wrapped her arms around Mark and said softly, "Don't torture yourself. It wasn't your fault. You didn't cause this." He nodded and then said quietly, "You're right, but what I know and what I feel sometimes don't line up side by side." "That is true of everybody, I guess," said Sarah. "So what do we do?" Mark said, "I guess we just keep plugging along. Some questions will never be answered. The best that we can hope for is a clear resolution of the matter. In my view, I'd rather see that sooner than later." "Me, too," Sarah added. After talking, they watched a little bit of TV and went to bed.

CHAPTER 59

When Mark walked into his office the next morning, Mack was waiting for him. They said their good mornings, snagged a couple cups of coffee and sat down in Mark's office. Mack started, "Mark, I have been thinking about this case all night. I couldn't sleep for hours last night. Finally, I came up with what I believe to be the next step in the investigation." Mark interrupted him, "Let me guess. You want to go see Miss Abigail and see what she has to say about what we have found out. Right?" Mack looked at him incredulously. "Do you have a spy in my head?" he asked. "No, Mack," Mark responded. "It is the same thought that I had in the middle of the night, too. Great minds run on the same track says the old adage." Mack mumbled, "Or broken ones." Mark grinned at the comeback. He said, "That is not far from the truth, I think." Mack said, "I think that it is the logical step to take right now." Mark said, "Let me call her and see when we can meet with her." Mack looked at him with a bulldog look and said, "I am the Sheriff of this county. She'll talk with me when I say so!" Mark said softly, "Do you intend to arrest her, then?" "Well, no. Not yet, anyway," replied Mack. Mark said to him, "I think that we should approach her a little more judiciously in that case. Requesting an appointment is better than demanding it. I know we have the authority, but I'd like to keep it low key as long as we can." Mack dropped his head and then looked at Mark out of the corners of his eyes. He then said, "You know, you're right. I don't have to tell you. I suppose it feeds your ego to hear it though." With that they both cracked up. "Let me make that call," said Mark. Mark picked up the phone and within a couple of minutes had an appointment set. He looked at Mack and said, "She can see us this morning at ten o'clock. Are you ready to go?" "I am; let's go," said Mack.

As they pulled up to the parsonage, they noticed that the pastor's car was gone. When Abigail answered the door, Mark noticed that she was thinner and didn't look like she felt very well, but she was as sweet and gracious as ever. She was dressed in jeans and a hoodie and didn't look anywhere near her age somewhere in the mid-seventies. She welcomed them into the house and then poured coffee. There were homemade cookies available for them to enjoy and they did.

After a few minutes of chit-chat, the pastor's wife asked them the purpose of their visit. Mark said, "Miss Abigail..." Mrs. Fogarty quickly interrupted him and said, "Please! Call me Cheryl. People don't call me Abigail anymore." Mark looked at her intently and asked, "Why is that, Mrs. Fogarty?" She gave him a sharp look and replied, "I asked people to call me Cheryl when I married Elliot. It seemed like a new start on a new life and I wanted a new name to go with it. It was my choice and people have embraced the change well enough. After all this time, you come back and call me Miss Abigail. It brings up painful memories." Mack asked, "What kind of painful memories?" She replied, "Memories of losing my Captain and other things that are best put behind me." Mark said, "Should we do this on another day? You don't act like you feel very well today." She replied, "I'm fine. I have felt out of sorts for a couple of weeks now. I have an appointment with my doctor this afternoon. He'll get to the bottom of it." Mack glanced at Mark and then said, "Mrs. Fogarty, I'm going to get right to the point. We have found two or three things in your background that make us more than a little suspicious that you might have done something terrible a few years back." Cheryl replied, "What in the world are you talking about? What terrible thing do you think I have done?" She was quite indignant. Then she burst out, "Do you think I need an attorney?" Mark stepped in and said, "Mrs. Fogarty, if you think you need an attorney then we should end the conversation right now until you have one." She smiled that sweet, innocent smile that she had and said, "No. I don't need an attorney. I have nothing to hide."

Mark turned to Mack and said, "Go on then, Sheriff." Mack continued, "I was part of the team that investigated this crime back when it happened. I had not been on the force for very long when It happened. I had just barely completed my rookie year. In fact, many still called me "Rook" at the time. The investigation that this new team is doing is beyond anything that I have ever seen as far as scope and detail. In the process, we have discovered first of all that your alibi does not hold up. You gave the impression that you were out-of-town back when the crime was committed when you were, in fact, here in town at your home. That alone would not have made you a suspect except that you did lie about it. Secondly, we couldn't find that you had the means to do such a horrible crime until we saw the nickname Deadeye in your high school year book. We looked up Howie Howard in your home town and he let us in on the fact that back in the day, you could outshoot all of your brothers and all of the men of the town. In fact, you won awards and trophies for your shooting." Cheryl interrupted him, "Is it a crime to be a good shot?" He smiled indulgently at her and said, "You know that it is not a crime. But it did add a bit to our suspicions because it proved that you could have done it." Mrs. Fogarty looked at Mark with a bit of shock. "Mark," she said, "did you come here to accuse me of murder?" Mark shook his head, "No, not today. We just came to talk." Mack said, "Mark, why don't you take over?" "Okay," Mark responded, "I'll take it from here. Mrs. Fogarty, Cheryl, there have been several questions that have come up in the scope of our work. For one thing we wondered how someone could be sure that the car would go far enough into the marsh to conceal it and not have it just drop down onto the bank. Then we found out that you had started as an engineering major and then switched to music because you loved music so much." She said sweetly, "There is no crime in switching majors, Mark." He replied, "Of course not. In fact, it is a time-honored tradition. The point was not that you switched majors, but that you had the sufficient knowledge to compute the trajectory to the point in the marsh where the car landed and could have computed the speed needed to get it there. There weren't many people in town that could do that. There probably still aren't." Mack picked it up again, "So you see, Miss Cheryl, we have means and opportunity. In some cases that might be enough, but in a case this old and of this magnitude we will have to nail it down or there will be questions forever." She looked at both of them with a questioning expression and finally asked, "So what is it you want from me?" Mack and Mark both looked at her innocent expression and it did not appear to be put on. She really seemed sincere. Mack said, "We were hoping for a confession." She looked at them with a truly mystified expression. She said, with real shock in her voice, "Do you think that I killed those girls?!" Mack said, "The evidence seems to point to it, but we can't prove it conclusively, yet." Miss Cheryl said scoffingly, "Well, of all of the crazy, trumped up ideas that I have ever heard, that one takes the prize. You men must be out of your minds! I'm going to ask you to leave my house, now. Don't ever come back unless my husband is at home." Mark and Mack got up to leave. "Yes, Ma'am!" they both said and walked out the door with no further conversation.

When they got into the car, Mack burst out, "Do you think we got it wrong? I mean she seemed so innocent and indignant at the idea that we suspect her!" Mark shook his head, "Nope, Mack," he said, "I think we got it right. There is something working here that I don't understand, but I think we got it right. I believe that she could pass a lie detector, but she is lying just the same. I wish we had brought Jay along. He can smell a lie a mile off. He would have known for sure, but I'm satisfied that she is lying. We just can't prove it. It's like she is two different persons. One is sweet and innocent, the other more crafty and sly." Mack looked relieved. He said, "She has me confused. Her denial seems so genuine and she showed no fear. I've seen the cornered animal look in the eyes of many a suspect and she showed none of that. She just looked at us with those innocent eyes like we were talking about someone else." "Yes, she did," muttered Mark. "I wonder about that." Mack looked at him and asked, "About what?" "Well," Mark said, "she should not be able to lie so naturally. I mean, she had to know what we were coming to and yet she sold that innocent little girl look by the pound. You know what I mean?" Mack nodded, "Yes, I do. What does it mean though?" "I don't know," said Mark. "If you come up with any bright ideas, let me know." Mack chuckled, "If you can't figure it out, fat chance that I will." Mark grinned, "I'll take it! At this point if anyone can figure it out, I'd be happy." They drove the rest of the way back to Pleasant Valley in silence, each of them occupied with his own thoughts.

CHAPTER 60

When they arrived at Mark's office they sat in the vehicle for a few moments. Mark finally broke the silence saying, "You know, there may be a thread of a motive that I had not given very much consideration, but listen to this. Abigail had seduced both Jack and Willy. They both said that she had designs on me. She never did make any moves on me that I can recall. It could be that I was so dense that I didn't understand her actions were seductive and I just thought she was trying to be nice, but I don't remember any overtly sexual overtures. I know that we never had any sexual relationship of any kind. What if, however, she thought of Esperanza and Cassie as competition for Jack and Willie, and Pauline as an obstacle to getting to me? Could that have been motive to kill them?" Mack was listening intently and thinking hard. He responded, "It would be really unusual for that alone to be motive to kill. Coupled with the death of her husband, however, it may have pushed her to such a desperate act. Don't you think it possible?" "Of course, it is possible," Mark replied. "It is clear that our notions of the times were way off, on the face of it. We thought in way too traditional concepts and it blinded us to the twists that the human mind and heart can take. We have been looking for a trucker or a trucking team, men on the fringes of society and such traditional suspects, when a non-typical one was right under our noses and we weren't even thinking in that direction. Knowing what we know and knew about Abigail Appleton, it was too ghastly to think. Now, however, we are forced to absolute reality, following the evidence if you will, and it is taking us where none of us would have otherwise gone. I frankly hate what I am thinking, but can't help it because the evidence is becoming compelling." Mack asked softly, "Do you want to arrest her?" Mark said, "We don't have enough to nail her. It would just cause a scandal and make it harder to get a conviction. I'd like to do it, but I'm not going to. I'd like to do it to get people started thinking along the line that we are thinking, but that would be tantamount to trying the case in the media. We're better than that, I hope." Mack chuckled, "You and your high ideals! I'd just like to get somebody convicted for this crime. It is more horrific than we ever knew way back when. We sold ourselves a sanitized version of it so we could sleep at night, but we had it all wrong."

As they finished their conversation, they were walking into Mark's office. The other members of the team gathered to see what they had found out. Mark and Mack briefed them on the information gleaned from Howie and why he had referred to her as Deadeye. The question came from Gina, "What's next then?" Mark said, "I don't think we have enough to get a conviction, given the years that Mrs. Fogarty has lived here and the fact that she has been a pastor's wife now for thirty-some years. Getting a jury to believe that she murdered those girls in cold blood and buried them under the school is going to be a tough sell. They could easily believe that it is just coincidental that she was in town and a crack shot. There were plenty of other crack shots in town that day that didn't do anything wrong." Mack was sitting with his head down, "So we need to prove that she knew about the haberdashery or had some other involvement. We need at least one more connection to the girls on the day that they disappeared." Mark nodded, "That is exactly right." Victor chimed in, "How are we going to find out if she knew something about the haberdashery? It is clear that whoever did this had to know about it, but how are we going to dig that out?" Mark said, "I don't know, Victor, maybe there will be another thread that will tie it together. We didn't expect to find out most of what we have learned. We just need to keep shaking the trees to see what falls out, I guess."

Tex said, "One thing that we haven't done is go door-to-door in the neighborhoods to see if anybody remembers anything strange on or around the day or night of the disappearance. It's a long shot, but we don't have many more shots until we're shot." Everyone chuckled or grinned at his play on words, but recognized that he spoke the truth. Mack said speculatively, "If Miss Abigail is the killer, she would have had to ride that bicycle back from the lake to her house. We could map out the routes that she could have taken and knock on doors and ask." Willie added, "That seems like a colossal waste of time!" Jay looked at her with a questioning look and asked, "Do you have a better idea?" She gave him a crooked grin and responded, "No, I don't."

Mark said to them, "Solving cold cases takes a lot of basic police work. It also takes a bit of luck. We have had more luck on this case than I can remember ever having on any case anywhere." They all nodded in agreement. "I guess it's time to do some good, old-fashioned, hard-nosed, grunt work." Mack spoke up, "I can spare some deputies to help with the canvass. If they find anything, we can have them hand it off to one of us for a more in-depth interview." "That sounds good," said Mark. "We'll have assignments in the morning. See you guys then." They all voiced their assent and went their separate ways.

CHAPTER 61

Mark and Sarah had a quiet evening at home enjoying a good dinner and a little TV. Sarah finally said, "Mark, you seem preoccupied this evening. It is as though you are trying to focus, but it is hard for you. Would you like to talk about it?" Mark replied, "I am sorry. I try hard not to bring the problems of the office into the house with me, but this is a tough one." "What is it?" Sarah asked. "It is Miss Abigail or Cheryl as she now wishes to be called." Mark answered. "What about her?" came the next question from Sarah. Mark hesitated and then said, "We confronted her today with our case. Mack and I were hoping that she would confess. We are convinced that she is the killer, but we can't prove it conclusively. On a case this old against someone as well respected as she is, we will need an iron-clad case. We have a good one, but not great." "What are you going to do?" Sarah asked. "It's going to take something that we haven't seen or, if we have seen it but don't understand, to break it open. Do you think it is possible that she had buried this guilt for so long that she really believes that she didn't do it?" Mark replied. Sarah said, "I don't know! It is so complicated. The human mind is capable of so many twists and turns that nobody can really understand." Mark said,

"Just thinking out loud, I wonder about the name change. What I mean is, I wonder when she started calling herself Cheryl instead of Abigail and why she was so adamant about it when Mack and I visited with her this time. She had never mentioned it before and we both have called her Abby or Miss Abigail. She didn't say a word about it then. It is curious to me." Sarah said, "I don't know and we probably won't figure it out tonight. Let's sleep on it and see how it looks in the morning." Mark smiled at the practicality of her suggestion and replied, "Agreed. Good night."

The next morning in the office, the team poured over maps of the area and assigned streets for canvassing. They were specifically looking for people who had lived in the area fifty years ago who were still there. It would be a small pool of people, but they were hopeful that it would be productive. It would only take one tidbit of information to tie it down. They didn't know what kind of information it would be. That was one of the interesting things about an investigation. Often when you were looking for one thing, you found something completely different or similar, but different enough that it took you down a road that you had not even considered before. After the assignments were given, the team split up and went out to knock on doors. The plan was to leave a door hanger where there was nobody home, and over a week or two, to speak with everyone who lived on those streets. Hopefully something would shake loose.

About four days into the effort, they received the news that Cheryl Fogarty had been diagnosed with a rare, rapidly advancing strain of leukemia. The doctors did not give her much hope of recovery nor did they give her long to live. Mark felt badly for her and if not for the fact that there were three murdered girls who deserved justice, he would have dropped the whole thing. In fact, Mack asked him if he thought that they should drop it and Mark said, "My compassion for Miss Abigail and her family says yes, but my sense of justice for three perfectly innocent girls, Pauline, Cassie, and Esperanza says absolutely not. I just hope that we can get an answer before she passes and leaves us with more questions than answers." Mack replied, "From your lips to God's ears."

About nine days into the canvass, the phone rang in the office one morning. It was Sarah and she said to Mark, "I have just been reading an article on multiple personality or syndrome. It fits many of the quirks of your case. Abigail might have felt so much guilt that she changed her name in order to move on as a different person. Could it work like that?" Mark said, "I don't know, but it is an interesting proposition. I will need to talk with a mental health professional, one of which I have on my team. Great Idea; thanks for sharing! See you this evening."

After hanging up, Mark quickly assembled his team. They had to wait for a couple of them to return from the field. When they were assembled, Mark said to them, "My wife called me this morning with an excellent question. Could the name change from Abigail to Cheryl be tied to strong guilt feelings that she needed to bury? Guilt so strong, she blamed the murders on her old self and reinvented herself as Cheryl?" Jay said, "You're talking about multiple personality syndrome. That is a possibility, but have there been any manifestations of the old Abigail?" Mark replied, "I'm not sure, but when I went out to interview her by myself, she acted very differently from the Cheryl that we have come to know as the wife of Pastor Fogarty. She expressed herself quite openly as a wanton slut. In fact, she exposed herself to me in very lewd and licentious ways. Mack had a similar experience, didn't you, Mack?" He replied, "I did indeed. She made sure that I had good views under her skirt and she was not wearing underwear. I think you could call that lewd." There were chuckles around the table. "I'll bet you don't go there alone anymore, do you?" said Tex. "No. After that experience we have partnered up when we go see her," replied Mack. "After our last visit, she told us to never come back unless her husband was home. Come to think of it, this Cheryl person is different from the woman I spoke to before. She was similar, but different." Mark nodded, "That is my experience, too. I just couldn't put my finger on it until Sarah suggested multiple personality. I think we need to go back even though she is sick. This needs to be resolved." "I think so, too," Mack agreed. "Maybe we can do it early next week. Since this is Friday, let's let it ride over the weekend," Mark said. They all agreed.

Late that afternoon Mark's cell phone rang. He answered to find it was Victor. He had found a lady who had an interesting story to tell. Mark drove right over to her house. Victor introduced him to Charlene Beatty. Charlene had grown up in that house and bought it from her parents' estate. She had never lived anywhere else except while attending university. She had come home, found a job in one of the local banks, and settled down. She married after her parents passed and was now in her late-fifties. Her home was just a couple of blocks from where Abigail Appleton had lived before marrying the pastor. Mark asked her if she would mind if he recorded the conversation and she consented. He began with the standard opening, "This is Mark Bellingham and I am speaking with Charlene Beatty…" He stated the date, time, and place and then asked her to state her full name and her maiden name, which she did. Then he asked her, "Do you recall the events of August 13th, 1968, when Cassie Patterson, Esperanza Chavez, and Pauline Franklin disappeared?" She answered, "Yes, I clearly remember that day and the events surrounding it." Mark asked her, "How old were you at the time?" She replied, "I was eight years old." Mark said, "Victor tells me that you have an interesting story to share. Would you tell me in your own words what it is that you remember?" She replied, "Yes. You know there are, and were then, many dogs in our neighborhood. Back in the day, people didn't keep their dogs in the house like they do now. Most of the dogs stayed outside in the back yards. At night, if something disturbed the dogs, they would set up a clamor of barking that would often awaken me and others." She paused and Mark asked her, "How does that apply to this matter?" "Oh," Charlene said, "There is more. Mrs. Appleton liked to go for walks at night when she couldn't sleep. I didn't understand at the time, but she must have been worried about her husband and she must have felt lonely, too. Well, when she walked, the dogs would set up quite a noise. My dad always called It the "Howlelujah Chorus". He thought he was funny." Mark interjected, "That is a bit funny." She chuckled, "I thought so too, but anyway, every night when the dogs awakened me, I would run to the window to see if Mrs. Appleton was out walking again. It was almost always her. On the night that the girls disappeared, the dogs were going crazy and I awakened. I ran to the window to see what it was and it was her, but she wasn't walking." Again Charlene paused. Mark tipped his head, "What was she doing?" he asked softly. Charlene replied, "She was riding a bicycle!" Mark was excited and asked "Are you sure it was her?" "Absolutely!" she replied. "There was a street light right in front of our house and I got a great look at her. I didn't know that she had a bike. I had never seen her ride it before. Actually, come to think of it, I never saw her ride it since either." Mark was excited, but he tried hard to be professional. He asked her, "Can you remember anything about the bicycle?" "Not really," she said, "it was a full sized one, but I don't remember the color or whether it was a boys or a girls."

Mark asked Charlene after they had finished the formal statement, "Why didn't you come forward back when they were doing the investigation?" She looked at him like he was from Mars and replied, "Nobody ever listens to kids! You should know that!" He pressed her a bit, "Did you tell your parents what you saw?" She said, "Well, sure I did, but they told me to keep my place. Nobody wanted to hear what I saw." Mark smiled at her and said, "I, for one, am very happy to hear what you had to say and only wish that someone fifty years ago had found you and the information that you have to share." She looked surprised, "Then you mean my statement is significant?" "Miss Charlene," Mark said, "I have never taken a more significant statement in all of my years with the FBI. It is one-hundred percent pertinent and significant." "Oh, good!" she replied, "I always hoped that I could help with something that mattered." Victor chimed in, "Lady, you hit the jackpot today. We really needed your statement to support something that we believed, but couldn't prove. Thank you for sharing." She smiled a beaming smile and said, "It was truly my pleasure. Thank you for asking. I have had that in the back of my mind all these years and wondered if it was important. Now I know."

As Mark and Victor drove back to the office, Victor remarked, "I thought you were nuts when you put us on this crazy quest, but once again, you have proved the effectiveness of thorough police work. This should have been done back in the day, but slipped through the cracks. Good on ya, Boss." Mark replied, "Thanks, Victor, that means a lot coming from a true pro like yourself. We have the proof that we needed. Now the question is what to do with it."

CHAPTER 62

Mark selected Jay to ride with him to the hospital to see Cheryl Fogarty. He wanted to use Jay's lie detecting skills. It was very difficult to do under the circumstances. Cheryl was very ill and would not recover. He was reluctant to even confront her, but felt that the families of the girls deserved closure. He was feeling like closure at this point was not as important as it had seemed a few months ago or even a few weeks ago. He had to steel himself with the thought that Abigail Appleton had almost certainly murdered three young girls, who trusted her, in cold blood. It still just did not seem to fit.

As they entered her room, Mark was shocked to see the change in her. She was thin and hollow-eyed. She looked really bad. He greeted her and she seemed happy to see him. She said, "I suppose you have found something else that you need to discuss with me. Am I right?" Mark smiled gently and replied, "Yes, Mrs. Fogarty. That is correct. We just need to cover a couple of things, but first, how are you feeling?" Mrs. Fogarty smiled the beaming smile that Mark remembered from her years as music teacher and said, "Thank you so much for asking! I guess I feel as well as I can expect to feel.

I am not going to surrender, but the doctors tell me that won't make much difference. It's a matter of days or weeks that can be gained by fighting, but eventually I will succumb to this thing that stalks me. I don't feel too badly though. There is no pain; I just feel weak and sick, if you know what I mean." Mark nodded saying, "I guess we've all felt like that a time or two."

"So," she said, "what was the big question that you wanted to ask me about?" Mark was slow to respond and she said, "Come on, Mark; do your job. What was it." "Well," Mark replied, "we found a witness that saw you riding a bicycle past her house on the night that the girls disappeared. She said she was sure it was you because she heard the dogs barking and got up to look. According to her, you frequently walked late at night. She had seen you because all the dogs in the neighborhood always barked. The difference this night was that you were riding a bike. She said it was the only time that she could remember seeing you ride a bicycle. Did you own a bicycle at the time?" Cheryl shook her head, "No, I didn't." Mark continued, "Whose bike did she see you ride, then? Do you remember." She replied, "I don't remember riding a bicycle that night. I never brought my bike over here from my parents' farm. I rode it when I went over there. I did walk a lot and jog a little back then." Mark pressed the issue, "Are you denying that you were riding a bicycle that night?" "No," she said, "I just don't remember." Mark said to her, "The reason that we need to know is that witnesses have placed Cassie's bike in the trunk of her car leaving town late on the afternoon of August 13th, 1968. This witness that we have found has you riding a bicycle toward your house between 3:00 AM and 4:00 AM. You can see why we need to talk with you about this, can't you?" "Oh, yes," she said, "I get it, but I did not kill those girls. I have told you repeatedly that I didn't do it. I wish I could help more but that's what I know." Mark gave Jay a side long glance. Jay had a studied look on his face. He gave Mark a nod and surreptitious thumbs up. Mark dropped the interrogation and just chatted with Cheryl for a few minutes.

As Mark and Jay were taking their leave, Mark said to Cheryl without any emotion, "Oh, by the way, the next time I come, I would like to speak with Abigail. Please let her know." Cheryl's reaction was almost startling. She bristled and then replied in a harsh voice, "Don't be ridiculous! That's impossible!" Mark said, "I don't think so. I think I saw her that day at your house. Do you remember?" Cheryl blushed a deep pink and just shook her head, but didn't respond. They left without further words.

As they drove back to the office, Jay said, "She was telling the truth about her, Cheryl, not killing the girls. Her reaction to your request to speak with Abigail was crazy. She reacted almost violently. I think it was Abigail who responded. It was almost a different voice. It was similar, but different. I was shocked. I think you are on to something. Good call." Mark replied, "I would love to nail this down before she passes. She doesn't have much time and I need to get this verified before she dies. No pressure!" Jay chuckled at that and then said, "Mark, to tell you the truth, I thought you were overrated. Now I believe that quite the opposite is true. You have made us all better by the way that you have worked this case and it is no surprise that you have one of the best cold case solve rates in the history of the FBI. It was not a fluke." Mark looked at Jay and said, "Well, thank you, Jay. Those are mighty kind words."

"Let me put it like this," Jay said, "any time you need a wing man, just call. I'm in."

CHAPTER 63

There was a lull in the case for a few days. The team was digesting what they knew and trying to figure out how to nail it down. They were satisfied that they had uncovered the truth, but couldn't put it completely together, yet. For example, it was hard for any of them to believe that one woman had accomplished the crime and the cover-up without help. The physical strength needed to bury three bodies, dispose of the car, load and unload the bicycle, and kill three active girls was making their conclusions look somewhere between unlikely and impossible. On top of that, how did they find the haberdashery? Some of them were still looking for a partner. Mark was leaning toward one person with incredibly good luck. He was most confused about how they found their way to the haberdashery. Both of the other guys, Willy and Jack, swore that they never told anybody about the place.

Victor had finished his deep dive into the life and times of Abigail Cheryl Jensen Appleton Fogarty. Most of what he found was consistent with what they knew of her. There was, however, the hint of a dark side. There had been a few incidents of violence that had been sort of swept under the rug. She had beaten up a girl who tried to flirt with her boyfriend Hoss. It appeared that the reason that he had broken up with her was that she was so violent over this girl that he wanted nothing to do with her. The incident had been overlooked because of her father's standing in the community. There were hints of other outbursts as well, but no specific records. It was certainly something to ponder.

Mark and Mack were due for a meeting in about fifteen minutes. Mack was stopping by again. It seemed like he had almost taken up residence in Mark's office lately. Mack was convinced that they were on the verge of cracking the case wide open and he wanted to be there when it happened. He kept saying that he had waited fifty years to see the truth come out and had really given up hope that it would happen. Now they knew the truth, but just didn't have enough facts to propagate it.

At ten o'clock Mack walked into Mark's office. They shook hands and got fresh coffee and then sat down. Mack started, "Mark," he said, "when we reopened this case, I was convinced that it was an exercise in futility. I never expected that we would know the truth about what happened that day. Even though we don't have the full story, we know who did it. I did not expect this. To be perfectly honest, I wish I didn't know in some ways." Mark nodded solemnly, "Me, too," he said. "Miss Abigail is the last person on the face of the globe that I would have suspected of doing this thing. I am as shocked as I have ever been in my entire life. But, the evidence points to her with ever more revealing light and convincing weight. I did not see this coming, not even a little bit." Mack was quiet for a long moment and then responded, "I don't think anybody did see or could have seen this coming. There was never anything in her conduct that even hinted at such an atrocity. It is mind boggling. To think, that she has been living among us all these years without even a whiff of suspicion." Mark added, "It does defy credulity. I wonder how she could go on living with herself without breaking down and going absolutely crazy. I mean that would be a monster of a memory."

They sat quietly for a few moments and then Mark said, "Well, Mack, old friend, what is on your mind today that you wanted to meet?" Mack replied, "The county board has met and has decided that we should disband the team, now. They are of the opinion that the work is basically done as far as the investigation goes. They are probably right about that. So it's time to break it up, I guess." Mark said in reply, "I have been expecting that for a while now. It's a little surprising that it didn't come sooner, but I am glad for the extra time because we were able to generate the Info about the bicycle and shooting skills. Those are key pieces of evidence. Anyway, how long do we have?" Mack replied, "I was told to give them two weeks' severance and send them home." Mark said, "Okay, I'll tell them. Do you want to speak to them, too?" "Yes, I would," responded Mack. Mark said, "They are all here; let me call them in."

When the team was assembled, Mark spoke to them saying, "We have done nearly everything that we set out to do when we took this case. I had hoped for a trial and a conviction. It appears that we are going to get cheated of that closure as our only suspect, the only suspect ever, is dying of cancer. It appears that she doesn't have long to live. We won't be able to present our evidence to a jury and see justice done, but it always gets done eventually. I want to thank you for your diligence but also for the excellent work that you have done. I have no doubts that this is the best cold case team in the world. Nobody else could have done what you have done. I want to say thank you and hope that we can do it again sometime. Sheriff Mack has some words for you." Mack cleared his throat, "A few months ago when Billy Patterson found Cassie's 1968 Mustang in the swamp, I would not have given a plugged nickel for the chances of solving this case. It had hung around our necks too long and there wasn't even a whiff of a suspicion on anyone. You guys came into town and turned the file inside out and shook out what I would have called a few useless, meaningless pieces and put a case together. Not only that, but you didn't give up until you had uncovered the truth. I am so impressed with the work you have done. You all are the best at what you do, but together you are the proof that the whole is greater than the sum of the parts. With my thanks and congratulations and the thanks of the county board, I have to announce the dissolution of this team. We are paying you two weeks' severance and shutting you down as of today. I have your checks in my possession." Tex spoke up, "I don't have anywhere to be right away. Do you mind if I hang around for a while?" Mack replied, "The rent is paid on the house through the end of August. You can stay that long, if you so desire." Tex beamed with pleasure, "Thanks, Mack. I'll hang around for a few weeks and see what happens. Mark, if you need me for anything, I'll be around. I'll work for free just to see how this one shakes out." The others all chimed in that they were staying, too. Jay summed it up for all of them, "Mark, if you bring this one home, I want a front row seat. I'll be right here, if you need me." The applause said the rest. Mark thanked them for their loyalty, knowing in himself that there came a point where it wasn't about the money any more.

CHAPTER 64

It was a Friday afternoon when Mack had paid the team off and announced the disbanding of the team, or task force, which was the official name. They were all seated around a table at the Wascally Wabbit talking and laughing. Mack was with them and Mark had called Sarah to come and join because he was not sure what time he would be home, so she was there as well. The conversation flowed back and forth and all around the various discoveries that they had made as they investigated. Finally, Victor spoke up with a question that maybe all of them had been thinking but didn't know how to phrase it or were just hesitant to raise, "Do you guys believe that the dead girls had anything to do with the way this unfolded?" Everyone looked at Victor, and as one, all eyes turned to Mark. He said, almost defensively, "Don't look at me; I don't know anything about such things!" Victor nodded and said, "I know; really nobody knows for sure about such things, but what do you think?" Mark looked at him for a long moment then his eyes went around the table. Finally he said, "I'll go last. You guys give me your impressions first. You've been in on this from the beginning of this investigation, as have I. Your impressions are both important and of interest to me."

"Okay," said Willie, "I'll go first. There has been something about this case from the beginning that is different from any other case I have ever worked. Just let me say that any time you are putting together a team, Mark, I'm in. This has been one of the most unique and interesting experiences of my life. By far, it has been the most interesting case I have ever worked." Mark nodded his acknowledgement and she went on. "I found myself praying that we would find even a small shred of evidence that would keep us moving forward, rather than in circles. It seemed like every time we were at an impasse something would turn up. The funny thing about the investigation is that these small clues that probably would have felt insignificant in any other investigation, felt bigger and more important in this one. Maybe, because it was so old that we didn't expect much, so everything seemed like more that it was or maybe there was a sense of destiny that I was feeling. I couldn't help but feel that we were going to find out what happened. I wasn't surprised when we found the bodies. I wasn't surprised when we found the gun. I wasn't surprised when we found the killer. I was surprised at who it was, though. I must confess that I was not expecting that. It just felt like it was time for justice in this case. Does that make sense to anyone?"

Tex spoke up saying, "It makes lots of sense. You didn't say whether or not you thought the girls were involved in the way that the case unfolded, but I'm going to just come out and say it. I think that they were looking over our shoulders the entire way and trying their best to point us in the right direction. I think that the injustice of what was done to them has carried on long enough. It is time for the truth to come out. Some might think that with the fifty-year anniversary of the crime coming up that it is high time that the light is shined on the killer and the case be finally put to rest." Mark replied, "So, Tex, you are a definite yes as far as the dead speaking to the living in one way or another to bring justice?" Tex smiled and said, "Mark, any other time I'd think I was losing my mind, but the things that I have seen and felt while working this case have left me with the impression that there are influences that we can't see, who from time to time, point us in a direction that we would not naturally take in order to bring justice to those who have been so terribly wronged." Mark nodded slightly and said, "I don't disagree with you, Tex." That brought what looked like a relieved look across the face of the Texan.

Jay spoke up next saying, "I was convinced the day we walked into the haberdashery. That place was alive with the dead!" His way of expressing it brought a chuckle to all, but they all had felt the watching eyes, with the exception of Mark. Jay went on, "That was really freaky to me. I have never felt anything like that in my life. Also, I couldn't get Billy's dreams out of my head. One of the girls actually told him that she had seen Mark the day before in the haberdashery. How crazy was that? I am not a timid person. In fact, I think that I am as bold as anyone else, more so than most people. There was, however, something about this case that, at times, made me feel like taking a step back. I didn't do it, but a couple of times it got so weird that I was thinking about leaving. The thing that kept me from doing that is the fact that the case was so interesting and there didn't seem to be anything threatening us. There was something out there that felt menacing, though. Do you know what I mean?"

Gina spoke up about then, saying, "I understand what you are saying and what you were feeling. Sometime during the process of this case investigation, I came to the realization that we had help. I felt the threat, but did not feel threatened. Does that make sense?" They all nodded and leaned in a bit. She went on, "I think the threat we felt was unsatisfied justice. Over time, unsatisfied justice becomes impending judgement. As time went on, the weight of impending judgement grew more and more intense. I still feel it and I don't think that it is finished, yet. I don't know what is going to happen, but I do think that there is at least one more play in this game. I just don't know whose it is. It may not be ours to make. What do you think?"

Mack, who had sat without saying anything, finally added his thoughts. "When we closed down the original investigation I vowed that I would never forget or let this case rest until it was solved or I was dead. Over the last few years it seemed like the latter was more likely than the former. I had resigned myself to dying without resolving this case. Then they found the car. Mark said something intriguing early on in this second investigation. He said, 'whoever did this had to have incredible luck to pull it off and not leave a trace. We will need incredible good luck to figure out what happened.' He was right and we have had it. We have had good luck at every turn of the road. Having said that, the team has made good, no… great decisions as far as the investigation strategies. Even with the good work done by this team, we still needed incredibly good luck to get to where we are. We know who did it, we just can't advertise it because we can't prove it in a court of law. Well, maybe we could, but our suspect probably would not survive the ordeal. I guess what I'm saying is this is good work and I, as Sheriff of this county and as a member of the original task force that worked on this case, am appreciative of the work that you have done. I told Mark this, but I'm going to say it in front of all of you. When we hired him, I thought that he was probably the best qualified but, most likely, overrated person for the job. I could not have been more wrong. This man is everything that the FBI advertised him to be and is actually better than their reports. I have never witnessed a more determined and better focused investigator in my life. He is one of the people who is actually better in real life. Thanks, Mark." With that the Sheriff sat down.

Everyone in the Wascally Wabbit had heard the Sheriff's speech so the place erupted into applause. When it died down Mark said, "Thanks, Mack, I appreciate those good words, but your friendship means more to me than all the words in the world." Mack interrupted with, "See what I mean?" There was more applause. Mark said, "Alright, stop it now! To address the question that started this discussion, I don't know whether or not we would have ever found the graves of our victims had Billy not had his dreams. He was told where they were and there we found them. It is uncanny. It is unconventional. But it is not impossible. The facts of this case bear out that it is not impossible. Was he visited by his sister or was it merely a dream where he recalled something he had heard or seen when very young, a repressed memory if you will? I don't know. Maybe we'll never know. I do know that we have found our killer. I don't feel like we can do anything with it as long as Cheryl Fogarty is alive. It would hasten her demise and cause pain to those who love her. They have done nothing to deserve the pain it would cause them. Even though it wouldn't be our fault, we would still knowingly be party to it and I don't wish to do that. Are we in agreement about that?" Mark looked around the table at all of the faces. There was no disagreement, but their faces did not convey very much pleasure in the fact. Tex said, "We usually get closure by nailing the SOB that did the deed. This time, it appears that she is out of our reach. That stings a bit, but I think you are making the right call. Anyone disagree with me?" He, too, looked around the table. "Okay, then," Mark said, "we can rest our case and our work. Thanks again for your excellent and tireless work." Mack said, "I second that." There was a warm feeling around the table. Mark and Sarah got up to leave. The others stayed to have a few more drinks. Mark had given up alcoholic beverages several years back due to a trip to rehab. He had managed to stay dry for seven years.

CHAPTER 65

Sunday morning found Mark and Sarah back in church. They had been going to church more consistently the last few months than in the past several years. It felt good and right, so they kept on doing it.

At the morning prayer time, it was announced via a general request for prayer, that the pastor's wife was in very grave condition. It seemed that there was not much that the doctors could do to help her. There was a feeling of sadness over the congregation because Cheryl was loved among the church people. Pastor Fogarty preached. Some of the usual spark of his personality was subdued, but there remained a certain quiet strength. Mark felt sadness for the man in more ways than just his personal loss. Mark was quite certain that Pastor Fogarty had no idea what kind of person he had married.

When the service ended and the people were filing out, Mark greeted the pastor and asked, "Pastor Fogarty, how is your wife doing." The pastor responded guardedly and stiffly, "she is dying and seems very restless in her spirit. Something is bothering her, but she will not say what it is. Thank you for asking." Mark said, "She was very close to us when we were young and she was very helpful to our band back in the day. There would have been no First String but for her guidance and training. She, in many ways, made us happen. We are very sad to see her suffering. I sincerely hope she finds peace." Pastor Fogarty relaxed and smiled. He said, "Thank you for that. I was under the impression that you were angry with her about something. I got that from something that she started to say and then would not finish. I was clearly mistaken." Mark realized at that moment that Pastor Fogarty was totally in the dark as to what had been going on over the last few months. Mark determined that he was not going to be the one to enlighten the Pastor. He could not imagine the shock that man would undergo when that truth landed on him, if ever.

Mark was quiet on the drive home and through lunch. He went out and sat on the porch pondering what he knew. Sarah came out and sat. She said, "Something has you in that pensive state where it feels like we are living in different worlds while occupying the same space. Do you want to talk about it?" Mark responded, "I was just thinking about what a shock Pastor Fogarty has coming if he ever finds out what his wife has done. I feel very sad for him, the poor guy." "Are you sure that she did it?" Sarah asked. "Is there no chance that you are mistaken?" Mark shook his head sadly, "If this were any other case, we would have called the DA to come and file charges. She would not survive the trial. We just don't see any point in going through that at this point. I talked with Billy and the other siblings of the dead girls. They see no point in going through a trial. They would like to see her punished, but know that she is beyond our reach. Mack and I have gone around and around with this. It seems like everyone agrees that if we can't put her in prison, there's no point in having a trial." Sarah scowled, "What are you going to do then? You can't just let it go?" "If I thought there was something constructive we could do, I would do it in a heartbeat," replied Mark. "Putting a pastor's wife on trial while she is dying of a horrible disease when she has apparently lived an exemplary life and was never even a suspect in anybody's wildest theory is crazy. We would wind up looking worse than she does even if we got a conviction and that is no slam dunk." "Don't you think you have a case?" Sarah asked aghast. "The evidence is in our favor," replied Mark, "but facts that appear so solid before trial become quite malleable in the hands of a good defense counsel. No, if we can't nail her, we don't want to just sully her memory. That would accomplish nothing." Sarah asked in a frustrated voice, "Why should she have a good legacy when she did such a horrible thing?" Mark nodded, "That is an excellent question and a valid point. The fact is that she has done much good in her life. She was a great teacher and mentor. She has been a fine pastor's wife. She has done much good to many people. I don't want to sully those memories for nothing." "But, at least people will know!" Sarah nearly shouted. She was quite passionate. "That is not the point, though," replied Mark, "it is not about exposing her, but about justice for the lives cut short. If we can't get that, there is no point in just taking vengeance." Sarah flopped back against the seat back and regarded Mark for a long moment. "No wonder you have been quiet. That's a lot to think about. So what's next?" Mark said, "I don't know. If she continues to get worse, we have a very short window before there is nothing that we can do." Sarah gave Mark one of her "I've got an idea" looks and said, "Maybe you could write a book." "Somebody will certainly write a book about this case. It is way too fascinating not to write it up. It would be easier to write the book, if there were a verdict or a confession. Mack and I went to see Abigail to see if we could get a confession out of her." "Are you kidding me?" said Sarah in an astonished voice. "Did Pastor Fogarty know about that?" "I don't think so," Mark replied. "He was not there at any of the meetings we had. I don't think she wanted him to know that she was our one and only suspect." "Wow! Oh, wow!" Sarah was overwhelmed with that thought. "He is in for a shock that is beyond belief," she said. "What is he going to do when he learns the truth?" Mark shook his head slowly and said, "I don't know. That is one of the reasons that we, Mack and I, decided that if he doesn't hear it from her, he is not going to hear it from us." "I get it, now," said Sarah. "What else can you do?" "Exactly!" replied Mark.

CHAPTER 66

Monday morning found Mark back at his desk in the office that was no longer open. As he sat there, the team started filtering in. They sat around the conference table just chatting. Mack walked in and looked around. He said, "I thought this place was closed, but then I saw Mark's car and decided to pop in. What's going on?" "Nothing, really," replied Willie, "we're just relaxing and chatting. What are you doing?" He responded, "Nothing, just exactly nothing, to be honest. I wish there was something I could do. I feel really off and I think it's because there is no closure in this case. When you have worked a case as hard as we have worked this one you want closure. I, personally, have carried this case with me every day for fifty years. That's a long time to have an unresolved injustice that you carry in your spirit. It's starting to feel like heartburn." There were sympathetic chuckles and other forms of commiseration around the table. Tex said, "I think we are all feeling that but probably not to the extent that you do. The thing is, I don't have any idea what to do about it. We have discussed it amongst ourselves and collectively we have no idea what to do about it." Mark spoke up and said, "We could invite the District Attorney to come in and review our case. We are pretty sure that they will conclude what we have found to be true. Do you think that idea has any value?" Mack said, "I have already run it by him. He won't try the case for exactly the reasons we suspected. I didn't telegraph my own opinion or our conversations, Mark. He came to the same conclusions on his own that we came to collectively. He asked me if I agreed and I told him that I didn't want to, but his process was on the money. They were amused that we came to exactly the same conclusion. They told me that we should be lawyers." Mark grinned and replied, "Well, I am an attorney and a member of the bar. I went into the FBI rather than the practice of law, but I haven't forgotten everything. I guess that answers that question regarding the DA." There was a general agreement around the table.

"So, what's next?" inquired Victor. "Where do we go from here?" Everybody looked around; the question written in all of their eyes. Mark, after a long moment said, "I'm going to do something that I have never done before. I trust this team like I have never trusted another. You guys are all the best of the best. So, my Hail Mary is to just turn you loose on the case to look where your instincts might take you. It goes without saying that you will be discreet, but I said it anyway. I would ask that you avoid talking with Mrs. Fogarty. She is in a bad way and will probably be gone within the month. Let's give her peace if she can find it." There were grunts around the table that indicated doubt that she was going to find peace, but that was her problem. Without saying anything further, they began to filter out until there were just three left, Mack, Mark, and Gina. Gina gave a long sigh and got up saying, "I think that I will give the file one more thorough review." Nobody said anything as she walked out of the conference room. Mack looked at Mark and asked, "What are you going to do?" Mark replied, "I think that I'm going fishing. I can think things through better when I'm fishing." "Want company?" asked Mack. "Sure, but I'm not sure I'll be very good company. I have a lot to think over." Mark replied. "It's okay," Mack replied, "I don't really feel like talking anyway. Let's just fish." "Good deal," replied Mark. "Let's go."

Mark and Mack spent the afternoon fishing. Very little was said between them. Mostly they chatted very sparsely about fishing and the water conditions. As the afternoon waned, they packed up and headed back to the boat landing. Mark had kept two medium sized small mouth bass that he had caught and released the others because he didn't feel like cleaning a whole mess of them. When they loaded the boat back onto the trailer, Mack asked, "Any solutions?" "No," Mark replied, "but I am going to meet with Billy, Jack, and Willy for a chat. I owe them that. Also, I would like to make one more effort to find out if Abigail ever owned the murder weapon. I think that she did, but it was probably in somebody else's name. I just don't know who owned it." Mack nodded and said, "I might be able to help with that. I have tons of contacts in the county, but also state wide. I'll pitch in on this because it is important. As far as Billy, Willy, and Jack, you are on your own." Mark gave him a sardonic grin and replied, "You're a real buddy, you know."

Mark called his three old friends and arranged to meet for lunch the next day and then headed home. He had called Sarah and told her he was fishing with Mack so it was okay that he was running a little bit late. When he walked in Sarah asked him, "Did you catch any fish?" Mark replied, "Yes, I have a couple of nice small mouth bass here. They are all filleted and ready to freeze." Sarah said, "We're not going to freeze them. I'm going to cook them for dinner. We can freeze the leftovers if there are any." Mark grinned, "That sounds wonderful to me. The fresher the better is my opinion when it comes to eating fish." Sarah smiled sweetly, "I know. That's my favorite way, too. If you hadn't brought any home, I had a couple of burgers ready to pop into the pan but this is much better." Mark replied, "I prefer it as well."

In a few short minutes dinner was ready and they sat down to a wonderful dinner of baked small mouth with baked potatoes and a nice salad. Once dinner was over, Mark helped Sarah wash and dry the dishes and clean up from dinner. As they sat down in the living room, Sarah asked, "So, what's going on with the case?" Mark shook his head and replied, "We know that Abigail did it. We can even prove it, but we're not sure that we would get a guilty verdict. At this point, there is as much sympathy for her, if not more, as there is for the dead girls. We're too far removed from the outrage. Many of the people around here were born after the fact and it just seems like a story they've heard all of their lives. It's a little bit like remembering an old movie. It seems real, but doesn't feel real. Does that make sense?" Sarah gave him a sympathetic look, "It makes all the sense in the world. What can you do about it?" Mark shrugged his shoulders, "I don't know," he replied, "it seems hopeless at this point. Cheryl knows that we aren't going to prosecute." "Did you tell her that?" asked Sarah. "No, but we didn't have to say it. She is sick and most of the sympathy is going to be for her. After all, she has spent years living in this community doing good work as a teacher, pastor's wife, and all-around good person. I wish I knew what to do. I wish that I could appeal to her conscience, but that doesn't work. I already tried. I would scare her if I could, but she is already facing death. It seems odd to me, though. She acts like Abigail was a different person and that she, Cheryl, is not Abigail. That seems a little strange to me but I can't make anything of it." Sarah just nodded her head and said, "Hmmmm." It wasn't terribly helpful.

CHAPTER 67

The next morning, Mark did not go directly to the office. He went instead to speak with Pastor Fogarty. The pastor was cordial, but reserved in his reception of Mark and Mark didn't blame him. What was happening to him with his wife being sick was awful enough without a bunch of ex-FBI agents hounding her to death's door. Mark felt sorry that he had to do it, but it was his job and he intended to do it to the best of his ability. They sat down in the Pastor's home office and began chatting. Mark, never one to make a lot of small talk, said, "Pastor Fogarty, I want to get right to the point. I know that you have many other things that you would rather be doing and please believe me, I feel the same way." He relaxed and asked, "What is it, Mark?" "When you first met your wife, was she still using the name Abigail or had she begun using Cheryl?" The pastor regarded Mark for an extended moment and then said, "The first time that I met her formally, she told me that her name was Cheryl, which I thought a bit curious because I had heard others calling her Abigail and Abby, but I soon forgot about it. I have only known her as Cheryl. Why do you ask this?" Mark hesitated and then replied, "I'm not even sure myself. Sometimes in my career as an investigator, I have followed a line of investigation just out of curiosity. It's that type of thing right now. I guess I wonder why she changed to using her middle name. What was the impetus behind that, I wonder." Pastor Fogarty replied, "Why does that have to be a reason? Maybe she just preferred her middle name and decided that it was time to make a change." "That could be," said Mark, "but I recall that she loved the name Abigail. She once told me that she was named after her favorite aunt and loved her name. I can't imagine what would cause her to change it. Maybe something happened to her aunt." Pastor Fogarty said, "Now I understand your curiosity. What do you want from me?" "Well," said Mark, "you could do me a favor. Try to ask her why she changed her name and what happened to Abigail." "That seems to border on the bizarre," replied the pastor. "Yes, I confess that I thought so, as well," said Mark, "but I have not been able to shake the thought that there is more to the story. Would you be willing to ask her those questions?" The pastor slumped in his chair and replied, "I guess so. You actually have made me a bit curious, now. I, too, wonder why someone would abandon a name they love. What would bring that about? I guess I'll have to find out. Do you want me ask her now?" Mark smiled, "Oh no," he said, "do it in a more relaxed setting. Think it over so you can ask without a demanding attitude. That would be counter-productive." "Yes," replied Elliot, "I can see the wisdom of that. You have a certain wisdom about you that is admirable." Mark smiled and thanked him. Then Mark asked, "Elliot, how is your wife doing?" After a long moment and a deep quivering sigh, the pastor replied, "Barring a miracle, she is not going to make it. What disturbs me is that she is very restless. She refused sedation because she says that she is not in pain. She doesn't sleep much and she is very restless. I'll wake up in the middle of the night and she is standing staring out the window. I ask her what she is doing and she just looks at me with an almost blank but tormented stare. I wish I could know what is behind the curtain." Mark thought he knew, but didn't say, 'You're better off to not know.' He did say, "Pastor, I have taken enough of your time. Please know that I am so sorry for what you are going through and I hope that you find some comfort and peace in the middle of all this turmoil." Elliot dropped his head and then looked Mark in the eye and said, "Thank you. I know that you mean that. Even though you suspect my wife of murder, I respect that you are only doing your job. I this case, I really don't envy you that job. It's a losing proposition all around, isn't it?" Mark nodded and replied, "Pretty much. I don't see any winners in this situation." They shook hands and Mark left.

Mark headed to meet his old buddies for lunch. This was not going to be pleasant, but it needed to be done. He arrived at the Wascally Wabbit a few minutes after the other guys. They looked up and grinned and Willy asked, "Are we being fashionably late today, Marky?" Mark replied, "I was never sure what that meant. I think it was an excuse for people of influence to be late without consequences, because for a subordinate, there is no fashionably late." They all chuckled at that and they shook hands all around. Mark noticed that Billy was not wearing his old jacket. Even though he was shaggy, Billy looked remarkably neat. "Billy, do you have a girl friend?" Mark asked him. Billy dropped his head and turned red, "You always could read me, Marky. Yeah, I have been seeing Lydia Johnson. She lost her husband a couple of years back and we have been seeing each other." "Good for both of you, Billy,"

Mark said. "You guys order, yet?" Jack said, "No, we just got here ahead of you. Let's get an order in now, I'm starved." Willy waved the waitress over and they all ordered. Then Billy asked for all of them, "Mark, why did you want to meet today?" Mark said, "Let's eat first, then I'll tell you." They made small talk until their food came and then they got serious.

When they were finished eating and the waitress had cleared away the plates, Billy again said, "Okay, Marky, now give; what's up?" Mark took a deep breath and settled himself in his seat. He said, "I need for you guys to get control of yourselves and don't let your emotions get out of hand here." Jack scowled, "What do you mean?" Mark replied, "I mean we know who killed the girls. We don't know exactly why, but we know how. I need for you guys to get ahold of yourselves while I line it out for you." They were all ears at that point, "Okay," they all said. "Here's the deal," said Mark. "The killer is not going to be prosecuted because of several issues." Billy said urgently, "Tell us who it is." His eyes were so intense. "Okay," said Mark, "You guys are not going to believe this." "Tell us!" they nearly shouted and every eye in the place was on their table. "See," said Mark, "you can't keep a lid on your feelings. Now everybody in the place is looking over here." Willy looked as contrite as only Willy could look, "Sorry." he said. "Okay," said Mark, starting again. "The person who killed Cassie, Hope, and Pauline is none other than Abigail Appleton!" The three of them looked at Mark with stone faces and then, as though on cue, said, "I don't believe you." "That's what I told you would happen," said Mark. "That isn't possible! We knew her! She wouldn't do that!" burst out Jack. "What he said," added Willy. Billy just sat in stunned silence. "She hugged me at the memorial and told me my sister was alright and that if I ever missed Cassie, I could go talk with her," Billy said softly. "How do you know? You wouldn't joke about something so serious, so it must be true, but how?"

Mark started at the beginning and outlined the details of the case as clearly as he understood them in chronological order. He explained the time line as completely as he understood it. There were gaps that had not been filled in, but there was enough. He explained the gun and Abigail Jensen's extreme skill in shooting. They chuckled at the idea of a girl winning shooting tournaments over the men and the boys of the farming community where she grew up. At the time, it was remarkable. Every generation likes to think of itself as more enlightened than the previous one. There was some joking conversation about the men and boys of the town being bested by a girl must have been embarrassing to them. The recitation took quite some time. When Mark was finished, he sat back in his chair and looked around. There were three sets of very intent eyes staring back at him. Finally Billy said, "You're pretty sure about this, aren't you?" "I am," Mark replied. "In fact, I am certain of it." Jack looked at him with a furrowed brow and asked, "Well, then why don't you or won't you prosecute? You have everything you need. This lady needs to pay!" Mark nodded, "I agree with you, Jack. Our reasons are not sentimental. She is dying of leukemia and is in the last stages. She probably has weeks, at the most, months, to live. This trial is going to be a long drawn out affair. She probably would not survive it. There is always the danger that she might gain jury sympathy. After all, she has lived an exemplary life and has never had a hint of anything illegal or immoral that anybody knew about. It makes prosecution delicate. The decision wasn't mine. It was Sheriff Mack and the District Attorney that decided that they would not prosecute." Billy asked quietly, "Then how do we get justice for Cassie and the other girls?" Mark dropped his head, "Billy, that is something that I have not figured out, yet. I hope that there is a way to get the story out but I just don't know. Maybe we'll have to write a tell-all book, but that wouldn't get them justice, it would just get the story out. It will look like we are just trying to capitalize on the case to make money. It will be hard to do it without looking bad." Billy responded, "Yeah, I see what you mean. I guess just knowing will have to be enough for us." Jack and Willy burst out together, "It just doesn't seem fair!" Mark agreed, "It isn't fair, but sometimes that's all we get. We know who did it, but for various reasons we don't get a conviction. We are really fortunate that Billy found the car and we have the insights that we have. A year ago, it was still a big, dark mystery. At least now we know."

There was a general feeling of an unrequited sense of justice. They all wanted more, but were at a loss as to what could be done about it. Even though it was an old, cold case, they all had a personal stake in seeing it resolved and justice served. It appeared that it wasn't going to be resolved to their satisfaction and it did not feel good to them. They weren't wrong, but there didn't seem to be any path to a satisfactory resolution. Mark felt a keen sense of disappointment as he drove home from the meeting. He knew that the others were going through similar struggles. As he passed the Memorial Gardens, he saw that Billy's car was there and that he was standing beside his sister's grave. Mark pulled into the drive and stopped his car. He slowly strolled out to where Billy was standing. He heard Billy talking, apparently to his sister. He was saying, "It doesn't look like there is going to be a trial. She is just going to get away with it because she is sick and can't stand the stress of a trial. She probably wouldn't survive a trial anyway. Sorry we couldn't do better for you." As Billy finished, he wiped a tear from his eye and turned to Mark. "I saw you pull in. Thanks for giving me a couple of minutes with Cassie. I try to let her know what is going on with their case. She probably can't hear me, but it does me good to talk and get it off my chest. I always feel like she is listening, even though I know in my head that she can't hear me." Mark shrugged and replied, "Billy, it can't hurt to get it off your chest. Who knows what goes on over there anyway. Maybe she does hear. I don't know anymore." "Me neither," Billy replied. They both walked back to where their cars were parked, shook hands without another word and got into their cars and drove away.

When Mark arrived at home, he told Sarah that he had talked with Billy, Willy, and Jack and told them what they knew for sure. He explained that he had also told them that there would not be a trial and they had not been happy about that piece of information. When they understood why, they had accepted the decision of the DA and the Sheriff. The county felt that they had already spent enough money on the case. They knew the truth; they just couldn't do anything about it.

Mark awakened with a start, his sleep troubled with strange and disturbing dreams of Miss Abigail, the three girls, the band all packed into Cassie's red Mustang. It was strange. He got up and walked out into the living room. He grabbed a pad of paper and sat down. He felt like he used to feel when he had a song coming on. He began writing and within a few minutes, he had lyrics on the page. It felt so strange, but good, to be writing again. He looked at the clock and since it was only three fifteen, he decided to crawl back into bed.

CHAPTER 68

He had just dozed off or so it seemed, when the phone rang. He grabbed his phone and walked out of the bedroom trying to keep from waking Sarah. It was Pastor Fogarty on the line. He said in a rather desperate voice, "Is this Mark?" "Yes, Pastor," Mark replied, "this is Mark. How may I help you?" "You can come to the hospital immediately," he replied. "Something really weird is going on and I don't know how to explain it, but my wife insists on talking to you and she says, 'now!'" Mark replied, "I'll be there as soon as I can. Is there anything that you can tell me?" The pastor replied, "I would not know where to start. This woman who is my wife is unknown to me. I have never seen her like this in the forty-six years that we have been married. Please hurry!" Mark had been getting dressed while they had been talking and replied, "I'll be there as fast as I can safely make it."

Sarah was sitting up in the middle of the bed staring at him with owl eyes. "What is going on at this hour of the night?" she asked. Mark replied, "I just got a call from Pastor Fogarty. His wife is asking to see me and he says it is really strange. He says he doesn't even know the person his wife is right now. I can't explain it, but I need to get there. I'm going to call Mack and ask him to meet me there." Sarah asked, "Do you want me to go with you?" Mark replied, "This is work. I'm not telling you no, but it most likely won't be pleasant. We are not visiting the sick. We are confronting a murder suspect. I expect that it may get contentious, but it must be done." "I think I'll go back to sleep, if possible," she replied. Mark smiled gently and said, "Good idea." He gave his wife a quick kiss and walked out the door. He was punching Mack's phone number into the phone as he walked to the car. Mack answered on the second ring just as Mark was starting his truck. Mark explained the situation and Mack said that he would meet him at the hospital. For Mark it was a fifteen minute drive. For Mack it was about a thirty minute drive so he would be fifteen or twenty minutes behind Mark.

Upon arrival at the hospital, Mark made his way to the cancer ICU. Elliot Fogarty was waiting for him in the waiting room. He seemed very relieved to see Mark walk in. "I am so glad you are here. Thank you for coming. I don't know what to do; I have never seen my wife like this in all the years we have been together. It's like she is a different person!" All that poured out of the pastor in a flood of words. Mark asked, "What happened?" Elliot said, "We had gone to bed and it was like she was having a bad dream. She was twisting around and talking in her sleep. I remember she said, 'You can't be here; you're dead!'. Then there was a lot of moaning and gibberish. I shook her to wake her and finally she awakened, but she was different. She even had a different voice than I remembered so I brought her to the hospital. Could it be the disease?" Mark replied, "I don't know. What do her doctors say about that." Elliot replied, "They don't think it's her disease or the medication. They think something else is bothering her. They said that when people get close to the end, sometimes things come back that they have buried in their past and they need to get it off their chests. Do you think that is what is going on?" "I don't know," Mark replied. "It could be what the doctor said or it could be something else. Do you want me to talk with her?" "I wish you would. She has been asking for you so I think she has something that she wants to say to you," Elliot said. "Why do you think that she is not the same person that you have known all these years?" Mark asked. Elliot replied, "When she saw me in her room she said, 'Mr. Fogarty, how nice to see you.' It was like she didn't realize that she is my wife. I found that more than a little bit disturbing." Mark nodded sympathetically and said, "I can see why you might feel that way." An idea was beginning to grow in his mind. Just then Mack walked in. He was not in uniform and the pastor looked at him somewhat askance. Mark said, "I called Mack. He has been in on the matter since day one and deserves to be here." Elliot hesitated and then said "Okay, let's go." He seemed a bit grumpy about it, but resigned to the idea.

When they walked into the hospital room, Mark was loaded for bear. He had briefed Mack, so Mark took the lead. He said, "Miss Abigail! It is so nice to see you after all these years!" She smiled the old smile that Mark remembered, "Mark!" she said. "You told Cheryl that you wanted to see me. Nobody has asked to see me for a very long time. I was surprised and she was frightened. I was beginning to think that nobody remembered me." Mark smiled, "I remember you, Miss Abigail. You were my favorite teacher." She smiled and replied, "You were my star student of all time. I never found another like you. You were destined for greatness. What happened?" A shadow crossed her face. Mark very gently said, "Why don't you tell me what happened? I wasn't there so I don't know. How did you find out about the haberdashery?" She smiled and said, "I followed you boys back when you were in the seventh grade and discovered where you were going when you disappeared. I never told anyone, though." Mark changed tactics a bit responding with, "You threw Elliot a curve ball when you greeted him." Abby replied, "Sorry about that. Cheryl married him. I never did. My husband was killed in action in Vietnam. I will never marry again!" Elliot was standing in the corner of the room. His face was a mask of shock. He looked at Mark with a questioning look. Before Mark had a chance to respond, Mack walked into the room.

Mark held up his hand to Mack and hoped that he understood that they would talk later. He addressed Abigail, "Why have you decided to talk to me now after all this time?" He was hoping that she would remain and talk to him. They really needed a confession. He noticed that Mack had a video camera and was recording the scene. Abigail gave Mark a furtive look and replied, "I didn't have any choice." Mark said, "So it wasn't just because I asked to talk with you?" She shook her head, "They came to see me!" She spat the words out in almost a stage whisper. Mark knew but wanted her to say it so he responded, "Who are you talking about?" Abigail gave him a pleading, rather desperate look and said, "You know! It was the girls and after all these years. For the first couple of years it really bothered me, but Cheryl rescued me. She took over and she was such a good person that I was forgotten. Until you asked to talk with me, nobody had even thought of me in years, as far as I know. After that, though, things started falling apart. Cheryl kept saying that she couldn't cover for me anymore and she was crying all the time. When she got sick, she became very scared. She insisted that we had to tell the truth, but I kept fighting her. This evening, though, they came. All three of them were there and they were all bloody just like that day. They told me that if I didn't tell the truth, I was going to hell. I never believed in that before, but suddenly it all seemed very real. I asked Pastor Fogarty to get you so we could talk." Mark said, "Miss Abigail, Pastor Fogarty is your husband." She replied angrily, "No he is not MY husband. He is Cheryl's husband. By the way, don't you think that it was quite sly hiding the gun in the church? It was several years before anybody found it and they had no idea whose it was or anything about it. Cheryl was married to the fool by then and he suspected nothing." She chuckled at her own remarks.

Mark said gently, "Miss Abigail, why don't you tell me how you worked out the plan to kill the girls. There had to be so many details that you planned. In all my years in law enforcement, I have never seen a plan work so smoothly." The pastor's wife looked at him with surprise and replied, "There was no plan. It just happened. I wanted to get rid of those girls because they were standing between you boys and the greatness that you had in you, but I didn't have a plan. The girls stopped by the school just before they left town and I was there. We started talking and I told them about the haberdashery. They said that they always wondered about it. I told them to wonder no more; I would show it to them. They were hooked, I can tell you that. So I grabbed a flashlight and took them down there." Mark asked quickly, "If you didn't plan it, why did you have a gun with you?" She smiled, "Oh, that," she replied, "I always took that with me down there because I had seen a couple of snakes down there and I hate snakes. It was in my desk and I stuck it in the waist band of my jeans. I really hadn't even thought of using it at that point. They asked me about the gun and I told them about the snakes. None of them were afraid of snakes so it didn't make sense to them. So we went under the gym." Mark was a bit shaken by the cold way she told her story. It was almost like a book report on a not particularly interesting book. He said softly, "Please continue." "Well," she responded, "when we got down there I realized that I would never in my life have a better opportunity to liberate you guys from the clutches of these anchors to your success." Mark couldn't resist, "Did the fact that you were having sex with Jack and Willy have anything to do with your decision?" She looked at him out of the corners of her eyes and gave him a sly grin, "Probably, because I wanted all three of you boys for myself. I knew that as long as you were in love with Pauline, I would never pry you away and you were going to settle for a very average life probably right here in your home town. I couldn't let that happen, if it could be helped. I tried to entice you, but you were oblivious. That made me so mad. The other two were easy, but you were so wrapped up in Pauline that you couldn't see any other female. Hundreds of girls, myself included, would have gladly spread their legs for you, but all you could see was Pauline. I came to hate her!" The venom of that last statement was shocking coming from a lady who had always been so sweet and helpful. Mark took a deep breath and said, "So you were in the haberdashery. Take us from that point." "So, we were in the corner near where I buried the girls and I just took my gun out and shot them. I didn't really think about it; I just did it. It was over in fifteen seconds. I almost panicked initially, but then I thought about it and realized that if I could get rid of the car, nobody would ever figure out what happened to them. The haberdashery was way too well hidden and nobody knew about it. It was like a place that didn't really exist. So I gave the car some thought and knew that if I could get it out into the marsh around Patterson Lake that nobody would ever find it. Who knew there would be a three-year drought and the car would emerge from the mud after all this time?" Mark mused, "Who knew indeed. So then what did you do?" She smiled her old, sweet smile and said, "I knew that I would need a way back into town so I grabbed Cassie's bike that she had left at the school and put it in the trunk. Then I drove out to the lake." Mark scowled, "Didn't you bury the girls first?" She giggled. "They weren't going anywhere, Silly," she replied. "I buried them after I buried the car." "Okay," replied Mark, "tell me about the car." "Well," she said and settled herself in the bed. She seemed to be drawing energy from the telling of the story. "I did some calculations and knew that the car would need to reach around fifty mile per hour in order to be propelled far enough into the marsh to be covered. There was somebody fishing on the lake so I had to wait until they left. While I was waiting, I took the bicycle out of the trunk and devised the mechanism to hold the accelerator down. Since the transmission was automatic, I didn't need to worry about getting the car in the higher gears. As the car gained speed that would take care of itself. Once the lake was clear of fishermen, I backed up the hill by the road and tied the steering wheel in place with the front wheels straight. I pointed it toward the lake and started it rolling down the hill. Then I jammed the gas pedal to the floor and locked it with a stick, dropped it into drive and rolled out and watched the result. It was really a beautiful thing to see. The car sped across that meadow and hit the lip of the ridge over the lake. It was flipped up into the air and soared out over the lake. I heard it hit and walked to the edge of the lake to see where it had hit. In the dim light of dusk I could see that it had landed in a place where it would soon disappear and never be seen again." Mark said, "So the hard part was done?" She replied, "That's what I thought, too, but I was wrong." "How so?" asked Mark. She looked at him with an expression that he had never seen. It was one of tortured horror. She said in almost a whisper, "After I buried the girls, I could not get them out of my mind. It kept going around and around in my head. I didn't mean to hurt them. It was a moment's impulse. It's not something that I would normally do. The gun was like an anchor around my neck. Cheryl kept telling me that I had gone too far this time and deserved to die. Finally, Cheryl started going to church which was something that we had never done. My family wasn't churchy. Then one day she took the gun, wiped it clean and hid it in the church. She would not tell me where she put it or I would have moved it. She is so weak!" Mark asked, "Were you aware that you broke your charm bracelet when you rolled out of the car?" "That's a funny thing," she replied, "I never even missed it. Cheryl never liked it anyway; maybe that's why she never found it. She sort of took over after that. She said we needed a new life and that she was best equipped to make that happen. So she married Elliot and I stayed in the background. I hated it! I did come out when you came to the house and Elliot wasn't home. That was fun, fruitless, but fun." Mark interjected, "You also met Mack when he came over, right?" She smiled a slow, sexy smile and said, "Yes, I guess he told you." "Yes," Replied Mark. Sheriff Mack looked uncomfortable which made Mark grin. He continued, "That explains why Cheryl fooled our human lie detector. She was telling the truth. She didn't kill the girls; you did it." "That is the truth," she replied. Mark said, "That had me confused for a good while. I didn't think of multiple personality syndrome for a long time. I'm not sure what pushed my mind there, but once it occurred to me, it made more and more sense." Abigail replied, "So that is why you told Cheryl that you wanted to talk with me. She tried to cover, but I told her she looked and sounded sneaky when she denied it. She gave us away didn't she?" "She just confirmed what I had already decided must be true," replied Mark. "Wow," said Abigail, "I knew you were smart, but I didn't think anyone would figure it out after all this time."

Mark decided it was time to change the subject. He said, "Tell me about the visitation from the girls. Was it a dream?" Abigail looked fearful and replied, "Oh my God, no! I was wide awake. I just pretended to be asleep. They walked right into my room just as bold as you please. At first they were young and pretty like I remember them, then they started changing. They changed so that I saw the holes and the blood. That was awful. They kept saying that they had come for me. Finally I ginned up the courage to ask why and they said, 'to take you to hell!' Now that scared me. Then they started changing to look like the most horrible creatures I ever saw. I was so scared! That's why I told Elliot that I needed to see you. I had to confess and get this off my chest. It does feel better just getting it off my mind." Mark glanced over at Elliot. His face was drawn and haggard. He looked awful, like he had seen a ghost. It was clear that he could not believe what he was hearing. He knew from the conversation that his wife was the "good" one, but the shock of having been married to and living with a murderer for forty-six years was almost more than the old man could handle. He staggered over to a chair and sat down. Mack was standing there with his mouth hanging open. He shook his head and said softly, "It was everything that we suspected even down to the incredibly good luck. She was even luckier than we thought."

Mark looked at Abigail, "Is there anything else?" he asked. She said, "I am dying. I was hoping for some peace of mind. I don't know that I can face death with this on my conscience. What should I do?" Mark replied to her. "Miss Abigail, I am not the one to talk with regarding matters of the heart. I am a criminal investigator, not a pastor or priest. You should talk with your husband about that. I'm pretty sure that forgiveness is God's providence. For my part, I hold no malice at this point. I am just relieved to know what happened. Well, I knew but could not confirm. Thank you, for opening up your heart and telling the truth." "Well," Abigail replied with a hint of huffiness, "I didn't exactly open up. I was forced by those girls. How did they find me anyway?" Mark replied, "I'm sure that I can't answer that question. Unless there is something else, I'll be going, now." Abigail replied, "It's okay; I've said everything to you that I need to say. Thank you for coming." She turned to her husband who had aged ten years before their very eyes. "Elliot?" she said and the voice was Cheryl's again. He came slowly to her side, "Yes, my dear." She asked him pleadingly, "Do you think that there is any chance that there is forgiveness for me?" Mark and Mack walked out of the room and did not hear his response.

CHAPTER 69

Mark looked across the conference table at the members of his team. Also present were Sheriff Mack, Billy Patterson, Jack Franklin, and Willy Hill. There was an air of curiosity in the air. Mark started the conversation by saying, "Fifty years ago a terrible incident occurred here in our small town of Pleasant Valley. Most of the people who were around when it happened are gone now. Those of us who were young are now old. The investigators at the time concluded that three young girls who never gave any indication of discontent with their lives had suddenly, and without warning, left town never to be heard from again. That explanation became the refuge for frustrated investigators who had been beating their heads against a wall. The wall gave no indication of cracking or moving so they gave up. There was one young deputy working the case who never accepted the explanation. In the face of a complete lack of evidence, he continued to believe that there had been heinous foul play at hand. He voiced his disagreement, but was ignored and silenced. This young man went on to serve the county and was eventually elected Sheriff in his own right. It was he who reopened the investigation as soon as there was evidence that the girls did not leave town of their own volition."

Mark went on, "That is where we the investigative team, the best cold case team ever assembled, in my opinion, came in. Mack contacted me and asked me if I would head up the re-investigation of this horrible crime. Jack, Willy, Billy, and I all lived through those awful days. Well, we have an announcement to make and I'm going to hand it off to Mack. It is appropriate that he would be the one to break the news. Mack?"

Sheriff Mack stood up and cleared his throat, "I didn't know that I was going to have to do this. You didn't warn me, Mark." Mark responded, "I didn't want you to think too much about it. Just tell your story." Mack nodded, "That makes sense. Fifty years ago this town and the entire region underwent a shock from which we have never really recovered. Whenever there is a tragedy we mainly seek two things, justice and closure. When they both come together, that is the goal, but it doesn't always happen. In this case, fifty years ago, we got neither. That is hard to live with if you are the investigator or the victim. In this case, we were both, so it was extra hard. For fifty years there have been conversations and theories about what happened. I had no idea that there were so many possibilities. For my part, I was convinced that they were dead, but we could not find even a hint of a clue as to what happened to them. At the end of the investigation, I almost left the Sheriffs Department for some other kind of work. The truth is that this is the only job I ever wanted so I could no more leave than I could lasso the moon. I stayed and over the years I have spent enough hours to fill months, maybe years, working the case over in my mind. I thought that I had considered every possible suspect and every possible motive, but I was so very wrong." Mack paused to take a drink of water. "When Billy discovered Cassie's car out in the marsh, it was like a bolt from the blue. In my wildest dreams I never expected that. I thought that someone might come forward and confess if they were facing death, but I never expected to re-investigate the loss. Yet, that is exactly what happened. At first, I felt defensive and resentful that you guys were having success and were finding answers where we never did. I resented that you were going over the same ground and not trying to build on our previous work. I understand now. I thought that our work was pretty thorough, but you guys redefine the word. You looked at everything that we looked at and all the sacred cows, too. The way you took fragments of evidence which led nowhere and slowly with patience pieced the case together. I understand why you had the best cold case solve rate in the history of the FBI. Your work speaks for itself." He took another long drink of water. "You know that we know who did this thing, but knew that we could not prosecute because of Miss Abigail's physical condition and the fact that she has been an exemplary individual for many years in the area. We had about given up until Mark received a call from Elliot Fogarty last night, or rather, early this morning. Mark called me and I met him at the hospital. To make a long story as short as possible, we have our confession and I am going to play the tape for you." With that, he sat back and punched a button and the room was filled with the recorded scene from the previous night.

When the tape was finished, Mark looked at Billy who had a strange expression on his face. "Billy," Mark said, "what were you doing in the graveyard the other evening when I saw you?" Billy looked at Mark and then around the room with a haunted expression on his face. He replied, "I was telling Cassie that if we didn't get a confession from Miss Abigail, we would never have complete closure. That she is sick and going to die and would take her secrets to her grave. I told her that it was up to her because we couldn't do more than we have done." He turned to Mark, "Do you think that's why the girls went to her?" he asked. Mark replied, "I don't know, Billy. A year ago I would have told you that it was impossible, but that was a year ago. This case defies logic in so many ways. For example, why did the marsh dry up in time for the fiftieth anniversary of their disappearance? Why have there never been manifestations and dreams before? I don't know, but it feels or seems like somebody or something is trying to bring justice and closure to those of us who are still here. If that sounds crazy then maybe I'm losing it." Mark threw his hands in the air and allowed them to fall, smacking his legs with his hands.

Victor said, "I am probably the most hard-bitten sceptic in the room, but I don't think you're crazy. Something is going on there that conventional explanations do not cover. Whatever it is, I'm glad they were on our side. I know that I felt a presence under the school where we found the remains. I have never felt anything like that in my life. I can't say it was scary, but it was definitely creepy. Anyway, for what it's worth, this has been a ride that I'm glad I was on. It was the experience of a life time in many ways. Just so you know, if you need my services again, I am available. Anytime you call I will make myself available." The rest of the team chimed in with "Hear, hear!", "Me, too", "Right on" and words to that effect.

As the meeting was breaking up, Mark grabbed Willy and Jack and asked them, "You guys want to come over and tune-up in my garage?" The look on Willy's face was pure joy. Jack was more reserved but looked very pleased and said, "I'm game if you are. How about you, Willy?" Willy replied, "I'm in like Flynn. Just tell me when!" "Let's do it tomorrow afternoon and I'll throw some steaks on the grill. I have a new song that I want to try out." Jack was the one who got excited at that. "You're writing again? That's great! I'll be there," he said. "Me, too!" added Willy. On impulse, Mark texted the entire team and Mack to invite them for steaks on the deck the next evening. Then he headed home.

CHAPTER 70

The next afternoon Jack and Willy showed up at around one-thirty. They just could not wait any longer. Their reasoning was that Mark didn't set a time and it was afternoon so… They ran through some of their old songs and it was amazing how quickly they jelled and much of the old sound was back. Mark showed them the new song that he had written. They read over the lyrics:

It was in the springtime of our lives

When dreams were dreamed and hopes were high

And skies were clear and breezes soft, the storm drew nigh.

It wasn't something that we did

We didn't cause the dark that fell

How could we know the buried hate, that would unleash such hell

Time has passed like the waves of the sea

Days, weeks, months, and years have rolled over me

I've learned to cope, survive and live

I've learned to say, I forgive.

The pain, we've carried far enough

The anger and hate have done their best

To wear us down and crush our hope

But we will give our loved ones rest…..

I forgive.

They sang through the song several times, but it just didn't click the way Mark had imagined it. Finally he said, "Oh, well, it was just a thought. Let's forget it. I need to get the grill fired up." Willy said, "Before we give up on this, let's try it in a minor key." Jack replied, "We have never sung in a minor key before. Why start now?" Willy said, "This song needs a minor key to capture its pathos. It is a passionate, but understated lyric and it needs a minor to give it life." Mark shrugged, "It's okay with me. In fact, I think it might be your first great idea, old buddy." They all laughed at that with the love of old friends. They set a key and slipped into the song and it was instantly different. There was a haunting magic that touched their emotions. When they finished, they were all very quiet for a moment. Then Jack said softly, "I think that's it. We just need to clean it up and polish it. I think, otherwise, it is just about perfect. Marky old buddy, you have done it again. That is a great song. Just like that, after fifty years, you pull one out of your hat." Mark was quiet for a long moment and then said, "Thanks, Jack. Do you know that I have never played music with anybody but you guys? In all these years I have never even sat in on a jam session with anybody. I have played at home by myself and played along with albums, but you are my music guys. Playing with you is magical for me. I guess I'm trying to thank you guys." They all hugged and then Willy piped up and said, "Let's get that grill going. I'm hungry!"

As they were preparing the grill and seasoning the meat, guests started arriving. It was mainly the team along with Sheriff Mack and Billy Patterson. Billy brought his new lady friend. She was known to all of the local people and was soon introduced to the team. Dinner went well with lots of laughter and discussion of the case and other topics of interest. Tex said, rather loudly, "I don't know what I think about all this ghostly stuff. It seems a bit strange." It got very quiet for a few minutes and then Billy spoke softly, "I understand your skepticism; I would normally have been skeptical myself. Just let me say that I never said that I saw my sister nor any type of manifestation. I said from the beginning that I had a dream. My dreams may be attributable to the subconscious mind. But whatever Miss Abigail saw in her home and hospital room was different. She insists that she was not asleep. Maybe you could say it was drug induced. It is really weird that it happened the next day after I had visited my sister's grave and spoke about what was going on. I'm not saying anything except that is a lot of coincidence to explain." Tex acknowledged, "You are right, Billy. That is a lot of coincidence. I felt something in that crawl space just like everybody else. I just don't know what to think about it or how to explain it." "Why do you need to explain it?" asked Billy. Tex gave Billy a sardonic look and replied, "That is a good question. I feel driven to understand, but truthfully, there is more that I don't understand than what I do. I guess this will just be a mystery, won't it?" "Maybe so," replied Billy.

From there the conversation drifted from subject to subject. Groups broke off as they will at any gathering. Suddenly somebody noticed the musical set-up in the garage. "Hey!" shouted Jay. "Have you guys been playing?" Mark replied, "For the first time in fifty years, we got together and worked on some stuff we used to play." There was an immediate clamor for a song. The three of them looked at each other and shrugged. "Keep in mind, it has been fifty years since we last did this," Jack said. Gina laughingly said, "We give you dispensation to be less than perfect, but just a little." "Mark said, "Okay, we'll do a couple of songs." They started on one of their old songs and the practice of the afternoon showed its value. With an audience, even a very small one, they played better and were more conscious of their sound. Sarah called out, "Play that last one that you did this afternoon." Once again, the three of them shared a glance, and Willy said, "This is a brand new song. It is the first one that Mark has written in nearly fifty years. Here goes." They strummed the chords and realized that they had not even worked out an introduction, yet. So they strummed the chords again and Mark just started singing. The minor was perfect and the other two just slipped naturally into the harmony parts. The song was slow and almost excruciatingly beautiful. When they were finished there was silence. Jack looked at everyone and asked, "That bad?" Willie responded, "No. That good! It was beautiful! It was haunting. It was mournful. It was a tribute with a path forward. Wow! We never knew that side of you, Mark. What a gift!" Then they all broke into applause.

The party broke up and almost everyone went home. Billy stayed and helped clean up. Most of it had been done, but there was the grill to clean and the patio. As they worked, Billy said, "Marky, you could have written that song just for me. I have not been able to let this go for my whole life. The loss of my sister had been like a stone tied around my neck. I'm going to let this go. Now that we know what happened and who did it, I suddenly don't want retribution. I just want to let the hate go and move on with my life." Billy walked over and took Mark's hand and then said, "No, that is not enough!" and pulled Mark in for a big bear hug. Mark felt Billy's pain because he, too, had struggled with his own feelings for years. "I don't know why the song came, but you are right about one thing," he said, "it is high time to move on. Let's go in the house." They went in and the girls were chatting in the living room. They got up as Mark and Billy walked in. Billy said, "Are you ready to go? I think it's about time." There was a good feeling in the room that only old friendships can bring forth.

As Mark and Sarah watch their guests walk to their car, Sarah said, "Mark, your new song is an amazing piece of work. It is, in my opinion, the best thing that you ever wrote. You guys should consider recording it. It is really that good." Mark smiled at his wife and said, "Your opinion is more important to me than any or all others. Thank you." Mark thought as they prepared for bed that they were a long ways from being ready to record anything, but he kept his thoughts to himself.

CHAPTER 71

Mark was dreaming of a pitched battle. He could hear the artillery shells bursting around him. He was hunkered down trying to assess the situation. He looked around and there was nobody with him. Something didn't seem right, but he felt the fear and tension of battle. Through the noise he heard a ringing sound. He slowly came awake and realized that his phone was ringing. He grabbed the phone and as he answered there was a sudden flash of lightning and clap of thunder. He realized that was the artillery that he had been hearing. He shook his head as he answered the phone, "Hello, this is Mark." He heard a desperate voice on the other end. It was a voice that he had come to know, Pastor Fogarty. "Mark?" he said. "Yes, Pastor Fogarty, this is Mark. What's up?" The pastor said, "I am so sorry to call you at four o'clock in the morning, but my wife is dying and she wants to see you before she passes. "Okay," Mark replied, "I'll be there as soon as I can. It'll probably be around a half hour before I get there." Sarah was awakened by the phone and the conversation. "What is it, Mark?" she asked. "It's Mrs. Fogarty again. She is dying and she wants to see me. I need to go to their house. She has hospice and Mr. Fogarty thinks that she is dying," he replied. She looked at him solemnly and asked, "Do you want me to go with you?" "How quickly can you be ready to go?" Mark asked. "Five minutes," she replied as she was already moving. Mark finished getting ready and looked at his watch. It was exactly five minutes since their conversation and Sarah walked into the room with her jacket over her arm. Mark said to her, "You are amazing, my Dear. Let's go, if you're ready." "I'm ready," she said.

As they drove, there wasn't much to talk about. They arrived at the pastor's home and knocked on the door. The home care nurse answered the door and ushered them into the living room. Elliot Fogarty came out of the bedroom. His stress was evident on his face. Mark felt sympathy for this good man who found himself in a tragic situation. Elliot asked, "Do you think me evil for standing by my wife given what she did?" Mark shook his head and said, "No, Pastor Elliot, I would think you evil if you abandoned her at this point of her life. What happened was a long time ago. The person that we know as Cheryl could never do what Abigail did. That's why she changed her name. A part of her could not live with what she did. You're a good man and you have had good years with this woman. Honor the good that you know and don't try to explain the evil that you never saw in her." Elliot swallowed a lump in his throat and said, "She wants to talk with you." Mark took Sarah by the arm and took her in with him. Cheryl was very pale and weak. She managed a faint smile when Mark and Sarah walked in. "Hi, Mark and Sarah, thank you for coming. I want to tell you something and ask an enormous favor of you." Mark looked on the person who had once been so full of life and energy. She seemed just a shadow of the person that she had been. It made his heart ache to see her so weak and wasted by disease. Mark said, "If it is within our power, we will do it." Cheryl smiled, but her eyes smiled more than her face. It was like she was just too weary to smile. Mark asked, "What is it, Miss Cheryl?" "Always so polite, you were always like that. Billy came by to see me. I thought that he was going to hate me, but he didn't. He told me about the song that you had written and how it touched him. He said that he forgives me even before I mustered the courage to ask him. Now, it comes to you. Will you, Mark Bellingham, forgive me for the awful wrong I did to you? I know that I broke your heart and stole music from you for many years. Can you find it in your heart to forgive me?" she said with tears streaming down her face. Mark did not hesitate, "I forgive you, Miss Abigail, Miss Cheryl, Mrs. Appleton, Mrs. Fogarty. I forgive all of you." Cheryl Fogarty was now sobbing as Mark's words washed over her. Sarah was sobbing at Mark's side. Pastor Fogarty had tears streaming down his face and Mark had tears brimming over his eyelids. It was, as some say, a moment to be remembered. "I have one more request," Cheryl said. "What might that be?" Mark asked, although he had a suspicion. She gave him a pleading look and asked, "Would you play your new song at my funeral?" Mark paused a moment and then replied, "I will. I can't speak for Jack and Willy, but I will even if they won't play it with me. It was written for you; it's your song in a way." She suddenly said, "Elliot?" He moved quickly to her side. "What is it, Darling?" he asked. "Good bye, Elliot!" With that she gasped and stopped breathing.

Mark stepped to Pastor Elliot's side and put an arm around his shoulder. They stood together sadly, two men who had loved the same woman at different times and in different ways, but sharing the pain of her loss nonetheless.

Mark and Sarah walked out of the house in silence. They got into their car and sat for a few moments before Mark started it. Sarah finally broke the silence, "That was one of the most amazing things that I have ever witnessed!" "Why do you say that?" Mark asked. "Did you see the relief and peace that came over her face when you said that you forgave her?" she asked. Mark nodded, "I did. I've seen that before on the faces of criminals on death row when their victims' families forgive them. It is a powerful moment." Sarah laid her hand on Mark's arm and said, "Thank you for taking me and allowing me to witness that beautiful moment." Mark gave her a lopsided grin, "It could have gone either way, you know. She could have come unglued and cursed me for still being alive and reminding her of what she did. People are weird," he said. "In this case, though, good things happened. I am particularly glad that we didn't have to arrest her and put her on trial." Sarah gave Mark and impish look and said, "I'm hungry; let's go get some breakfast.

CHAPTER 72

The funeral for Abigail Cheryl Jensen Appleton Fogarty was a simple affair, but huge in its attendance. The pastor chose to have the funeral in the church because it was larger than the chapel that the funeral home had to offer. The church would seat five hundred comfortably, but they were not seated comfortably on this day. There were by actual count six-hundred twenty-seven people in attendance plus those on the platform. All of the participants in the service were seated on the platform in order to accommodate the large crowd.

Word was out that Abigail Appleton had confessed to the killings of the three girls. Reporters were there in force and they were all trying to interview Mark and Mack. They had both refused interviews until after the funeral and burial. In fact, they had both told the reporters that they would not speak to them until the day after out of respect for Pastor Fogarty and those close to Cheryl Fogarty. It just didn't seem right to air the town's dirty laundry right in front of the church where her services were to be performed. It was on the verge of being turned into an all-out circus. Nobody in town wanted that. Well, at least those responsible. Mark thought that the Mayor secretly wanted the town to get as much publicity as possible and that he was possibly behind the attack dog attitude of some of the media people. Mark had already decided that he was going to choose who he spoke to and what he shared. They could ask what they wanted. He was going to say only what he chose to say. Mack, too, was an old hand at handling obnoxious news hounds. Mack had the unique position of being the only member of the original team that was still working and involved in the cold case investigation. Mack had a deep sense of satisfaction that human beings rarely get to feel. A quest of a lifetime had been completed. Even though he didn't complete it on his own, he participated and he was there. He felt so vindicated for the many times that he had stated his doubt of the original disposition of the case and was told to, "Shut up!" It really felt good to be right in this case.

Mark's feelings could be better described as closure. The girls had been close friends of his. Pauline was his first real love and he always felt like he had failed her in some way. This put that feeling to rest and he felt closure for the first time in fifty years regarding the loss of his friends. Others were feeling similar emotions. Billy had grabbed Mark's hand and just squeezed. He held on for the longest time without saying a word, but none were needed. Mark felt his thanks and reached out and gave Billy a big hug. Billy finally spoke, "I wish we could have shared this day with mom and dad. I think somewhere they know what is going on here. Thank you, Marky. You are the best." Mark just squeezed Billy one more time and let him go. People had been coming up to Mark since the confession. Everywhere he went people wanted to ask him questions and congratulate him. He understood it, but really did not feel like he should be getting the credit. Billy found the car. If it weren't for Billy's dreams and him hearing the word haberdashery in his dream, they would have never thought to look under the gym for the girls. There were just too many things that happened that were "lucky" or "supernatural" to take credit, but that didn't stop people. Mack and the team didn't help much either. They kept bragging on the "brilliant" leadership that he had provided and the "thinking outside the box" that had turned up some of the evidence. Mark was pretty sure that the confession would never have happened without the "visitation" that Abigail had. He finally relaxed, realizing that people had to have somebody to focus on, so they could stand around and marvel at the fact that the truth had finally come out. They didn't know about the visitations. Neither the team nor Billy was talking about them. How do you tell people about something like that? It sounds so crazy. It would be crazy, if it were not true.

The service started with a prayer from one of Pastor Fogarty's colleagues. There was a song from some of the church people. The church people were stunned to realize that for forty-plus years, their pastor's wife had been a murderer and nobody had ever sensed anything off about her. They were troopers, though. They felt they owed her a proper send-off and they were doing their best to hold it together. After the song, there were several eulogies. Everyone scrupulously avoided the elephant in the room. There was no open mic for people to speak. It would have been nice, but it was too risky. Pastor Elliot sat on the front row with their children. They kids looked just shell shocked and Mark's sympathy flowed out to them. They had to be wondering what was happening to their world. They were all grown and had families of their own. Looking at them, Mark wondered if they were thinking, as he often did, "What would it take for me to do something like that?" He told himself, as did most everyone, that he never would do anything like that. He knew that Miss Abigail would have said the same thing up until the moment that she did it. Things like this were just confusing to people. He was reasonably sure that they were feeling very confused about now.

The band was the last part of the service. Their song was to be the final farewell to Miss Abigail from her students, to Cheryl from her husband and church, to mom from her kids, and to grandma from her grandchildren. There was something about this funeral that was not like others that Mark had attended. It had a different atmosphere. It was like people were really connected emotionally. The tributes were heartfelt and kind. The eulogies were about the qualities of Cheryl Fogarty. The memories shared were many and good. It felt almost cathartic. It was definitely unlike any funeral Mark had ever attended.

The plan was that the final prayer would be given and then Mark and his friends would play their song. Mark had misgivings, but Miss Abigail had asked for it sort of like a last request. He didn't feel like he could refuse. As the service wound down Mark, Jack, and Willie kept glancing at each other. Cassie's older brother Peter had come in for the funeral so they added him at the last rehearsal, so they would have the added support of the keyboard. Finally, the pastor stepped up to the microphone and said, "We are going to pray a final prayer, but please remain in your seats for one more musical presentation." As he began his prayer, Mark, Willy, Jack, and Peter took their places. As the prayer ended, the strains of the music of the First String began to be heard in public for the first time in fifty years. There was an energy in the room that was palpable. Mark began singing:

It was in the springtime of our lives

When dreams were dreamed and hopes were high

And skies were clear and breezes soft, the storm drew nigh.

It wasn't something that we did

We didn't cause the dark that fell

How could we know the buried hate, that would unleash such hell

Time has passed like the waves of the sea

Days, weeks, months, and years have rolled over me

I've learned to cope, survive and live

I've learned to say, I forgive.

The pain, we've carried far enough

The anger and hate have done their best

To wear us down and crush our hope

But we will give our loved ones rest…..

I forgive.

The plan was to sing through the last four lines three times at the end of the song. The second time through, something happened that was so unexpected. Suddenly from three parts of the auditorium, the areas where the remnants of the families of the three girls were setting, three young girls got up and moved toward the center aisle. They met and hugged in the center aisle and turned to face the band. At that moment, Mark, Jack, and Willy saw Pauline, Esperanza, and Cassie smiling up at them as they had so many times in the past. They waved and turned and walked out the door. Not knowing what else to do, they kept singing. That's what they did. The show must go on and all that stuff. They finished the refrain for the last time singing, "But we will give our loved ones rest… I forgive."

Mark looked back at Billy and he was as white as a sheet. He looked at Mack and he was sitting down. He looked at his team and they all had stunned looks on their faces. He locked eyes with the band. They had all seen them. He looked at the rest of the crowd and realized that just a few of them had seen what happened. He just shook his head. Nobody was going to believe this.

The End